THE TRITON ULTIMATUM

THE TRITON ULTIMATUM

Laurence Delaney

NEW ENGLISH LIBRARY/TIMES MIRROR

First published in the USA in 1977 by
Thomas Y. Cromwell Company Inc
First published in Great Britain in 1978 by
New English Library

First NEL Paperback Edition May 1979
Reprinted October 1979

NEL Books are published by
New English Library from
Barnard's Inn, Holborn,
London, EC1N 2JR.
Made and printed in Great Britain by
Hunt Barnard Printing Ltd.,
Aylesbury, Bucks.

45004086 0

Especially for
Arlene and Deborah
&
Tiger, Morris and Henry

Glossary

ARASS   American Rocket and Space Systems. A government-controlled combine established from major electronics and weapons manufacturers when scandals and national economic disasters jeopardized their existence, and the government nationalized the entire industry under the guise of protecting national security. Development and production contracts were no longer awarded outside the combine, and all peripheral companies were at the capricious mercy of the first recognized military/civilian industrial complex.

basket leave   Unofficial leave where authentic leave papers are filled out and approved, then left conveniently in the yeoman's 'in' basket and forgotten, and therefore it never officially counted against later annual leave periods.

BIWI   Slang for British West Indian (which includes Jamaicans, Bahamans, Trinidadians, etc.).

boat   Submariners always refer to their vessels as 'boats' never 'submarines'.

broom to the scopes   A ritual used by returning submariners to signal that they had sunk an enemy vessel. A 'clean sweep' sign.

Chief-of-the-boat   Senior enlisted man on board.

COMSA   Computer Characteristic Sound Analysis. A computer program to identify ships by their characteristic sounds. Similar to a voice print, each ship has her own unique sound generated by her propellers, engine defects, etc.

cruise missiles   An updated version of the German buzz bombs. With a range of over 3,000 miles, its 'terrain-following' computer keeps it hugging the ground below radar contact, to within yards of the target.

Crypto Room   A top secret area where communications are

coded and decoded by various secret apparatus.

curtain   A picket line of Hunter-Killer submarines 'on station' at a secret perimeter hundreds of miles off each coast to defend against the intrusion of enemy submarines into United States waters.

Fleet Boats   Pre-nuclear diesel electric submarines, similar to the ones used during and after World War II.

grunt   The unaffectionate name given to the tough, coldly efficient Marine guards in charge of the prison.

H-5s   Sikorsky anti-submarine helicopters armed with ASW homing missile torpedoes.

Hunter-Killer   A submarine whose primary mission is to seek out and destroy other submarines.

looking for O'Rourke   A term seasoned sailors use to describe the action of bending over a railing or any other convenient place to relieve seasickness.

main induction valve   A huge shaft that runs into the boat to supply fresh air for ventilation and for the auxiliary diesel engine. The only time it's ever open is when the boat is on the surface.

March Hare   Nickname for a submarine decoy device which sounds and acts like a submarine and whose purpose is to lure homing missiles, etc., away from the actual submarine.

MIRV   The Poseidon's warhead. Multiple Independently Targetable Re-entry Vehicles. Fourteen thermonuclear warheads released from the original Poseidon and rocketed independently to separate targets or used as decoys to mask the ultimate targets of other missiles in the launch.

Mustang   Slang for an officer who has come up through the ranks.

Nimitz, Eisenhower and Vinson   The three largest nuclear-powered aircraft carriers ever built. They each measure 1,092 feet long, 252 feet wide, with crews of 5,400 men and 300 officers. They only needed nuclear refuelling once every twelve years. The *Nimitz* was commissioned

8

on May 3, 1975, the *Dwight D. Eisenhower* in early 1979, and the *Carl Vinson* in early 1982.

Nixie   An acoustic projector that transmits sounds that will temporarily confuse torpedoes that home in on a boat's sound.

Nukey Bogie   Navy slang for unidentified nuclear radiating contact.

oxygen generator   One of the submarine's miracles of engineering. From seawater, it eliminates salt and other impurities, and converts the pure water into gas. The gas is then pumped through a series of cells where the oxygen is separated from the hydrogen. The oxygen is added to the atmosphere inside the submarine, giving it independence from having to surface to renew their oxygen supply. The negative side of this miracle is the by-product – pure hydrogen. Lethally explosive, it is normally discharged over the side, but if the discharge valve fails it builds up and an explosion is inevitable.

percolator   Slang for the nuclear reactor.

plank owner   A certificate issued to crew members commissioning a new ship.

pumps   After a missile is fired, before the tubes can be closed, tons of seawater flood in. Massive pumps in the bilges automatically drain an equal amount out of the trim tanks, or the added weight would quickly sink the boat.

sail   The superstructure above the main deck that forms her unique silhouette. The designating numbers are painted in the side of the sail, and it is the last thing visible as the boat submerges.

sanitary tanks   All sewage aboard submarines is stored in tanks that, once filled, are discharged overboard by compressed air.

scrubber   A unit that works in conjunction with the oxygen generator. It cleans carbon dioxide and other impurities out of the atmosphere within the submarine. Once 're-cleaned' the old oxygen is circulated back into the boat with the new oxygen from the oxygen generator.

Seal School   The school from which the Navy graduates its super-elite Underwater Demolition Teams.

Sea Spider   Code name for a sonar network on the ocean floor. The system distinguishes sounds of passing ships, submarines, explosions, earth tremors, and other sea noises and returns the data to a computer center. The network includes systems in the Caribbean, the coasts of Britain, Denmark, Portugal, and Turkey, the eastern end of the Mediterranean, and the ocean floor west of the Hawaiian Islands and south of Mexico.

sea trials   Each ship that comes out of a Navy shipyard is given a short period at sea to check her seaworthiness.

ship over   Navy slang for 're-enlisting' for another tour of duty.

superstructure   A submarine is like an iceberg for, even cruising on the surface, most of the boat is submerged. The crew lives and works in a long tube of thick, pressure-resistant alloy called the pressure hull. The ballast tanks, high-pressure air lines, etc., that run outside this are hidden by the superstructure which also gives the boat her sleek silhouette.

tank tops   The top of the ballast tanks, which when flooded cause the boat to submerge, meet just below the superstructure, forming a small sloping area that it is possible to stand on.

Tiger Team   Computer experts whose job is to try to penetrate the elaborate security systems of various highly complex and secret computers, and who, in most cases, are successful.

trim manifold   The control manifold through which tons of water are pumped from tanks in one part of the boat to another. By this pumping – or flooding – the boat can skilfully be 'hovered' or balanced at one location and depth with no movement or noise.

tubes forward   Slang for forward torpedo room.

ULMS-11   Undersea Long Range Missile System. An advanced missile developed in the early 1980s with range of over 10,000 km. (6,000 miles).

1

The giant Triton submarine lay snuggled up outboard the gray submarine tender like a huge pregnant whale. Few lights were shining from the tender and most of the portholes were dark. Only the gangway lights leading down to the Triton from the huge ship twinkled in the tropical early morning blackness.

On the deck of the black Triton, Bobby Quillen, the nineteen-year-old bleary-eyed topside watch, sipped from a heavily sugared cup of lukewarm coffee as he paced the deck, praying he'd be able to stay half awake until his relief showed up at 0345.

The son-of-a-bitch'll probably be late, he thought. Figure 0400. Maybe even a little later.

Normally it wouldn't bother him. But they were getting underway at 0600 and his relief would only have to stand a half watch. And that really pissed him off.

Sighing loudly to break the silence, he craned his head back and looked up at the millions of stars shimmering in the moon-less sky.

Streaking across the heavens, two dying shooting stars fell in a gentle arc against the roof of the black night.

Better make a wish, Quillen thought as he followed their brief fiery suicide. Shit! he groaned. Maybe I just better wish I can stay the hell awake.

He walked back toward the bow of the boat.

Can't understand why the hell they figure they need a topside watch in the first place, he thought. Especially on an island in the middle of the Pacific. And tied up outboard another ship that's already got a watch, and a goddamn jarhead security detachment as well.

Maybe that's it. He chuckled to himself. To protect the boat from the goddamn jarheads.

As a swabjockey, Quillen instinctively hated jarheads. Even though his father had spent almost thirty years in the Corps. And he'd grown up almost exclusively on Marine bases.

Leaning back against the dull black sail, he reached in his pocket for a cigarette and thought about the patrol that was starting tomorrow.

Christ! he thought disgustedly. Three months at sea submerged under half the goddamn Pacific. No liberty! No mail! No new movies!

After Sub School in New London, Connecticut, he'd hoped to get a Hunter-Killer out of the East Coast where he could go on a few Med cruises. Maybe even hit a few ports in the Caribbean.

Instead, the sons-of-bitches sent him to Bremmerton, Washington, in time to become a plank owner of the pride of the fleet. The newest, biggest, and deadliest weapons platform known to man. The Triton submarine *Lewis & Clark*.

Shit! he thought, tossing the half-smoked cigarette over the side.

At first he'd been excited. The Orient! Hong Kong! Japan! They'd for sure have some spaced-out chicks running around those places. And they'd sure be cheaper than the French chicks. Or even the BIWIs.

But shit! Agana, Guam?

This wasn't exactly Quillen's idea of a tropical paradise. It might be to the goddamn gooks that flew over every week from Tokyo on the tours. But to him it was shit.

He turned and walked aft toward where the superstructure dropped into the black waters of the bay. Moving aft, he unconsciously counted the dark, hopscotch-like outlines on the deck that marked the missile tubes.

He hadn't seen many. Mostly pictures. But these were twenty-four of the biggest sonsabitchin' missiles he'd ever seen. One of his buddies told him each of these new missiles had at least fourteen different warheads in them.

Jesus! he thought. That's over . . . He unsuccessfully tried to multiply twenty-four by fourteen. But as maths, especially mental arithmetic, had never been one of his natural gifts, he quickly forgot it.

Standing in the shadows on the outboard side of the sail, hidden from view from the tender, he unzipped his pants and sent a warm fountain of urine spiraling toward the water almost fifteen feet below.

The cascade had hardly splattered against the water when he heard someone from the tender step onto the gangway and start down toward where he was supposed to be on watch.

His bladder ached as he zipped his pants back up. Hoping he wouldn't dribble all over his only clean pair of whites and look like he'd pissed his pants, he quickly came around the sail as two men reached the deck.

12

In the dark, Quillen could see the first one was a lieutenant-commander, wearing gold submarine dolphins above the decorations on his left chest.

He was taller than most submarine officers. Probably a Mustang, Quillen thought, as the handsome, dark-headed lieutenant-commander came toward him.

Definitely not Annapolis, he thought as the lieutenant-commander smiled. Those assholes never smile at whitehats.

The other man, dressed in the white overalls and white hard-hat of a factory technician or scientist, was sweating from the struggle of bringing a heavy metal equipment case down the gangway.

Probably one of the civilian factory reps, Quillen thought. They'd been hovering around the new boat like a bunch of mother hens. So many civilians onboard the last couple of weeks, you damn near need a scorecard to figure who the hell's crew and who's out here on a goddamn expense account.

'You the Topside Watch?' asked the lieutenant-commander.

'Yes, sir,' Quillen answered, saluting casually. 'Sorry, sir. I was taking a leak,' he said with a smile that usually guaranteed his getting the girls in the few ports he'd been in, and few, if any, of the shit details that the chief-of-the-boat was always handing out to unsuspecting seamen.

'I understand,' the lieutenant-commander chuckled as he stretched like he'd just been awakened. 'Listen. This gentleman's from ARASS. He has to sign off the final missile fire control alignment.'

'Yes, sir,' Quillen nodded. 'I'll call the OD for you.'

'Don't have to be bothering him if he's crashed out,' the civilian said in a preachy Texas drawl that reminded Quillen of a skinny Billy Graham.

'Sorry, sir. But . . . well . . . ' Quillen looked at the lieutenant-commander knowing he'd understand that if he didn't wake the OD it'd be his ass, 'I gotta let him know you're onboard.'

' 'Course you do,' the lieutenant-commander confirmed smiling. 'No sweat. You go right ahead.'

Quillen swung up through the access hatch into the dark sail. Inside he reached for the intercom switch that when depressed, would connect him to a below-decks watch in the control room.

The Below-decks Watch, an equally bored first-class electronics technician, was reading a paperback novel propped up on the cushioned seat in front of the diving station.

Quillen reached for the cold, smooth, waterproofed gasket

that covered the IC button when he heard a strange, harsh noise, like someone sneezing directly into his ear, roaring through the back of his head – the sound of the rapidly dissipating gases screaming through a silencer mounted on the end of a small black custom 9 mm pistol.

The hollow-pointed bullet shattered Quillen's skull, erupted into his brain, and broke into a hundred pieces before lodging behind his left eye and bulging it out.

His hand jerked away from the IC button as he sagged to the deck. His body shuddered in several involuntary spasms before finally becoming still.

The lieutenant-commander watched for a few moments as blood from his crushed skull and jugular vein turned the Topside Watch's white uniform an ever-darkening shade of red.

God! he thought, gritting his teeth to hold down his nausea as he watched the seaman's convulsions subside. I'm sorry. I'm truly sorry.

Paul Morgan, the lieutenant-commander, stepped away from the access hatch and put the dull black automatic back under his clean, starched uniform.

Will Adamson, the civilian, took a miniature transmitter out of his breast pocket and put it to his mouth.

'Runner's on first,' he said in his soft Texas drawl into the tiny condenser mike.

Adamson put the transmitter back into his pocket and quickly moved to the gangway. Pulling out a pair of insulated pliers, he snipped the wire to the gangway lights.

He stopped for a moment as his eyes adjusted to the dark. He scanned the decks of the tender above him. But they were deserted.

Quickly he returned to the sail where Morgan, trying not to get blood on his khakis, had rolled the seaman's body up into a sitting position. Swinging the lifeless arms up, he put his shoulder under the seaman's chest and heaved him over his shoulder. Kid died badly, he thought. But does anyone ever do it well? Carrying him to the inboard side, between the Triton and the tender, he lowered him over the side onto the tank tops.

Adamson followed, once again struggling with the heavy equipment case. He lowered the case down to Morgan who had jumped down on the tank tops and was standing next to the body.

Morgan opened the case and took out a six-foot length of braided steel wire. With the wire out of the case, it was obvious why Adamson had to struggle with it. It was filled almost to the top with concrete.

Morgan took the wire, wrapped it around the seaman's feet several times, made a loop, and secured the wire to a ring embedded in the concrete.

This done, he pushed the body over the side into the water. As the body drifted toward the bottom, he lowered the case over the side and let it go.

Like a rock, it skidded along the side of the ballast tanks and dropped to the bottom of the bay, yanking the dead seaman after it.

Sixty-five feet beneath the surface, a cloud of silt blossomed up as the case hurtled into the bottom. After a few moments, the silt settled and the only movement was the gentle rocking motion of the tethered body as it swayed back and forth in the current.

After watching the body disappear into the dark waters, Morgan hurried back to the sail and quickly climbed up to the bridge to join Adamson.

From the bridge Morgan and Adamson watched as two shadowy silhouettes came quickly down the dark gangway.

The two men, each carrying a heavy seabag on his shoulder, glided silently down the deck to the access hatch in the sail.

Heaving the seabags up to Adamson, the two men quickly swung up into the sail where Morgan was waiting next to the hatch which led down into the quiet interior of the boat.

2

In the control room Karl Beasley, the electronics technician, looked up at the sound of something scraping along the outside of the ballast tank.

He slipped his paperback into the rack under the operations table and listened.

Except for the hum from the blowers circulating fresh air throughout the boat, it was once again quiet. He listened several moments longer to the normal, predawn sounds, then shrugged.

Some asshole from the tender probably shit-canning something over the side. Should tell the topside watch to yell at them. But what the fuck! He's probably crashed out, he thought, remembering the many hours of midnight watches he'd suffered before finally mastering the art of sleeping half sitting, half standing against the sail.

He'd tell the kid's relief watch and let it go at that.

Beasley picked up the duty clipboard which had to be kept by each watch to record air tank pressures, bilge levels, temperatures, nuclear reactor levels, etc. He checked his watch. Time to make his last inspection round before waking the relief watches. But first, a quick trip to the head. Then for a fresh cup of hot coffee.

He stepped through the hatch into the warmth of the crew's mess. At the corner table nearest the galley, one of the cooks was taking a break from his nightly baking chores.

Across the compartment, a mess cook just out of Sub School in New London was whistling as he emptied vanilla ice cream from the churning stainless-steel ice cream machine into five-gallon containers.

Beasley nodded to the cook as he walked over to the giant coffee urn. He took out a heavy white crock mug from the storage bin next to the urn and turned the spout.

'Fresh pot?' he asked.

The cook, tattooed arms, apron and shoes covered with a film of white flour, nodded as he inhaled deeply from a cigarette that had a dangerously long ash drooping from it.

Snuffing out the cigarette in one of the ship's monogrammed

ashtrays, the cook looked distastefully at the mess cook across the compartment.

'Only two kinds of people whistle in the Navy, old son,' he said. 'One's a bosun's mate, the other's a cocksucker. Now I happen to know you ain't no bosun's mate,' he smiled, sarcastically.

The mess cook's face turned flame red. 'I'm not the other either, sir,' he said sheepishly as he quickly put lids on some of the containers.

Beasley snickered and shook his head as he bent down to open the small refrigerator next to the coffee urn.

'Whatta ya got for a sandwich?' he asked as he searched through the cluttered refrigerator.

'Horsecock, same as always,' answered the cook.

'Jesus! We ain't even underway and we're already down to horsecock?' he asked in mock sarcasm as he took the twelve-inch length of bologna out of the reefer.

'Well,' said the cook. 'Till we get underway, I gotta keep the good shit locked up or frozen. Otherwise those pussy officers skarf up anything that isn't nailed down or painted gray. I told that Chief Steward fucker that I was going to start wiping my ass on everything I left out. I figure that'd sure cure 'em from stealing crew's shit for the Wardroom.'

'On second thought, maybe I'll just have some of that bread you got cooling off in there,' Beasley said, putting the bologna to his nose to check whether or not the cook had carried out his threat.

The cook roared a tubercular-sounding laugh and nodded approval. 'Sure! Go ahead! That's what it's for.'

'There's new cookies, too!' added the mess cook as he opened the deck hatch that led down into the food storage locker and massive ship's freezer.

'Cookies! Why thank you, sweetheart. Ain't he just the sweetest little pussy we had aboard in a long time,' Beasley said as he put the bologna back in the reefer and took out a two-pound block of cold butter.

The mess cook's face turned flaming red again. This was his first cruise and he wasn't used to the familiarity everybody seemed to show. Embarrassed, he quickly lowered the ice cream into the storeroom, hurried down the ladder, and opened the heavy freezer door.

'Close the hatch, goddammit!' the cook screamed in mock

2

exasperation, ' 'fore some innocent son-of-a-bitch falls through and breaks his ass.'

The mess cook scurried back up the heavy metal ladder. 'Sorry,' he said with a sheepish grin and closed the hatch after him.

'Good kid,' the cook smiled at Beasley. 'But I figure you gotta break 'em in right.' Beasley nodded his agreement.

'By the way, Pappy,' Beasley asked, cutting a thick slice from the piping-hot loaf. 'You hear anything banging against the inboard side of the boat?'

The cook shook his head. 'Naw! But with that fucking ice cream machine running, you can barely hear yourself scratching your own ass.'

Topside in the sail, the two new arrivals, dressed as seamen, were opening the seabags next to the conning tower hatch. One of them contained breathing devices similar to those worn by firemen.

From the other seabag, the other man took three steel cylinders equipped with valves and directional nozzles.

Morgan quickly stripped the plastic wrapper off one of the shiny new breathing units. He tapped Adamson on the shoulder and handed it to him.

Adamson quickly slipped it on as the two seamen followed suit, adjusting straps and securing the units snugly on their backs.

'Sure hope this shit'll do the job,' whispered one of the men anxiously as he picked up one of the steel cylinders.

'I guarantee it,' Morgan said quietly.

The man nodded.

'OK,' Morgan said. 'Jones, you take the main induction valve. Rap twice on the tank when you're in position and ready. Nardulli, you and I'll take the conning tower hatch.'

Jones nodded, picked up the cylinder, and squeezed into the darkness of the sail behind the bridge.

As he disappeared, Nardulli took the nozzles of the remaining cylinders and dropped them over the lip of the hatch so they pointed straight down into the boat.

From the darkness behind the sail, Morgan heard the muffled signal indicating that Jones was in position and ready to release the gas into the main induction valve.

Morgan turned and nodded to Nardulli, who rapped twice in response.

Holding up his mask, Morgan took a deep breath as Nardulli

strained to crank open the stubborn valves, and the hiss of the escaping gas dissolved into the night.

In the eerie glow shining up through the conning tower hatch, Morgan watched the gauge on the tank slowly unwind as the contents of the cylinder was sucked down into the massive ventilation system and rushed via the air-conditioning into every compartment and space in the giant Triton.

Morgan hated the sound. It reminded him of a hissing death rattle. He had hated that particular noise since he was eleven years old and had seen his father die.

Before his death, Morgan's father had been a touring golf pro. Though never a big money winner, Remmie Corona was tremendously popular with the galleries and television audiences because of his sometimes emotional, mostly comic outbursts during the quiet, straight-laced tournaments.

Smuggled into the United States near Mexicali from the heart of Mexico, Remmie, his mother, and sister, Claudia, trekked north to a barrio on the outskirts of Santa Ana, California.

After weeks of sleepless nights, waiting for the Border Patrol to catch and deport them back to Mexico, Remmie's mother went to work as a day maid on Lido Isle, the wealthiest of Newport Beach's fashionable islands.

Despite not having the 'green card' which would allow her to work as an immigrant, and having to work for less than half of the going rate, she kept her kids fed, clean, out of the barrio gangs and almost put them through school.

Remmie was her pride and joy. But he almost broke her heart when he quit school and went to work at a driving range for sixty-five cents an hour and all the golf balls he could hit.

A naturally gifted athlete, in less than two years he was able to qualify for his PGA card and became one of the youngest pros on the tour.

Unfortunately, the tours brought to light several flaws in Remmie's character. He loved the ladies, booze and the nice hotels with their twenty-four-hour room service. And mostly, he loved the limelight.

One day he'd shoot a round that would tie or break the course record. That night he'd celebrate with loud music and louder women. And the next day, suffering from a tremendous hangover, he'd bogie his way out of the top money.

Leading one year at La Costa, he was studying a relatively easy approach shot when he spotted a spectacular redhead standing near the front of a group of fans following him around the course.

'Wot jew theenk?' he asked her, giving her his most roguish smile and thickest accent which all the ladies seemed to adore.

She smiled and shrugged.

'I theenk I batter finish queek so we can half deener. Wot jew theenk?'

'I theenk you pretty damn full of crap,' she laughed, mimicking his phoney accent.

He roared through the rest of the course. Led at the end of the day by two strokes and withdrew from the tour the next morning so as not to interfere with their sometimes tender, most times wild, sometimes violent, rarely sober affair.

Three months later she called him in North Carolina and told him she was pregnant. Though wild as the March winds and sexually insatiable, she was brought up a good Irish Catholic and drew the line at abortion.

Two weeks after little Paul was born, she left him with Remmie's sister and they never saw or heard from her again.

As a child, Paul was as much a free spirit as his Irish mother and as vibrant as his Mexican father.

He was happiest when they were driving around the tour together. They were great pals. And Remmie treated Paul more like a younger brother than a son. Whatever Remmie did, wherever he went, little Paul did and went.

Unfortunately, the years weren't kind to Remmie. The women, the booze, the travel, the days on end without sleep, living on amphetamines and junk food were slowly destroying him.

On the outside he sparkled, but on the inside, he ached.

In the muggy heat of the Master's in Augusta, Georgia, Paul was tagging along behind him on the second round when all of a sudden Remmie keeled over.

The gallery oohed and ahed. But they knew his reputation. And they figured he was joking again. Trying to clown his way into a few minutes' rest in the stifling heat.

But this time Remmie didn't move.

He was strangely quiet. After a few moments, his caddy dropped his golf bag and ran to him.

'Oh Jesus!' Paul heard the caddy mutter and watched, in a trance, as he turned Remmie over onto his back and tried unsuccessfully to give him mouth-to-mouth resuscitation until help could arrive.

Paul stared as the sweat from the black caddy's forehead dropped in sparkling rivulets onto his father's pallid face. There was a faint hiss from Remmie's throat, and he was dead. A massive coronary at forty-one years old.

The PGA flew his body and Paul back home to Santa Ana. And he was buried in a little cemetery in the shade of a Saddleback Mountain east of the coast.

Though not yet twelve, Paul refused to go to the funeral. He still couldn't accept that Remmie was gone. If he didn't go to the funeral, or see him in the coffin, or the gravesite . . . maybe it wouldn't be true.

His grandmother, old and broken by her son's death, protested. But his aunt understood, so he stayed behind in his grandmother's little shack in the barrio.

He watched them go. And felt himself starting to cry. But if he cried, then he'd be crying because Remmie was really gone. And he wasn't. So he wouldn't cry.

Almost two hours passed and he'd hardly moved when he saw the battered limousine from Gonzalez's Casa de Paz bringing them back.

They stopped in front, next to Remmie's old, faded Volkswagen, plastered with bumper stickers, heralding his support to 'save' just about everything.

He watched as Aunt Claudia's husband, a tall arrogant-looking Anglo, got out of the limo and helped his grandmother across the brown, dried-out lawn onto the porch and into the small living room.

'Wait on the porch, Paul,' his Anglo uncle said.

'I want to talk to your grandmother about what we're going to do with you.'

'Si, Uncle,' he mumbled as he quickly darted out through the screen door into the front yard.

He didn't like this tall Anglo his aunt had married. He always lorded it over them and thought he was better than they were because he had a little money. It bothered everybody but Remmie.

Before he died, Remmie laughed at him and his money.

Remmie always accused him of driving through life and never bothering to look around at the beauty or smell the flowers.

His Anglo uncle told him if you wanted to make it through to the end of the highway, you had to keep your eyes on the road and both hands on the wheel.

It looked like his uncle had been right.

'Have to get rid of that accent,' his uncle said to his grandmother. 'Only people in our neighborhood with accents are the hired help.'

She nodded through the tears. Though she shared her dead son's belief about this man, she was grateful to him for providing a way out of the barrio for her young grandson.

'And if he's going to live in my house, we're going to do something about his name, too,' he added, laying out the ground rules for the young boy he'd agreed to shelter as a second-rate son.

A year later, in a stark courtroom in Santa Ana, in a meaningless civil ceremony, his uncle took away his father's name and made him a Morgan.

3

In the crew's mess, Beasley, the electronics technician, was trying to spread the cold butter onto the soft, hot, doughy bread. He squinted from a sudden pain that shot through the front of his brain.

Jesus! he thought setting down the knife. By now his ears were starting to ring and he felt nauseous.

What the fuck's happening? he thought. He raised his hand and felt his nose. Son-of-a-bitch! It felt tingly numb. Like somebody had given him a massive shot of Novocain. His face was flushed. It felt like it was burning and he couldn't seem to catch his breath. He was terrified.

Jesus, sweet Jesus! I must be having a heart attack. But Christ! his mind screamed. I'm only twenty-sev . . .

Before he could finish the thought, his head snapped back and the last thing he remembered was how the soft lights in the overhead suddenly seemed painfully blinding. And how quickly the floor seemed to rush up and smack him in the face.

In the glow from the conning tower hatch, Morgan reached down and tapped the gauges on the two cylinders a couple of times. Both registered EMPTY. He turned off the valves and turned to Nardulli.

'Ready?' Morgan whispered.

'Ready as I'll ever be,' Nardulli nodded, picking up one of the seabags and dropping it down the hatch into the boat.

'OK!' Morgan whispered. 'Hit it!'

Adamson and Nardulli inhaled and exhaled several times to make sure their gas masks were working, then quickly dropped down into the gas-filled submarine.

After Jones had followed the other two down the hatch, Morgan took out a tiny transmitter and quickly depressed the key.

'Bases loaded,' he said.

Moments later two more ghostlike figures scurried down the gangway from the tender.

Giving the dungaree-clad figures a thumbs-up signal, he

23

grabbed the seabags they were carrying and dropped them down the conning tower hatch.

'Barth,' he whispered. 'You and Nichols get the lines singled up. Stand by to get this thing out of here.'

'How we doing, Pablo?' the paunchy, balding Barth whispered anxiously. Over the years, Barth's once-trim midsection had slipped and now hung over his belt like a drill sergeant's.

'No hangups so far,' Morgan whispered down to his old friend. 'But be ready to cut the damn things if we have to get out of here in a hurry.'

Barth moved quickly back up the gangway and made his way up the deck to a giant iron cleat where one of the lines that moored the Triton to the tender was coiled.

Below him, on the bow of the Triton, Nichols loosened the heavy line. It went slack and Barth pulled it free and let it fall into the dark water below.

In tandem, they quickly worked their way aft, repeating the procedure with each line. When the last hit the water, Barth trotted back down to the Triton and disappeared into the dark sail.

On the bridge, Morgan depressed the intercom switch the seaman had died for earlier trying to reach.

'Home run! Home run!' he said quietly into the mouthpiece.

In the control room, two decks directly under the bridge, Adamson acknowledged by clicking the IC switch over the operations table several times.

'Jones,' Adamson said. 'Take the helm. Nardulli, you start taking care of the crew. I'll be aft in maneuvering,' he said as gave them the thumbs-up.

Through their masks, which gave them the appearance of bug-eyed insects, the two seamen broke into wide grins.

Jones quickly slipped onto the seat in front of the diving station and punched a switch that lit up the panel indicators. Pushing several others, he energized the massive hydraulic system that gave him total power over the ship's steering and diving controls.

Adamson, rushing aft, wound his way through the sparkling-new submarine. Through compartments, down ladders, past hydraulic and high-pressure air lines, past unconscious crewmen, he finally came to the missile compartment, which on the first missile submarines had been nicknamed 'Sherwood Forest'.

He was halfway through the compartment before its technical grandeur brought him to an abrupt stop.

My God! he thought. He'd been on missile boats before. But not a new one. He was completely unprepared for its glistening new chrome-and-brass toy-store look. The back of his neck tingled with excitement. It was almost like being in the presence of something divine.

His face flushed from his pounding heart as his eyes drank in the seemingly haloed steel rows of tiered vaults that sheathed the dormant missiles.

He unconsciously counted the number of tubes.

Twenty-four! They were all there!

He smiled and rubbed his hands together, like a gleeful child before rushing on aft.

Passing through the tunnel that led through the reactor compartment and into the maneuvering room, he softly hummed an old gospel hymn to himself.

The maneuvering room was a brightly lit compartment from where the nuclear-powered steam turbines that propelled the sleeping giant were directed.

Quickly, he expertly pushed buttons, depressed switches, and aligned levers until the various gauges reached their operational levels, and warning and safety lights blinked out on the panel in front of him.

He quickly glanced over all the dials and gauges to double-check everything one last time.

Finally satisfied, he reached up and depressed the IC button over the computer console.

'Ready,' he said quietly.

On the bridge Morgan replied by clicking the switch several times. Leaning over the side, he looked aft. 'Cast off the stern line,' he whispered through cupped hands. A few seconds later, he heard the heavy line fall into the water.

'Back one-third. Left full rudder,' he said into the IC and several clicks told him Jones at the helm and Adamson in maneuvering had heard and were responding.

He looked aft and after a few moments, could see the water starting to move as the huge boat started backing slowly away from the tender.

Still held to the tender by the umbilical bow line, the stern of the Triton started to swing in a slow, lazy arc toward the bay. As the angle and the distance from the tender grew, Morgan clicked the IC switch.

'Rudder amidship,' he said into the mouthpiece. And again he heard the answering clicks as Jones acknowledged his order. 'Let go the bow line,' he said to Nichols in a voice just loud enough to carry to where he was standing on the bow.

Nichols quickly slipped the heavy line free and let it drop over the side.

'Right full rudder,' Morgan said into the IC.

Back on the bridge, both Nichols and Barth took binoculars and climbed back into the lookout stations.

If anyone on the tender or any other part of the sprawling Navy base happened to see them leaving, the boat would appear to be leaving on a routine patrol like the dozens of others that came in and out of the harbor every week.

By now the Triton was moving away from the tender in a straight line toward the middle of the deep channel that led to the open sea.

'All stop,' Morgan said. 'All ahead two-thirds,' he added without waiting for the first orders to be acknowledged.

A few moments later, Morgan could feel the faint vibrations running through the boat as the giant propeller changed direction and reversed the flow of water. The boat slowed its backward motion and glided to a dead stop in the water.

Then, ever so slowly, it started forward.

'Left full rudder,' he ordered. Looking down, he saw the illuminated rudder angle indicator in the deck next to the compass swinging toward the left full that he'd ordered.

Slowly the giant boat gathered speed and swung away from the tender toward midchannel.

'Rudder amidships,' he ordered, and again he saw the indicator move back parellel to the hull.

As the submarine gathered speed, the only sound the three men topside were aware of was the sound of the boat's bow softly breaking through the calm waters of the dark, empty bay.

The cool predawn breeze in his face reminded Morgan of being at the helm of a huge phantom sailing ship as it plowed silently through a dark sea.

By now they had left the tender sleeping quietly in her berth. On the port beam, Morgan could see the distant twinkling lights of the sprawling Navy base.

Farther down the beach the distant lights of Agana, Guam's sleeping capital, looked like the shimmering lights of some vacant stage as they pointed the way to sea.

Morgan looked down at the speed indicator. A little over fourteen knots.

'All ahead full,' he said loudly into the IC so he could be heard over the noise of the wind.

Leaning over the bridge and looking aft, he could see the glow from those mysterious, low order sea creatures as they flared up in the wake of the Triton seemingly in protest as they were churned up by the huge brass alloy propeller.

The make-believe Milky Way kicked up by the whirling propeller reminded him of a windy, star-filled sky years earlier coming into Gibraltar.

4

His submarine put into the British Royal shipyards at the foot of the 'Rock' after making the Atlantic crossing on their way into the Med for a four-month patrol.

Shortly after tying up, Morgan came ashore armed with 'civvies' and a ten-day basket leave that didn't start until the following Monday.

Saluting the topside watch, he walked down the narrow gangway and hopped on an aging bus that the crew, dipping into their slush fund, had hired to take them across the border into Spain to a bullfight.

The crew cheered heartily as he was the last to get on and they were getting impatient to 'hit the beach'.

Morgan bowed graciously and slumped into the lumpy seat before the cheers could become jeers and catcalls.

'Whatta ya wantta do after the bullfights?' A young sailor sitting behind Morgan asked a younger but already 'salty' Barth.

Barth didn't answer. He was busy figuring out if there was a way to dump this young snotnose once the *corrida* started.

'Hey!' the striker whispered enthusiastically. 'How 'bout we find us a couple locals? Buy 'em a few drinks and get us some cooze?'

'Not me,' Barth said, staring out the window. 'I'm gonna find some poor old broken-down hooker 'n camp out with her for the weekend.'

'A whore?' the sailor asked like he had a bad taste in his mouth as the bus shuddered through its lower gears.

'Damn right! That way I can spend equal amounts of time on poontang, and the other equal amounts on serious drinking.'

'But why bother with whores when you don't have to pay for no local stuff?'

Barth took out a small, ugly, black cheroot and peeled off the yellow cellophane. 'Listen, sonny,' he said, lighting the vile little cigar. 'First off, I've been in this part of the Med so many fucking times I've lost count. So you can consider me somewhat of an expert as to what's available. And what I'm telling you is that with the locals you're gonna be running into chances are you'll more than likely end up in the toilet with your dick in your hand.'

The bus turned up a narrow street and headed for the sentry gates in the distance.

'Second thing,' Barth continued, 'with a hooker, we know it's gonna cost twenty for her and five for the room. Right?'

The sailor nodded.

'Goddamn right!' Barth emphasized. 'Now with the "locals," it's gonna cost three, maybe four, drinks. A lot of bullshit small talk. And, you can bet your ass, at least dinner. You spend the twenty you'da spent on the whore and there's still no guarantee you'll get any pussy. Chances are, you'll end up with no money and no ass,' he finished, as the bus hissed to a stop next to the sentry headquarters at the main gate.

'With a hooker, believe me, you'll have both. And probably end up saving a few bucks,' he added as he took out his ID and liberty card.

'But ain't you 'fraid of getting the clap?' the sailor whispered, not wanting Morgan, their Division Officer, or the Royal Marine who came down the aisle to hear what they were talking about.

On his way back out of the bus, the muscular, red-hatted Royal Marine gave their IDs a cursory glance.

' 'Ave a nice time, lads,' he said as he stepped back off and motioned them through the gate. 'There's a couple of busloads already on their way to the same place yer going,' he added in an unspoken warning against their running into the much hated 'surface-craft sailors'.

'Thanks, mate,' shouted Barth as the bus creaked and moaned off down the narrow street. 'But if it's anything less than a whole fucking squadron, not to worry!'

The burly Marine grinned as the bus disappeared. He liked the two-fisted drinkers that invariably came off the American submarines. Reminded him of his own Royal Marines.

'Ain't you 'fraid of getting a dose?' the sailor asked again as he thought about how the evil, infectious disease could leave his beautiful young body looking like a leper's. 'I mean . . . they say there's not a whore in the Med that don't have it.'

'Listen, sonny,' Barth sighed. 'If a hooker gets a dose, she knows what the hell it is. But the "local", she don't know shit. She'll go four, maybe five weeks before even telling anybody. And you wanna know why?'

'Yeah! Why?' the sailor asked delighted that Barth was going to share some of his worldly experience with him.

' 'Cuzz she's too goddamn embarrassed to do anything about it. So . . . don't ya see? It's the goddamn fucking locals that're giving it to half the world. Not the self-respecting whores. No siree! They're running a business. And looking for the "return trade".' Looking up, he winked at Morgan who'd turned to listen to this amazing bullshit-filled lecture.

Morgan shook his head in disbelief and laughed. Barth was one of those marvelous characters who could find the logic in anything.

A few hours later, Morgan was sitting in the front row on one of the hard seats as the late afternoon sun beat down on the crowd sitting in the little arena near the ocean.

Sitting next to him was the grateful Barth, whom Morgan had taken pity on and rescued from the puppylike sailor.

It was the last bull of the day, and the crowd was jeering and throwing seat cushions at the picador for almost butchering the attacking little black bull.

From where he sat, Morgan could see the blood streaming down the shoulder from the large muscle that formed the hump high on the neck that was the characteristic of the Santa Brioso fighting bulls.

The first part of the *corrida* had been spectacularly uneventful. The bulls, though spirited, were no match for the flashing capes, the picadors, or the deadly swords.

But this last bull, small and coal black with a slash of white circling his neck like a wreath, was different.

Before he was released, with a great show of bravado, the novice matador had gotten down on his knees. And with a flourish, he spread his cape on the ground in front of the chute the bull was about to be released from.

The previous five bulls would have seen the cape, charged past it, and would have been off and running. But this little devil charged out into the sunlight, saw the flashing cape, and drove over it and the matador like a fast freight train, almost trampling him to death in the process.

Then before the dust could settle, he spun and was after the fallen figure. Instantly, the other matadors jumped into the arena and distracted him long enough for the young matador to scramble to a red-faced and rather undignified retreat over the *barrera.*

The rapidly aging young matador dusted himself off and tried to regain a little of his lost composure. Cautiously, he returned to the arena and tried a few dancing, shakey, sporadic passes.

In a box, high in the stands, the judge saw from the way the bull was intimidating the young matador that a disaster was in the making. So he quickly raised his hand and had his trumpeters signal for the hated picadors to make their entrance.

The crowd booed and hissed, as the first picador trotted out on an ancient, bony mare and waited next to the *barrera*.

As soon as he spotted it, the bull charged. Hitting the feeble animal with one almost effortless lunge, he hooked a horn under the heavy protective pads into the horse's unprotected belly.

The blindfolded mare tried to rear away from the pain. But it was too late.

The heavy-necked bull plunged the horn deeper into the horse's belly, lifted and threw her and the picador backwards into the *barrera*. Unfortunately, the picador was on the bottom, as the already dead horse landed in a slow backward somersault on top of him, crushing his pelvis like a soda cracker.

Again the matadors reacted, leaping into the arena, yelling and flashing their capes to distract the bull.

The crowd leaped to its feet, howling as the bull prowled the ring like a raging monarch while several attendants worked desperately to free the unconscious picador.

Tears welled into Morgan's eyes as he watched the proud little bull. He didn't know why.

But every now and then, he knew he was exposed to something special in life. And this was one of those moments.

'Make 'em pay,' he yelled in a hoarse, screaming whisper. 'Make 'em pay.' But his voice was lost in the deafening roar from the crowd.

Suddenly the bull whirled. He had spotted the second picador trotting his blindfolded horse around the perimeter of the *barrera*, trying to get an angle on the bull that would be advantageous to him.

From halfway across the arena, the bull charged.

The crowd roared. The matadors tried in vain to distract him. To slow or break his charge so the picador could easily place the pike in the heavy neck muscle.

But the bull would have none of it and without slowing, hit the horse head-on.

Its heavy shoulder pads absorbed most of the shock, and were too thick for his stumpy horns to penetrate, but the force of the charge folded the horse up like an accordian. Not feeling any heat on his horn from any penetration, the bull bellowed and whirled like some bloodthirsty beast as frothy saliva flew from his mouth.

Finally the matadors distracted the bull long enough for the attendants to drag the picador from under the horse and get the shaking animal back on its feet.

From that moment on, every soul in the arena and in the stands was aware of the explosive danger and phenomenal spirit of this remarkable animal.

But, as is the nature of bullfighting, it was doomed.

Savagely wounded over and over by the terrified picador on the shaking horse that had to literally be held up by four attendants on the side away from the bull – and worked at a disgracefully safe distance by the matador – the bull fought on . . . and on . . . and on.

Finally, the judge signaled for the kill.

The crowd roared its protest. And almost instantly thousands of white handkerchiefs waved hysterically, frantically signaling for the judge to spare the little bull.

The matador, thankful for surviving the seemingly endless onslaught from the black devil, came to the *barrera*, raised his cape and sword, and gestured for the judge to spare him.

Morgan looked back over his shoulder at the judge sitting above him in his box halfway up the arena. He seemed almost Caesar-like in the midst of the sea of waving handkerchiefs as the roaring masses pleaded for the life of their favorite gladiator who had fallen to be spared.

Morgan could see his eyes searching the crowd.

Finally, they stopped on a once-handsome and terribly overweight man in his mid-fifties sitting several seats away.

The man was Enrique Vasques, manager of the Santa Brioso and a once-famous matador himself. He studied the bull circling the far side of the arena. It was apparent the little animal was exhausted and had lost a considerable amount of blood from the picador's deep, grinding wounds. But he was still willing to fight anything that would challenge him.

Several other people were sitting quietly with him respecting the difficulty of his decision.

Between him and Morgan, sitting next to Barth, was an incredible-looking young woman with dark hair cascading down her backless dress.

There was no doubt about the way she felt. She was screaming with Morgan and the crowd and waving her brilliantly colored Givenchy scarf for the bull to be spared.

Finally, almost imperceptibly, Vasques shook his head.

The judge nodded in resignation and again raised his hand for the trumpeters to signal for the kill.

Morgan was stunned. The young woman wasn't though. For above the din, Morgan could hear her cursing and raging unmercifully at the red-faced ranch manager.

In the arena, the matador nodded in resignation. And while the attendants distracted the exhausted bull, walked to the center of the arena, where with a great show of bravado, he dedicated the kill of the black blood-stained animal to the crowd.

They roared. But it was impossible to tell if they were roaring thanks or protest.

The dedication over, the matador walked cautiously toward the rear of the bull who was charging wearily back and forth between the capes thrown at him by two assistants from behind the safety of the *barrera*.

He positioned himself and raised his sword, sighting down it as it hung over the front of his cape. Finally, he took a deep breath to calm his jittery nerves, flung a quick prayer to the heavens, and called softly to the bull.

On hearing the sound, the bull spun around to face him. Sides heaving and gasping painfully for each breath, it hesitated just long enough for the matador to lunge forward with the sword.

With a great deal of luck, mostly provided by the straight-charging bull, the razor-sharp sword sliced down between the shoulder blades, through the heart, and out through the bottom of his chest.

The perfect kill! And the little animal fell like a rock. Dead before he hit the hot sands of the arena.

There was a stunned silence. Then, the crowd exploded with applause.

The din of noise became suffocating for Morgan. Unable to bear their disloyalty, he raised both arms and shook his fists at the unseeing crowd. 'Sons-of-bitches!' he raged. 'Sons-abitches!'

The judge, to keep the crowd's attentions from the fallen bull, awarded the matador both ears.

The young boy was tearfully stunned. Overwhelmed. He couldn't believe his good fortune. This was the extraordinary stroke of good luck from which careers were launched.

As the disbelieving young matador started his triumphant tour around the arena, Morgan slumped into his seat, his eyes riveted on the little animal. In death he seemed somehow even smaller. His heaving sides were finally quiet. His eyes stared unblinkingly

3

into the dazzling setting sun. The streams of blood that had gushed from the deep neck wounds were already drying, staining the once-pure white slash around his neck into a bright red wreath, like some macabre Kentucky Derby winner.

The gates through the *barrera* opened and a team of mules were led in, their harness bells jingling gaily. The shabbily dressed attendants quickly hooked a rope around the bull's once-dangerous horns. A whip cracked behind the lead mule and the team was off at a trot dragging the bull behind them.

Quickly they disappeared into the dark chute that lead under the arena. The *barrera* and the gates swung shut. The dust settled. And the little bull was gone.

The only thing that remained was a large black pool of blood from his final, massive death wound, and a deep furrow in the sand that had been plowed up by his horn as he was dragged out.

Within moments, red-shirted attendants tossed new sand over the stain. Another attendant with a rake quickly smoothed away the furrow. And suddenly, nothing remained but the memory.

'That, my friend,' slurred the bleary-eyed, half-drunk Barth, his once-white uniform wrinkled and dotted with red stains from his now empty *bota* bag, 'I believe, is the ball game.' He stood up and rubbed his ass to try to get some circulation flowing back to where his pants had stuck to his sweaty backside.

Morgan, his eyes taking in the applauding crowd, didn't answer.

'By the way, Lieutenant,' Barth continued. 'It's fucking unpatriotic to be pulling for the bull.'

Morgan didn't answer as he looked down at the matador who'd stopped in front of Vasques.

'You gotta remember things like that,' slurred Barth. 'The bull ain't supposed to win. You stick with me, kid, I'll teach you the ropes. Just remember, when in Rome . . .'

Morgan wasn't listening, but was watching the young matador who was bowing with elegant grace to the applauding little group sitting on the other side of Vasques.

Accepting their applause, the matador casually threw one of the severed ears toward the young woman next to Barth.

Morgan knew instinctively she wasn't going to even attempt to catch the gory prize. And quickly, with movements more graceful than might have been expected from a man of his size, he reached across Barth and plucked it out of the air for her.

Morgan offered the gruesome trophy to her. She acknowledged the honor from the matador with a nod. But she declined to take the ear from Morgan.

'Thank you,' he said to her as he let the ear drop back into the dirt of the arena below them.

She smiled slightly to show her appreciation.

'Make sure that fat old bastard pays,' he said, taking her completely by surprise by his bold though crude honesty.

She watched in stunned amusement as the tall, athletically graceful American wove his way through the crowd streaming toward the exits. Finally, he dropped down into one of the dark tunnels and disappeared from her view.

As the black rounded bow of the Triton plowed effortlessly through the growing swells of the open ocean, the wind carried the spray back across the bridge like a gentle misty rain.

Morgan lifted his arm and checked his watch. A little after 4 am. It's over! he thought. At least the hard part.

Another five minutes and they'd pass the sea buoy that marked the entrance to the channel into Guam's harbor. 'After the buoy we'll be in water deep enough to hide from anything in the world.'

He stared back at the disappearing island. In the distance, the tender had grown so small he could barely make out her twinkling lights or fading silhouette.

As they cleared the island, the Triton started to roll like some great black whale gently riding the swells of the ocean currents.

'Son-of-a-bitch!' he said quietly to himself as his mind relaxed enough to allow what they had just accomplished scream up through the tension.

Suddenly he whirled, almost scaring the shit out of Barth and Nichols.

'Goddamn!' he screamed to the two open-mouthed men standing in the lookout stations. 'We really did it!'

'They are gonna shit,' Barth screamed back. 'They are truely gonna shit!'

Morgan climbed back over the canopy and pounded them both on the back and shoulder. Pummeling them from the excitement, he grabbed their white hats and threw them over the side into the black ocean and messed up their hair like a deliriously happy schoolboy.

Finally, he held up both arms, and over the sound of the wind and crashing sea, screamed a monstrous, savage scream of joy.

5

'This is the President.'

'Klein here, Mr President. Sorry to disturb you. But I'm afraid we have an emergency that involves a nuclear weapons system.'

'Jesus,' the President sighed heavily. 'OK. I'm on my way,' and groped to replace the phone. God, doesn't it ever end, he thought, trying to fight off the craving ache to lay his head back down and go back to sleep.

He found the cradle and hung the phone back up. Quickly, he swung out of the warm bed. His wife rolled over and pulled the covers up against the chill of the early morning air.

'Mac?'

'Got a problem. Go back to sleep, sweetheart. I'll see you at breakfast.'

'One of these nights they're going to screw up and you're going to get at least half a night's sleep,' she mumbled almost to herself from the blackness beneath the blankets.

'That's something that would really worry me,' he lied as he slipped on his robe and quietly left.

Vince Klein was sitting with half a dozen other nervous, drawn men in the President's private study far removed from the Oval Office.

To the public and those who didn't know him, Klein seemed the most illogical choice the President could have made for his top civilian adviser. But those who knew him realized his disorganized appearance and abrasive manner were façades which hid a brilliant computerlike mind with uncanny powers of foresight.

A short fiery Jew married to a stubborn Polish Catholic half his age, most of his formal education had come from the streets. It started in the Marines where he made history by being one of the only casualties in the Lebanon Crisis in the late fifties.

He had spent the night before the landing shooting craps on a blanket below decks aboard a rusty troop carrier. He'd busted everyone but a Filipino steward's mate and an obnoxious master sergeant who kept trying to break his luck. The more he won, the more the sergeant seethed at the luck of this 'young shithead'.

The only thing that finally broke up the game was the dawn landing.

Klein felt like shit. But he took great satisfaction knowing he had won and won big. And the asshole sergeant was going to feel worse that he did. Especially since he was the big loser.

Klein didn't have any idea how shitty he felt until he stepped to the rail to go over the side. Looking over at the loading master, he saw it was the asshole sergeant from the crap game.

As Klein climbed over the side, the sergeant looked over and sneered. 'Have fun, pussy. Soon as you're gone, I'm gonna hit the sack.'

Klein gave him the finger as he climbed down the cargo net toward the waiting assault boats. Suddenly the pack on his back felt like it weighed a ton and his M-1 kept getting caught between his legs.

The next thing he knew, he was falling head first toward the water below. Fortunately, or unfortunately as the case may be, his right leg caught in the net a few feet above the water.

It broke, a spiral fracture halfway between the ankle and knee, just about the same time his helmeted head hit the side of the ship with a resounding ring. The last thing he remembered that day, hanging upside down in the net with a broken leg, was wondering whether he was going to drown first . . . or was he going to get crushed like a bug between the ship and the waiting assault boat?

Fortunately for him the boatswain's mate at the helm of the assault boat was an old salt from the Korean conflict and had the boat backing away as soon as he saw Klein falling.

They saved his leg, but the Marine Corps figured his beach-assaulting days were over. So they gave him a Purple Heart, a monthly disability check, and a free ride home.

Back on the streets in Detroit because he was a 'vet', and had received some good press, a local union leader gave him a job in a profession that would hold his fascination for the rest of his life – the United Auto Workers' Union.

He fell in love with the Union. It represented a force that could stand up to power, wealth, politicians. The Union took shit from nobody.

After thirty years, he wasn't number one. He never would be. He didn't have the polish or the independent money. But on the other hand, he had most of the power. Let the spotlight-minded assholes fight for the big desks, but he controlled the Union's hidden clout, the pension and strike funds.

And if anybody wanted to be number one, they had to 'sleep in his bed'. Everyone in the industry knew that. That's why the President had come to him before the last election and asked him to be his Chief of Staff.

In a lengthy tête-à-tête, the President told him how he felt it was vital to the country to have someone with Klein's expertise in a top advisory position.

'Bullshit,' Klein said. Without him, he wouldn't have to worry about any decisions. Because without his support, he wouldn't have any decisions to worry about, because he wouldn't be the President.

The President howled with laughter. 'That's why I want you,' he said. 'With that type of bluntness I'll never have to worry about bullshit in my staff meetings.'

Klein nodded, 'That's for sure.'

'I'm sorry I can't offer you the Vice-President's spot,' the President said. 'But I'm going with an old sentimental name. He's too senile for anything other than helping me win. Besides, to be frank, as VP, you wouldn't be able to use that honesty now, would you?'

They both looked at each other for a few moments.

'I want you to give it some serious thought,' the President said as he rose to leave. 'With the two of you, I can win.'

So Klein thought it over and accepted. And helped him win.

Klein could hear the rain splattering against the shrubbery next to the open window as they waited in the President's private study.

On the President's order, the window was always open. Even in cold weather.

One thing Klein would never get used to was this man's passion for fresh air. Oh, he knew all the bullshit about how he'd been born in the 'Big Sky Country', son of a rancher and the most important politician to come out of the Northwest. But if he wanted fresh air, he sure wasn't going to get it downwind from Capitol Hill.

The faces of the half-dozen advisors looked up as the President barged into the study. For a moment he didn't speak as he looked around at the red-eyed faces of men constantly awakened in the middle of the night.

'Good morning, gentlemen,' he finally said cheerfully. 'Glad to see everyone up so bright and early.'

Everyone mumbled acknowledgment of another night shot to hell by being dragged out of bed for their nightly crisis.

'Almost thought someone screwed up and forgot to schedule something for tonight,' he said, yawning and stretching his Gary Cooper body.

They all chuckled at his by now standard joke.

'OK, Klein. Gentlemen. What the hell's going on?' he sighed as he slumped back in a bright overstuffed chair next to his massive desk that his wife had picked out even though it didn't match the decor.

'I'm afraid a Triton submarine is missing,' said an immaculately dressed admiral standing next to Klein, coming directly to the point.

'Jesus Christ!' the President said almost inaudibly. He got up and went around behind his desk where he picked up an ancient, well-used pipe.

Klein and the others waited as he expertly filled the crusty bowl. When he was in public, true to his Western image, he traded his pipe for a can of Prince Albert and rolled his own.

He struck a sulphur-headed match and puffed quickly on the pipe. 'Which one?' he finally asked.

'The *Lewis & Clark* in the Pacific off Guam,' answered the admiral.

He settled back into the heavy leather chair behind his desk. 'How long's she been overdue and what happened?' he asked puffing nervously on his pipe.

'She was just going on patrol,' the admiral shrugged, handing the President a dispatch. 'We don't even know for sure she's down. But from all indications, we have to assume she's not only down, but lost.'

The President glanced quickly through the message trying to decipher the decoded mumbo-jumbo that made up most Navy messages.

TO CIC: OSCAR – OSCAR
FROM: COMSUBPAC VIA COMPAC VIA CNO

SSGN999 MISSING PRESUMED DOWN/NEGATIVE/REPEAT/
NEGATIVE DIVING COMMUNICATION RECEIVED/EN

'Isn't she the new one Congress bitched about spending so much for?' asked the President.

'I'm afraid so,' Admiral Whittiker sighed.

As Chief of Naval Operations, Whittiker was a no-nonsense, by the book disciplinarian. A lean, tan, ex-submariner himself, he had been appointed CNO by the President over many officers his senior.

The President was proud of this appointment as Whittiker had taken a Navy heavy in desks and light in ships, rampant with waste, political intrigue, and lazy, under-preparedness and turned it completely around.

The admiral's new Navy, although small in numbers and hardware, was once again respected as one of the deadliest and technically superior navies in the world.

'OK. Give me everything I'll need to know,' said the President.

Whittiker nodded and picked up a heavy folder marked 'Top Secret' and scanned through several pages.

'Commissioned last June, she was just out of the Yards at Bremmerton. Guam was her first stop after her shakedown cruise. She was armed with a full complement of new Poseidon ULMS-11s. Had the newest fire-control system. The best crew, 114 men, 14 officers. She's the newest of her class. All in all, just like a new penny.' The admiral rattled off mechanically from the file. He never wasted time mincing words or harboring unspoken opinions, which was another personal attribute respected by his colleagues.

'How many Poseidons?' asked the President.

'Twenty-four. All nuclear MIRVs,' he said, turning to the Top Secret Target Index at the back of the folder in a separate envelope. 'Let's see . . . sixteen are targeted for fourteen strike zones, 224 targets. All military in nature. The balance are programmed for sixty-four targets. All civilian in nature. Plus she had six torpedo launch cruise missiles, each targeted for six separate targets.'

'Son-of-a-bitch!' Klein whispered.

'Great God in Heaven!' said the President. 'She's really loaded for bear.'

The admiral nodded. 'Lots of bears out in the world these

days,' he said matter-of-factly.

'Any possibility of survivors?' Klein asked.

'I guess that should be our first order of business,' said the President. 'We should start notifying their families as soon as we get a roster.'

'I'm afraid that's out of the question, Mr President,' the admiral interrupted. 'At least for the time being.'

'I'm afraid I don't understand, Whitt.'

'Well, sir, the *Lewis & Clark* is a weapons system absolutely vital to national security. Until we've either located or isolated the area and determined whether or not anything is recoverable, it would be foolish to even let on the possibility exists that she's down.'

'I see,' mused the President. 'Gentlemen. Are we all in agreement?'

Taking Klein's cue, the other advisors nodded.

'What about the chances for survivors in something like this?' the President asked.

Whittiker shook his head. 'Two,' he replied flatly. 'Slim and none.'

'All right, Whitt. Find the damn thing and find out what the hell happened,' the President said. 'Anything else?'

'Yes, sir,' said Whittiker. 'I'll need your authority to release the operational area for the search units. And to confirm Bandit Time.' He handed the President the sealed envelope holding the Top Secret operational orders for the missing Triton.

'What the hell is Bandit Time?' he said, breaking the seal and signing the order.

'Well, sir, the *Lewis & Clark* wasn't due to get underway until 0600. According to ComSubPac, she evidently got underway around 0400. Western Defense and SEATO have operational plans based on her arrival and departure times. So any change by any ship or aircraft carrying nuclear hardware must be acknowledged within a certain time period. Or they'll consider her hostile.'

'You mean if she's not in trouble, and they don't hear from us, they'll try to sink her?'

'Yes, sir,' the admiral nodded.

'Were you aware of the change of departure time?'

Whittiker shook his head.

'Any possibility that she's not sunk, but suffered some kind of communications breakdown?' asked Klein.

'Absolutely not. She has too many alternate systems.'

'Well, goddammit!' the President said, getting irritated. 'Is it unusual for a nuclear submarine to get underway earlier than scheduled?'

The admiral shrugged and shook his head. 'It's not uncommon. The captain might have wanted to reach his diving area ahead of some nasty weather. Or a Russian might have been reported near that area. There're a hundred reasons he could have done so. In any event, the captain's solely responsible.'

'Well, goddammit,' the President suddenly got to his feet. 'She damn well better be sitting on the bottom of the ocean somewhere. Or that solely responsible captain's going to get his ass kicked up around his ears.'

6

The Triton glided through the ocean depths as effortlessly as an eagle riding invisible hot air currents high in a clear summer sky.

On the surface, bright with reflected sunlight, the temperature was creeping into the eighties. While 500 feet below the lazy, rolling swells of the surface, the water was achingly cold, and as totally black as a starless night.

Like a giant starship she glided through the heavy-pressured ocean depths with brutish, almost unlimited power. Power that was generated by the eerie blue glow from the nuclear mass housed behind tons of lead and polyplastic neutron shielding that made up the S7Z water-cooled reactor that fed her hungry steam turbines.

On the deserted, sparkling surface, it was ghostly quiet. There was absolutely no telltale trace of sound from the Triton as she slipped past in the depths below. But to the schools of gentle dolphins, flashing yellowtail, and clouds of snapping shrimp, the noise made as she passed blindly through their world was as deafening as a high-balling freight train roaring past a grade crossing, and the water churned up by her massive propeller left a swirling wake of turbulence miles behind her.

Inside the Triton, far below the rolling and pitching action of the surface, the ride was so smooth she seemed absolutely motionless. At high speeds the only clue that she might be moving came via the distant vibration generated by the glistening alloy propeller as it spun invisibly on the end of its finely tuned shaft.

In the control room Barth sat at the diving station keeping the bow constantly pointed to within a quarter of a degree of his prescribed course.

His eyes constantly checked the gauges on the manifold in front of the diving station: depth gauge, bow, sail, plane indicators, and compass heading. All of which he controlled with one wheel, similar to the way a pilot controls all angles and positions of his aircraft.

Behind him, Morgan was leaning against the operations table, thumbing through the electronics technician's forgotten paperback. Occasionally, he glanced up as Barth made a slight adjustment that kept the boat unerringly on course and depth.

Looking around the control room, through tired, bloodshot eyes, Morgan marveled at the technology billions of dollars of research and years of experience had purchased. Blinking lights behind shining pearl and ruby switches sparkled like some Mad Hatter's Christmas tree.

Some of the twinkling lights illuminated solenoid switches that controlled the various air systems. Systems with air pressures ranging from a mere thirty to forty pounds, all the way to a nightmarish 6,000 pounds per square inch. Air systems that could gently push warm water through a spigot . . . or crush plate steel or a seaman's body with an impartial ease.

Other switches controlled sophisticated sensory equipment that warned when critical parts or systems were reaching questionable value, or needed to be replaced. Other parts of the system analyzed breakdowns and ordered repairs.

Everywhere, from the gray panel that housed the controls for the massive hydraulic system to the fire control panels that breathed life into the sleeping missiles, to the ultrasensitive and infinitesimally accurate navigational system, green and red dials and gauges sparkled as the finely calibrated instruments displayed readout information vital to operating the boat safely.

Barth took his hands off the controls, stretched and groaned, trying to shake off his drowsiness.

Barth looked around at him bleary-eyed. 'I'm gonna have to crash pretty soon.'

Morgan nodded. Reaching under the operations table, he picked up the sound-powered phone and cranked the handle several times. He waited a couple of seconds for an answer and when there was none he cranked it again.

'Jonesey?' he said as someone came on the line. 'Morgan here. How you feeling?'

'Like shit,' Jones answered over the hollow-sounding phone.

'Yeah?' Welcome to the club. But I'm afraid it's time to disturb that beauty sleep. Barth's crashing out on me. Take the next watch, okay?'

'Okay, I'm on my way,' he groaned through a voice heavy with sleep. 'Let me grab a hot cup first.'

'Okay. Bring me one, too,' Morgan said, replacing the receiver. 'He's on his way.'

A few minutes later, a shirtless Jones came in from the Crew's

Mess carrying two cups of strong coffee left over from yesterday's pot. 'Black and bitter,' he said, handing one of the cups to Morgan.

He tapped Barth on the shoulder. 'Whatta ya got?'

'Oh, I make the depth at about six-five-oh. And a course more or less of one-four-two,' he said as Jones slipped down into the warm seat. 'If I get any calls I'll be sacked out up there in the officers' quarters. You'll know me right off. I'll be the only one with a hard on,' he said as he unbuckled his pants and pulled out his shirt.

Jones shook his head and grinned as Barth disappeared through the hatch leading forward toward the officers' quarters. As he leaned forward, his bare back made a ripping sound as it came unstuck from the slick plastic seat. He adjusted the lights on the control panel and slouched back. Morgan watched as the wiry little man made his adjustments and settled back into the seat nonchalantly taking over the controls.

As an auxiliary man, Jones claimed he knew every goddamn nut and bolt onboard. Tritons held no magic or mystery for him. He'd mastered the engines, pumps, motors, compressors, the maze of systems years ago at sea via countless hours in boring Navy and civilian contractor schools.

Morgan and this quiet, sullen little man went back a long time together. He could trust him. And he trusted Morgan.

Years earlier, he and Morgan had arrived on their first submarine the same day. It was an old Fleet boat that had been in mothballs and they went through three months of hell together recommissioning her.

Morgan seemed to be a young, bright-eyed ensign destined for command. And Jones was a high-school dropout with a brilliant mechanical aptitude who the Navy hoped to convert into a career man.

They probably would have succeeded had not one of Jones's boats returned to the shipyards in Charleston for an overhaul just in time for him to ship over a second time. As a reward, the Navy gave him a thirty-day leave and a shipping-over bonus that amounted to several thousand bucks which he immediately set out to drink up and fuck up as fast as he could.

A few weeks later, in a drunken melancholy mood, he married a flashing-eyed barmaid from one of the jukebox-blaring clip joints near the old slave quarters in 'Old Town' and set up housekeeping in a tiny, mildew-smelling, paint-peeling apartment located over an all-night liquor store.

Unfortunately, her flashing eyes didn't match her flashing brain. And when Jones left for sea trials, she mistakenly thought he'd left on another cruise. So, when he returned three days later, he found his place in the saddle had already been filled by a blond, crew-cut Marine MP from the Main Gate at the shipyards.

Not wanting to interfere in their marital problem, the Marine went out the second-storey window. It took most of the skin off his face and he broke his leg on the sidewalk after somersaulting off the liquor store's flashing neon sign before managing to escape the raging little seaman.

His rather undignified retreat left Jones's hysterical wife trapped inside the apartment where she tried to elude him by locking herself in the bathroom. It took three beefy local cops to pull him off her after he shattered the door, her face, and the toilet in which he was trying to drown her.

The cops, grinning 'good old country boys', took Jones downtown where they had to rough him up a little before he'd settle down. Then they listened in sympathy as the little man cussed his misfortune at marrying an angel that turned out to be an unfaithful wife.

They started to feel sorry for him and left him alone in an unlocked interrogation room for a few minutes to get him some black coffee and doughnuts and try to figure out how to cut him loose without charging him.

But they were wasting their time. When they came back with the coffee and doughnuts he was gone.

By the time they tracked him down, he'd caught up with his wife, who by then was feeling like she was caught in some bizarre, endless nightmare.

On catching up with her at the Greyhound bus depot waiting to go back home, he strewed her hastily packed cheap suitcase all over the station's filthy tile floor, ripped off her clothes, and with a can of model spray paint grabbed from the gift stand, sprayed a bright red 'Whore' on the white skin that ran from her bouncing little breasts to her little patch of soft pubic hair.

Then, dragging her screaming through the panicky crowd, he tied her spread-eagled across the hood of the police car he'd stolen when he escaped, and drove up and down the busy downtown streets with red lights flashing and siren blaring, with the hysterical girl trussed on the hood like some giant fleshy ornament.

The traffic jam he created just about brought the town to a

standstill, before the embarrassed cops could corner him again. By the time they got him back to the station, they'd pretty well proved they weren't the 'good old boys' they'd led him to believe they were.

The publicity created such a furor that the Navy wanted to deal with him themselves, and an obliging municipal judge, thankful to be getting rid of the problem, obliged.

Sitting at a stark table with Morgan, who had been appointed to handle his defense, they watched as the senior officers from the local submarine squadrons, who were to comprise the court-martial board, filed in.

'Don't look too good!' Jones whispered.

'Could be worse!' Morgan whispered back. 'They could be civilians.'

Jones nodded and smiled slightly. 'No need to be wasting too much of your time, Lieutenant. I know they've been told to get my ass and get it quick.'

'I wouldn't worry about what they been told,' Morgan lied as he looked through some of the defense papers he'd prepared. 'Only problem I can see, outside of the fact that you're guilty as hell, is the captain who's the head of the court. Iron-balled, by-the-book son-of-a-bitch! He's going to be our biggest problem.'

And he was. Even with Morgan's well-meaning defense, and a mostly sympathetic court, they couldn't keep Jones from being sentenced to the hellhole of all military prisons – Portsmouth.

The only thing that kept him from a life sentence was that his ex-wife was afraid that if she testified, someday he'd escape and come looking for her. So the only testimony against him came from the civilian arresting officers whose only charges against him were disturbing the peace, car theft, and escape.

While he was the 'guest' of the grunts at Portsmouth, Morgan made it a point to keep in touch with the little man. After he got out, despite his dishonorable discharge, Morgan made it possible for him to find a decent job and slip back into civilian life.

Jones never forgot his efforts and over the years his loyalty to Morgan was quietly fanatical.

'So, whatta ya think?' Jones asked, yawning, trying to wake up. 'We OK?'

Morgan nodded, 'You can bet your ass that by now they

think she's down. They'll have everything, anything that can fly or float out looking for her.'

Jones sipped from the steaming mug. 'Kinda quiet,' he said, yawning again.

'A little,' Morgan nodded.

'You sure everyone decided to stay?'

'I think so,' Morgan chuckled. 'Adamson's still watching the percolator. Nardulli's in tubes forward, and Nichols is in sonar.'

'He ain't gonna be able to hear shit in sonar until we turn north and slow this beast down and creep up to our operating area,' Jones said.

'Yeah, I know. But he says it makes him feel better if he keeps the seat warm,' he said, thinking about their circuitous course that would take them north of Australia, zigzag through the Solomon Islands before rounding the Fijis and turning northward toward an empty tract of ocean near Palmyra almost 1,000 miles south of Honolulu.

That area was the heavily traveled lanes where any noise they might make would be lost in the constant noises generated by the endless parade of ships traveling between the Orient and the States.

'I'm going to take a quick check through the boat. At 2400 Adamson's coming to "All-Stop" for an hour. That'll give Nichols enough time to give us a good sonar sweep and see what's in the neighborhood that we should know about. Take the trim manifold and keep her hovering around 500 feet.'

Jones nodded. 'You oughtta try to catch a little sack time yourself.'

'Thanks. I'm OK.'

'You wouldn't know it to look at your eyeballs. Look like they'd glow in the dark.'

Morgan smiled. 'You think they look bad from the outside, you should see what they look like from in here. Anyway, after Nichols makes a couple of sonar sweeps, I'll crash out for a few hours.'

7

An hour later Morgan had almost finished his inspection of the boat and so far all her systems checked out. He marveled at how the boat almost ran herself. The last stop on his rounds was the forward torpedo room.

As he came into the compartment, he saw the peaceful form of Nardulli sprawled across a mattress in the middle of the passageway in an exhausted sleep. Bending down, Morgan shook him softly by the shoulder.

At Morgan's touch, Nardulli erupted into a twisting frenzy. Rolling off the mattress, he swung up a small Israeli sub-machine gun that had been nestled in the crook of his arm and jammed it into Morgan's face.

'Jesus! Hold it! Take it easy!' Morgan screamed, holding his hands motionless above his head. 'Take it easy . . . ' Morgan whispered as he remained perfect still, waiting for Nardulli's sleep-clogged brain to clear.

'Oh God!' Nardulli said, lowering the gun in hands that were trembling noticeably. His heart was pounding and his nerves were jangling from the surge of adrenalin that had roared through his system. 'Goddamn! I'm sorry, Morgan. I must have crashed out. I didn't even think I was tired. Next thing I feel something shaking me . . . '

'No sweat,' Morgan said. ' 'Course, I must admit, you could tell I was getting a little tense when I shit in my pants,' he joked, slapping Nardulli on the back to show he really understood and to soothe his nerves. 'Anything stirring?' he asked, pointing to the hatch barely visible under the plastic-covered mattress that Nardulli had been sleeping on.

'No. I don't think so. At least not before I crashed out,' he stood up breathing heavily as his heart was still pounding. 'But it's still probably a little too soon, don't you think?'

Nardulli cautiously slid the mattress away from the hatch. Cocking the submachine gun, he quickly threw it open.

At the bottom of the hatch, a large storeroom was bathed in the bright lights from several spotlights hanging from the overhead. On the deck of the storeroom, crammed together like so many sardines, was the crew.

They were all still unconscious and had all been trussed up inside lightweight straitjackets with heavy leather straps which had been brought onboard in two of the heavy seabags.

Each man's legs had been taped to the man's leg on either side of him. And because their heads had been stuffed inside black cloth sacks, they looked like so many faceless, limp mannequins.

'Phewww!' winced Morgan as the stifling heat from the tightly packed bodies raced upward toward the cooler air of the upper compartment. 'Boy! There's no doubt about how effective the gas was.'

'Yeah,' said Nardulli. 'More'n half of 'em took a dump in their skivvies from it,' he said, wrinkling his nose.

'It reminds me of the old days when they used to call them "sewer pipe" sailors.'

'Why was that?' Nardulli asked, taking out a handkerchief as he tried to blow the stench out of his nostrils.

' 'Cuz you didn't have to see a submariner coming. You could smell him.'

'I can believe it,' he said, closing the hatch.

Suddenly the intercom crackled. 'Bridge? Sonar. I've got a contact.'

Instinctively, Morgan bolted down the passageway, leaving Nardulli standing over the smelly hatch.

Roaring through the control room, he shot down the chrome ladder, behind the diving station that lead down to the lower level.

'Take the helm, Jonesey,' he yelled as he passed Jones sitting at the trim manifold. 'Make your depth 1200 feet and ring up three knots.'

At the bottom of the ladder, he came to another hatch. Slamming it open, he dropped down into the silent, dark world crammed between row after row of gray panels filled with sophisticated electronic equipment that was affectionately referred to as the 'sonar shack'.

Nichols, the sonar man, was sitting in front of one of the consoles with a set of earphones hung partly over one ear and partly off the other. He was cranking a heavy chrome wheel that jutted out from the front of one of the instrument-cluttered consoles like the small, shiny steering wheel of a powerful racing car.

Like a driver rounding a high-banked racetrack, he trained

the wheel back and forth, scanning a distant sound source.

Back and forth. Listening.

Back and forth. Back and forth. Finally, he focused on one bearing. Adjusting several filters, he calmly looked over his shoulder at Morgan.

'Whatta ya got?' Morgan asked, panting.

'Don't know yet,' said Nichols, as he reached up and energized the target tracking computer.

'Shit!' Morgan whispered, not trying to hide his apprehension.

Once the TTC was energized the front of its panel looked like a fireworks display. Lights started flashing and computer read-out tapes started clicking as the computer took over and automatically started preparing the submarine to fire torpedoes at what might be an enemy target.

Deep inside the intricately woven circuits, microcosmic flashes darted from one part of the system to another, carrying preprogrammed commands within the Triton's fire control system that took complete control of the ship and started making minute alterations in depth, course, and speed automatically.

As Morgan watched, the lights from the fire control panel started their sequential blinking from red to green, which was the visual signal that the system was feeding updated target data to the sleeping torpedoes. The outer doors of the torpedo tubes were on standby and would open automatically when the fire control sequence reached its final countdown stage. The impulse air, that which expelled the torpedo out of the tube like a dart from a blowgun, had reached operational pressure. And, as Morgan watched, all the sequences registered their readiness on the panel by changing from a red light to a green.

Finally, only two lights – on opposite ends of the panel – remained red. One was the 'Fire' button; the other was the 'Override' button, which could override and abort any firing run.

'What's the range?' Morgan asked.

'About sixty-five miles, give or take five thousand yards or so.'

'Speed?'

'Wait one,' Nichols said, turning back to the wheel. He trained it back and forth as he relocated the center of the ever-moving target. He reached up and clicked on a stopwatch mounted on the bulkhead next to the console and silently counted the RPMs of the distant screws to himself.

After a few seconds he clicked off the stopwatch and punched the figures from the stopwatch and the screw count into the miniature calculator mounted on the console. 'Fourteen knots,' he read from the calculator's red digital display lights.

Morgan nodded, 'Can you tell what she is yet?' he asked, hoping it wasn't a warship. He knew they could handle any confrontation. But the time wasn't yet right to be put to any test.

Nichols spun the chrome wheel back and forth. After a few sweeps, he reached behind Morgan and turned on a tape recorder. In the dark, Morgan watched the almost hypnotic dance of the meters on the consoles as they silently beat out the rhythm from the sounds of the distant ship.

Nichols taped the contact for several minutes, stopped, and rewound the tape. He quickly patched the recorder into a filter system and adjusted several knobs until he could clear out some of the ocean garbage mixed in with the sounds from the distant contact as they floated through the dark ocean depths to the massive array of hydrophones built into the graceful bow of the black Triton.

'Small freighter. I'd say in the fifty-thousand-ton range. Riding kinda light. Probably half empty,' Nichols said, relieved, as he reached for a cigarette. The flare from his match lit up the space for a brief moment. In the glare he could see Morgan's mind clicking through all the possibilities. He shook his head in amazement at the way the man could still function and demand effort from his brain that hadn't been rested for untold days.

'A warship could sound like a freighter riding light,' Morgan said, pulling anxiously at his ear.

Nichols smiled up at him and shook his head. 'Sure. It could. But it's not. Propulsion's not right. This one's old and tired. Single screw. Shaft sounds like it hasn't been pulled in quite awhile and needs some work,' droned Nichols as he clicked off fact after fact of what that characteristic sounds from the distant contact meant to the trained ear.

'How about COMSA? You think she might be classified?'

Nichols shrugged. 'I don't know. Let's give it a try,' he said, as he took the tape from the recorder and placed it on the front of a small computer behind the ladder. He pushed the 'Run' button and the tape unwound through the machine at an unusually high speed. The tape had no sooner ended when the computer started clattering and a report started unrolling from a slot on the top of the machine. The clattering stopped and the machine turned itself off. Nichols tore off the report and glanced at it quickly. Shaking his head, he passed it to Morgan.

Morgan took it and read it. 'Nothing? Jesus Christ, it sure sounds noisy enough to have some characteristics that could give us her name.'

Nichols shook his head again. 'Well she might be some old bear they dragged out of mothballs. Or she might have just never been taped and classified.'

Morgan angrily rumpled the paper into a ball and threw it against the bulkhead.

'You sure she wasn't pinging or anything?' he asked, knowing that if the ship was, chances were she wasn't a civilian ship.

'Hey!' interrupted Nichols with a frown on his face. 'I know my job. If I'm not mistaken, that's why you invited me on this little buggy ride in the first place.'

'Yeah. I guess you're right. No, I know you're right,' he said as he rubbed his face with both hands trying to wipe away the exhaustion creeping back into his body.

Nichols leaned back, stretched, and took a deep drag from his cigarette. ' 'Course if you're really worried, we could go ahead and sink her,' he said, an elfish grin crossing his face.

Morgan didn't answer.

For a few moments he watched as the fire control systems kept electronically realigning themselves in anticipation of the 'Fire' command.

Nichols' grin faded as he waited apprehensively for Morgan to answer.

Finally, Morgan heaved himself to his aching feet and patted Nichols on the back.

'We'll wait this time,' he said.

Nichols breathed a quiet sigh of relief and pushed the 'Override' button that would start the abort sequence.

When the last fire control panel light finally flashed red, Morgan started up the ladder. Reaching the top, he opened the hatch and whispered back, 'Keep an eye on him for a while though. OK?'

'Fuck you,' moaned Nichols as Morgan closed the hatch.

8

The maneuvering room was uncomfortably chilly and as quiet as the inside of a crypt.

Adamson, the 'civilian' from the bridge, was hunched over a worn Bible under the soft, indirect lights that seemed to halo the spartan-looking panels that controlled the reactor.

Deeply engrossed in the Scriptures, Adamson didn't bother to look up until Morgan spoke.

'Everything OK?' Morgan asked, slumping down onto the upholstered observer's bench directly behind where Adamson sat.

Adamson looked up, and briefly scanned the instrumentation before nodding through a distant smile.

He returned to his reading as Morgan said, 'Contact was some old tramp on her way west to the east.'

Adamson looked up and briefly smiled again.

'Thought maybe that was it,' Adamson said, closing the Bible and laying it gently in his lap. 'When Jones went back to hovering. After ringing up three knots, that is,' he added.

Morgan started to respond but didn't. It was a son-of-a-bitch trying to make conversation with Adamson. 'He's like a dull book . . . he'll put you to sleep when nothing else will,' he thought.

Heaving himself up, Morgan said, 'I'm going to hit the sack for a couple of hours. You be OK back here till then?'

' 'Course,' he answered through the smile that was almost permanently frozen on his face. He picked up his Bible and walked with Morgan to the hatch that led forward into the next compartment which housed the missile tubes.

As Morgan disappeared through 'Sherwood Forest', the largest compartment on the boat, Adamson's gaze settled hypnotically on the complex of missile tubes.

Like a child with a new toy, he kept constantly checking the compartment to make sure everything was still there.

He clasped his Bible to his breast and prayed to his angry God that by the time they launched the missiles, his second wife would have read how he was part of the crew that was holding the world for ransom.

He smiled at the pleasure of how bizarre it would be if she could be in one of the target cities and die at the last minute while reading his name emblazoned in the banner headlines.

He had been madly in love with his first wife, Faye, a childhood sweetheart. But a hurricane had roared in from the Gulf of Mexico and when it left, Faye and their tiny trailer were never found.

Since her 'disappearance', there were many nights when Adamson was suicidal from the loneliness her death left him trapped in.

Finally, after an all-too-brief courtship, he married a girl he met at a Houston Oilers game at the Astrodome.

It wasn't long before he realized she wasn't Faye. And she realized he wasn't the submarine hero she thought she'd met at the Astrodome.

In his desperation to make the marriage work, he even tried experimenting with pot. Which was terrifying. Because, after all, he was an officer in the US Navy. And growing up in the Bible Belt, he'd been educated to believe that marijuana's roots were in hell.

It did relax him though. And it seemed to ease the constant agony of Faye's loss that tore through his guts every minute of his waking life. And people who turned on around him seemed enchanted by his preachings. His ramblings. His wandering, pleasing philosophies.

It wasn't until his last night with his new wife that he realized most of them were just stoned out of their minds. And would have been just as happy listening to a stuck phonograph record, which most of them considered him to be anyway.

That night, he and Jan stayed late at a party to visit some of her 'old school chums'. It was at the height of the craze when it was very fashionable to experiment with a variety of foods laced with the 'killer weed'.

So, after many dry, gritty pieces of newly-baked brownies, he started a sentence that went on and on and on. It went on so long that not only could he not figure out how to finish it but he lost track of what he'd started talking about in the first place.

Finally, he dropped into a stupor. A foggy, wandering haze, until he passed out on the floor next to the couch halfway under a shiny chrome-and-glass coffee table.

It seemed like years had passed when from out of the inky

swirling depths, he heard someone whisper, 'What about "Just Plain Bill?" '

The whispering voice seemed to float past in distorted bits and pieces like from out of the depths of some dark, endless tunnel.

'Don't worry about him. He's so stoned he's like a fucking zombie,' he heard another voice answer. He listened for several more light-years before opening his eyes ever so slowly to see who the hell was talking about him.

His eyes finally cracked open a slit.

'My God,' he thought in a panic. Through the haze it looked like the distorted voices had come from the core of some indescribable monster made up of innumerable writhing arms, legs, and heads interwoven into one repulsive ugly beast.

'You sure?' the voice whispered from the center of the writhing beasts. Forcing his eyes open a little more, he finally brought the monster into focus. Across the darkened room he could see that one of the voices had come from his wife lying entwined between two vague blobs that, when they moved, he figured out were two other bodies.

His heart roared like a blinding explosion when a paunchy, pimply shouldered man mounted his wife with jerky, sporadic thrusts. While at the same time, his wife's big-breasted 'old school chum' seemed hungrily to be trying to engulf as much of Jan's glistening naked body with her mouth as she could.

He watched as the veins in his wife's neck pounded with familiar excitement. Excitement he thought only he could arouse.

Slowly starting to reach the wonderful agony of orgasm, she started a low grunting sound that grew until it sounded to him like a pig caught in a mucky bog.

Adamson's heart was pounding so loudly he thought they would surely hear. He was humiliated. His face was so flushed it felt like he had a bad sunburn.

But he was so hypnotized by the sight that he couldn't interrupt. If for no other reason than they would know that he'd been watching.

Angrily, he squeezed his eyes shut as he tried to shut out the sounds.

But he couldn't.

They seemed to grow louder and louder until he thought his eardrums would shatter. Suddenly, he heard a new sound shattering the already excruciatingly painful sounds from the ménage à trois. Like a madman screaming in the midst of hysterical laughter.

The nightmarish screams and laughter went on and on and on and on. Until finally, when he opened his eyes to locate the screams and stifle them, he realized they were coming from his own throat.

Looking around hysterically, he realized his screams weren't really screams at all. But loud, snakelike hisses erupting up through a voice box paralyzed with agony and loathing and hatred.

Through tear-filled hysterical eyes, he saw that Jan had seen him watching and the mocking laughter was coming from her as she laughed out at him from her intricately woven sexual pin-wheel.

Now he was filled with new life.

Dear God, it was revenge. Yes. But it was called for in the Bible. It was in the Scriptures. A nuclear stoning for the nuclear-age adulteress.

He looked at the shiny metal tubes that housed the deadly missiles and smiled. Smiled at the thought of Jan, her big-boobed blonde friend and the nameless man locked in their lustful climax vaporizing from the ungodly heat in the mush-rooming holocaust he would soon unleash at them.

9

It was another hot, breathless day as the sun beat unmercifully through a crystal sky onto the blue waters of Tumon Bay on Guam's tropical western coast.

In the middle of the bay, the diesel engine of a small gray work boat clattered in what sounded like almost intentional disharmony as the boat putt-putted toward the island-sized submarine tender.

Sitting in the bow, two Navy divers in threadbare, bleached-out bathing suits occasionally jockeyed for a shot at the lifeless breeze, generated as the boat sluggishly made its way across the mirrorlike bay.

The older diver lit a cigarette from the one that had reached a precariously short length and shook his head as the breeze hardly had enough force to blow away his cigarette smoke.

In the stern a sweating, burly black bosun's mate cussed silently as he abruptly had to change course to avoid cutting across the path of two round-bowed Shark/Hooper Shadows on their way out the main channel.

The Shadows were the newest and most radical Fast-Attack ships added to the Navy in over fifty years. Based on the Winchester hovercraft originally developed by Britain, they had been added to the Navy's arsenal after a flurry of squabbling by 'traditionalist' admirals, politicians, and classic ship designers. They were finally added after a determined push by the new Chief of Naval Operations, Admiral Whittiker.

Almost three hundred feet long, powered by four Bristol/Vaught Proteus gas turbines and manned by a small élite crew of six officers and thirty-seven men, they were the new pride of the fleet.

The Navy acknowledged speeds of seventy-five knots and twice the range of the nearest diesel-powered ship, which meant they could do a lot more. They could turn on a dime, travel over shallow water, be maneuvered up a ramp and stored out of the water, eliminating costly dock and maintenance facilities.

They were billed as the wave of the new Navy's future. And there was a long list of volunteers waiting to serve on them.

Bristling with armament, which included surface-to-surface and surface-to-air missile launchers, they had also become the scourge of submarines.

Mainly because they were the only thing, outside of helicopters or fixed-wing aircraft, that could keep up with the speed of the submerged marauders. And they had the range that neither aircraft had.

The bosun's mate and the two divers watched as the Shadows cleared the harbor. Once clear of the breakwater, their gas turbines roared as the high octane fuel poured into the workhouse turbines. Higher and higher they shrieked, until the Shadows literally seemed to be skimming over the crests of the waves like some behemoth skipping stone.

On the stern of the sleek, uncluttered Shadows, the massive, two-storey aircraft-type rudder flapped slightly to port. The ships responded instantly and, in a blast of heat and spray, disappeared behind the jetty that jutted out into the ocean.

But the banshee wail from the guzzling gas turbines thundered across the ocean swells like thunder, long after they had faded from sight.

'Jeeesus!' mouthed one of the divers in quiet awe. 'Beeeutiful! Absolutely beeeutiful!'

'Makes your blood boil to go that fast on top of the water,' said the sullen bosun's mate from the tiller of the chugging boat that now seemed infinitesimally insignificant compared to the Shark/Hooper Shadows. 'All they is is goddamn airplanes tied on top of a couple of inner tubes. Goddamn rubberboaters!' he said, sarcastically.

'Yeah, but wouldn't you just love to be able to ride one of those rubberboats?' said the older of the two divers from the bow.

The black bosun's mate nodded through clenched teeth, knowing what the man meant. The asshole squadron commanders of the Shadows, like the submarine commands, didn't solicit or welcome blacks as crew members.

'Looks like the whole fucking squadron's put to sea,' remarked the younger diver leaning against the gunnel. His red hair matched his red freckly skin which was constantly peeling from hours of exposure to the sun and seawater of Guam.

Having red hair was something he'd had to live with. Especially when one day in front of his class at the Seal School in Virginia, one of the salty instructors said in a thick southern accent, 'Why, you little red on the head like the dick on a dog.'

His classmates roared. And after that, everywhere he went, someone would yell, 'Hey! Red on the head, like the dick on a dog.' A few weeks later, when they found out he was going to 'make it' through the grueling training, they did him a favor and shortened it to just plain 'Dogdick'. Since his hair was responsible for his one-of-a-kind nickname, he'd almost grown to like it.

'Both squadrons are gone. Scuttlebutt has it that new FBM went down her first day out,' the bosun's mate said as he skillfully guided the little boat down the side of the tender toward the stern.

'I sure wouldn't want to be out there with thirty or forty of those bastards screaming round the same part of the ocean all the same time,' said Dogdick as he picked up the bowline coiled under his feet and threw it up to a bored shirtless seaman waiting on the tender.

The line secured, the two divers set about readying their gear for the short inspection dive of the tender's propellers and ton of zinc plates that kept electrolysis from eating through the harder hull plates.

'Wonder why they even bother with all this shit. She ain't even been to sea in over three years,' the bosun's mate said. 'Probably sink if they cast off her mooring lines,' he added as he settled back under the canvas that served as a sunshade from the roasting late morning sun.

'I don't see why they don't just take the damn screws off and store 'em on the dock. That ways, you guys wouldn't have to get all wet,' he scoffed as he took out a pack of rumpled Camels from the sleeve of his white tee shirt.

'We got a strong union,' said Dogdick as he slipped the well-used tank of compressed air over his shoulders and adjusted the straps. 'We work by the hour. You know what I mean?'

'Sure as shit still seems like a waste of time if you ask me,' the bosun said, rearranging the cockpit cushions more comfortably under his rear end.

Dogdick grinned and pulled his mask down over his raw nose. He sat down on the gunnel and fell backward into the blue water. The older diver swung the gray work ladder over the side and stepped up on its tiny platform. He put on his fins and dropped into the water next to the waiting Dogdick.

'Don't run off now, you hear?' Dogdick yelled to the bosun's mate from the water.

Without looking up, the bosun's mate, who'd leaned back and

pulled his hat down over his eyes, raised his right forearm and gave the young diver the finger.

Smiling, both divers cleared their masks, checked their regulators and quickly slid beneath the surface that was shiny from the oil slick that constantly flowed into the Pacific from the myriad of Navy ships anchored in the harbor.

Once beneath the surface, the two divers drifted effortlessly down between gleaming bolts of soft filtered transparent sunlight that seemed to shoot down from the surface.

Drifting down to the brass propellers, they balanced like slow-motion high wire artists on the thick drive shafts that connected the screws to the giant turbines and checked the packing glands that kept the seawater from rushing in past the shaft and the huge bolts that held the propellers in place.

As the two divers worked, the noises from the ship, now awake and alive with thousands of men working in the confines of the miniature, capsulized city, filtered through the water like a distant radio program. The pounding machinery, the whirling of motors, even the sound of voices and footsteps filtered down from the tender. Magnified through the water, the depths were cool – but far from quiet.

Dogdick, his face a few feet from the hull, kicked slowly along the shafts behind the propeller blades that were taller than he was, and slowly drifted toward the bow of the ship. Not wearing a weight belt, he had to use his hands to push off and keep from scraping against the hull, as every few yards his natural buoyancy and the buoyancy from his air tanks kept lifting him into the tender's barnacled underbelly.

Everything checked out. The soft metal of the propeller blades was in good shape. Nothing fouled them, the shafts or the rudder. A quick check of the zinc plates and they could call it a day.

He kicked a little further forward under the tender's rounded hull when a bright reflection from the distant bottom caught his eye.

'Jesus!' he thought. 'What the fuck had they dumped over the side now?' The fucking bosun's mates had a bad habit of conveniently shitcanning the damndest things over the side. Especially things that needed working on. He shoved off from the barnacled bottom and lazily kicked down toward the object gently waving up from the bottom.

The frenzied action of hundreds of little fish feeding on the body of the dead seaman from the Triton floating several feet off the bottom stopped him cold in the water. The arms floating gracefully above his head seemed to be waving a friendly salutation.

'My God!' Dogdick yelled, accidentally spitting out his mouthpiece. He grabbed at it and in a panic dislodged his mask which immediately filled with water. Kicking viciously for the surface, he forgot he was under the tender and smacked into the heavy hull plates near the shafts.

In a daze, he floated toward the surface where the older diver saw him and swam quickly to his side.

'What the hell happened?' the bosun's mate yelled down as the older diver tried to help the choking Dogdick up the ladder into the work boat.

He tried to speak but could only sputter as he coughed up half the seawater he swallowed. 'There's a dead guy down there. Drowned or something,' he finally spat out.

While the bosun's mate helped him into the boat, the older diver cleared his mask and grimly slipped below the water, disappearing in the direction Dogdick had come from.

The bosun's mate helped the still-gagging Dogdick get his tanks and flippers off. He quickly lit a half-soggy cigarette and held it out to the shaking kid.

Dogdick shook his head and suddenly lunged to the side and started heaving up the rest of the oil-filled briny water.

The older diver's head broke the surface next to the ladder and he quickly climbed into the boat.

'Really a dead guy down there?' the bosun asked, not really wanting to know.

The older diver nodded grimly. 'You better move round to the dock,' he said as he unclamped the straps from his dripping tank and let it fall into the bottom of the boat.

'He's dead. And he didn't drown. Somebody put him down there,' he said.

'How long's he been down there?' the bosun asked, starting the little diesel.

'Hard to tell in these waters. Not too long. Couple of days maybe. But you best move your ass. The tender'll want to get him out of there quick 'fore the hungries have him all et up.'

Less than a half hour later, the railing of the tender was lined with white-hatted sailors and khaki-shirted officers of all ranks staring down at the filmy blue surface of the water below.

Two goggled heads broke the surface. 'It's there,' yelled up one of the frogmen to a group of officers waiting on the outboard side of the bridge.

The senior officer, evidently the captain, nodded.

'Bring it up,' he said grimly.

The two frogmen nodded and waited as a beer-bellied chief bosun on the main deck tossed down a smooth white nylon line. One of the frogmen grabbed the braided end of the new line and slid beneath the shiny surface.

'Of course it's there!' muttered Dogdick as he sat in the work boat, still tied up to the stern of the tender. 'Assholes!' he said disgustedly.

The older diver, exhaling smoke through his nose like an aging dragon, took a deep drag on his ever-smoldering Camel and nodded in agreement.

Halfway to the bottom, the frogman snorted to equalize the water pressure pushing painfully in on his eardrums. A few feet from the bottom, he trod water until he located the seaman's remains. Kicking gently, he moved silently through the water over the swaying corpse. Gently, he coiled the line around the dead man's waist and tied the end off in a beautiful butterfly motion that became a bowline knot.

Taking a pair of wire cutters from his weighted belt, he settled onto the mucky bottom so he could get enough leverage to clip through the cable. He had to grind and twist back and forth across the tough cable several times before it parted. As soon as the body was free from its tether, it drifted aimlessly in the gentle current of the ebb tide.

On deck, the chief bosun's mate felt the signal as the frogman gave a couple of sharp tugs on the slack line, and motioned for his gang of young seamen to start hauling up the body.

Watching the body disappear upwards like some grisly dead mackerel on the end of a hook, the frogman started to kick toward the surface. But he couldn't move his feet. For a split second he almost panicked. His flippers had sunk down into the bottom muck. He hated bottom muck. Always had and always would. He didn't like to get near it or touch it. And he guessed subconsciously he felt it would suck him down into its depths like the divers he had seen in the old Saturday morning matinees. Finally, he freed one of his feet and rested it on the concrete-filled case that had tethered the seaman to the bottom. Using the case as solid footing, he pushed off from it until his other foot was free and quickly headed for the surface. Looking back, he saw the case turn slowly over and could see stencilled letter-ing on its muck-covered side.

Rising quickly to the surface, he broke out of the water a few feet from the dead seaman. As much as the muck bothered him, he was hardly even aware of the grotesque corpse. He'd brought up too many other dead bodies. Most recently, the charred bits and pieces from oil drilling platform crews which environmental terrorists had recently taken to blowing out of the water like so many fiery roman candles. Mostly though, he dealt with the jet jockeys that had flamed out. Or fucked up, and had tried to ride their thin-skinned aluminum birds down to the safety of the concrete-hard surface of the ocean.

'You want me to bring up the case that was holding him to the bottom?' he yelled up, as he lifted his mask off and emptied a couple of inches of water out of it.

The captain nodded and motioned to the chief bosun on the main deck. Without a word another line whistled down and splattered into the water next to the frogman.

10

Keeping up with the sun, *Air Force One*, the newest version of the much-maligned SST of the late seventies, left a trail almost fifty miles long as it hurtled through the lower levels of the crystal clear ionisphere toward the great open skies of Montana.

Vince Klein was sitting in the deserted forward VIP lounge, finishing an overly rich and mostly unappreciated elegant lunch, when he was interrupted by the chime sounding on the forward compartment airlock which led from the communications center just aft of the flight deck.

He reached over and released the button which activated the lock from the ComCenter.

The automatic doors, which stayed open on a three-second time delay before mechanically reclosing and resealing, had been installed as a safety factor to maintain pressure, for at this altitude it would normally be fatal if explosive decompression occurred. The system was expensive, but for the President's safety it was cheap.

As the door whooshed open, a black Air Force colonel hurried through with a bright red Top Secret communications envelope. Handing the envelope to Klein and waiting as he signed for it, the colonel said, 'The General asked if you'd inform the President we'll be on the ground in fifteen minutes, Mr Klein.'

'Thanks, Everett,' he responded, as the colonel disappeared back through the lock.

Klein wiped some of the chocolate cake, which he liked to eat with his fingers, off on his blue linen napkin and slipped his fingers under the gummed seal.

His eyes narrowed until they became almost indiscernible slits as he mulled over the communication from Admiral Whittiker. Finally, he reached over and pressed the President's intercom button.

'Yes, Vince?' crackled the intercom that connected him to the President's private office several compartments aft.

'We'll be on the ground in about fifteen minutes, and . . . ah . . . I have a communication from Whittiker.'

'What's it about? Oh, that submarine thing,' the President's

5   65

voice sounded exceptionally clear over the speaker system.

'Yes,' Klein answered.

'Bring it back, will you, Vince? I'm in the middle of dessert.'

'On my way,' Klein said. He clicked off the intercom, stood up, and unconsciously fumbled with his top shirt button and adjusted his tie, a gift from his wife's mother that didn't match anything he owned. But he wasn't exactly known as a fashion plate, which was one of the reasons he had been so popular with his rank-and-file union members.

He pushed the button and the safety lock into the next compartment opened and he started aft. He made his way past the two matronly secretaries in their gleaming, efficiently compact cubicle. He quietly passed the First Lady, napping in the lavish 'formal lounge' which had been decorated to impress. And impress it did. For its decorations featured everything from a moon rock display and Martian soil returned by one of the first manned Mars/Explorer missions and a closed-circuit TV system the size of a wall that the President used to watch sporting events during the endless flights.

At the end of the gleaming passageway, he pushed the call button to the President's private cubicle, a cubicle that would automatically jettison and be parachuted to earth in the event of an emergency.

The President's cubicle was 'him to a tee'. Western artifacts were everywhere and included a number of original Charlie Russell letters from the President's personal collection. The cubicle looked more like a ranch foreman's office than that of the Chief Executive of the United States. Of course all the 'rustic' decor had been re-created for the sake of weight economics in the sophisticated aircraft. But to the visitor's eye, everything seemed absolutely authentic and original.

The door closed automatically behind Klein as he handed the President the red envelope. The high altitude flights always made him exhausted and he slumped into the overstuffed, full-grain leather chair across from him with a groan.

The President, savoring an after-lunch brandy, took the message from the already opened envelope and scanned it quickly. He tossed it nonchalantly to the green felt desktop.

'What the hell are you complaining about, Vince?' chuckled the President.

'Getting old,' he answered.

'Old? Bullshit! You're not any older than I am. You oughtta

try jogging or something. Then old age won't creep up on you like this.'

'Bullshit! Old age don't creep up on you. It roars up on you like a freight train,' Klein said, tugging at his tie to loosen it. 'The other day I looked in the mirror and there it was. Day before, I was a young man.'

'I'm afraid I know what you mean,' the President laughed. He'd also been seeing a lot of new lines and gray hairs that hadn't been there yesterday.

'Well, anyway, what's this all about?' he asked, motioning with his glass to the message on his desk.

Klein shrugged. 'Whatever it is, it's enough for Whittiker to chase after us himself.'

Through the tiny porthole in the SST the skyline of Billings hardly made a dent in the brilliant sky as it poked up sporadically here and there in the green distance.

Klein leaned back in the President's swivel chair and looked toward its horizon. Used to the roar and crowds of the big cities, he always felt insignificant in the presence of the quiet vastness of the open countryside.

The President had already taken the 'All-Terrain' vehicle he liked to drive himself, and had gone ahead with his wife and her party of friends to the ranch.

He left Klein behind to wait for Whittiker with orders to take the 'copter and join him as soon as he landed. So Klein decided to wait aboard *Air Force One* parked in a security area some distance from the main commercial terminal.

Several hundred feet south, Klein could see the old *Air Force One*. The one he'd flown on in the President's first years in office.

A hulking 747, it was now used for a bulging entourage and White House staff, the advance contingent of Secret Service men, press corps, lobbyists, senators, mayors, Miss Americas, movie stars, and wives. It could also, and often did, carry a collection of limousines, which varied dependent on where the President was going in the world and whom he was seeing. And it even flew the President's three old and cranky cats which had to fly separately because of his wife's allergies.

In the distance, a stubby-winger, needle-nosed Navy fighter slammed down on the end of the incoming runway. Telltale smoke rooster-tailed up in protest as the tires, icy cold from the high altitude flight, squealed against the eighty-degree concrete runway.

As Klein watched, the little plane's massive engines reversed thrust and black kerosene smoke roared forward against the wind, showing the blistering speed.

Simultaneously, a brilliant blue and white drag chute deployed, dropping the needle nose of the speeding aircraft almost to the splotchy cement hurtling past the nose wheel.

'Jesus! That's beautiful!' he thought as the black maria turned abruptly and darted toward the security area.

The sight of the menacing jet swelled a hawkish pride in Klein. A pride that once again his country was a strong world leader, and the number one military power.

'Yes!' Klein said as he answered the intercom chime.

'Admiral Whittiker's just landed, Mr Klein.'

The President was sitting in his small air-conditioned office inside the battered old two-storey barn that served as headquarters for the 'Western White House' while the President was in residence at his family ranch.

'Hijacked!' he choked in disbelief as the tall admiral, dressed in wrinkled khakis, nervously paced back and forth in front of the President's desk.

'I'm afraid so, Mr President,' he said.

'Good God, man!' Klein howled. 'You can't be serious.'

'I couldn't be more serious,' the admiral flushed angrily.

'You mean someone just waltzed into one of your bases and waltzed back out again with a whole goddamn submarine?' the President asked in disbelief.

The admiral nodded. 'Not as simply as that. But nevertheless, I'm afraid so.'

'Will you please explain why it took the Navy until now to realize this?' the President exploded in exasperated disbelief.

Whittiker shook his head and stubbed out a half-finished cigarette. 'We still wouldn't know if we hadn't accidentally found a body next to the sub tender in Guam this morning. He was a sonarman from the *Lewis & Clark*. And he was wearing the watch belt and .45 automatic which indicated he was the topside watch. He'd been shot in the back of the head,' he said, taking a deep breath to try to relieve the tension that was creeping into the back of his neck.

The President scratched nervously at the cigarette burns that marred the old desktop. There were so many of them, they almost formed a pattern.

'Any chance that he was just the victim of a good old-fashioned killing? Something that didn't have anything to do with the submarine?' he asked hopefully.

'Maybe this guy wasn't even missed when they left,' Klein added. 'I mean there're probably a couple of hundred guys on that ship. We got less staff than that around here. And half the time we can't keep track of them. Maybe this dead kid wasn't even missed when they left.'

'I'm afraid not, Mr Klein. If it were anyone but the topside watch, I might agree with you. You see, the entire crew has to be on board twenty-four hours before they sail. If the captain was missing someone, he'd still put to sea. But he'd notify SubPac before he was scheduled to reach his diving area. In addition to not reporting this man missing, he never transmitted a diving message.'

'I hope this isn't going to turn into one of those charades where some fucking ensign suddenly comes running in with some papers he forgot to file and the Navy discovers they just "momentarily misplaced" one of their damn ships,' Klein warned sarcastically.

'I wish it were that embarrassingly simple, Mr Klein,' the admiral said, 'but with the evidence left at the scene, we have to presume the *Lewis & Clark* has been taken by an unknown group or unknown government.'

Klein looked at the President, who was staring silently out the office window into the distant hills.

'Maybe as long as the President's available we should talk to Guam direct. Do you agree, Mr President?'

The President looked at him for a moment.

'Yes. Of course,' he finally said.

Whittiker picked up the phone and spoke briefly to the operator. After waiting a few moments, he pushed the button that amplified the call through a conference speaker. A voice came on the line. 'Admiral Towne, here,' said the distant Chief of Staff in Guam.

'Admiral Towne. This is Whittiker. Can you read me all right?'

'Yes, sir. I read you perfectly,' the admiral responded through the faint hollow echo that indicated they were transmitting through a scrambler.

'Admiral, I'm with the President and his chief advisor, Mr

Klein. We're in receipt of your message regarding the *Lewis &
Clark*. Any new developments since you sent this?'

' 'Fraid not, Admiral.' The line crackled several times and the
faint humming garble of the scrambler faded in almost to the
point where it was audible. Whittiker looked at the President
and at Klein. After a moment they both shook their heads.

'OK, Admiral Towne,' Whittiker said. 'The President will
order the appropriate action after we've discussed all the options
with the various national agencies. In the meantime, if anything
breaks there, anything, I want to be the absolute first human
being that knows just what the hell's going on. Do you understand?'

'Yes, sir. Absolutely,' he said briskly. 'I would suggest though
that the less delay the better our ability will be to respond.'

'Thank you, Admiral. No one's more aware of the danger of
the situation than the President,' he said. 'In the meantime, confirm, and I emphasize, confirm that bandit time has passed and
the *Lewis & Clark* is to be considered hostile. We'll be getting
back to you as soon as possible.' Whittiker hung up and the
conference speaker clicked several times until the Communication Center operator came on the line.

'Are you through, Mr President?' the bored voice asked.

Without answering, the President reached over and clicked
off the speaker, disconnecting the operator.

The President sighed as he got up and walked to the glass
partition that separated the office from the hay-strewn working
area of the barn. 'What's it going to mean, Whitt?' he asked
softly.

Whittiker took out another cigarette and put it to his mouth.
He struck one of the President's big sulphur-headed matches and
puffed it to life. 'I'm afraid it means the shit is about to hit the
fan,' he said as he stared out of the office past the open barn
doors into the distant shimmering purple hills.

'Well, gentlemen,' the President said as he turned to the waiting men. 'What the hell are we supposed to do in a situation like
this? There's not exactly a lot of precedent.'

Neither man answered. The only sound that penetrated the
gloomy silence was the vibrating of the airconditioner.

The President gave a little half-assed smile. 'I guess it's too
much to hope that the son-of-a-bitch has simply blown up and
sunk.'

Klein finally said, 'Because of the number of people in Guam
exposed to this situation, I suggest you restrict everyone to the

base. Men, women, children. Civilian personnel. Everyone. We have to isolate this right now till we know exactly who or what we're dealing with. Do you agree, Admiral?'

Whittiker nodded his silent agreement, knowing full well the President had no contingency plans. And he knew that if things were going to be kept from getting totally out of hand, firm military discipline would be necessary.

'Also,' Whittiker added, 'I feel strongly that you should order the combined forces to a stage three red alert.'

'My God,' gasped the President. 'Don't you think that'd be like waving a red flag as far as the press is concerned? Not to mention the Russians. I thought we wanted to keep this quiet?'

'The Russians won't know shit,' Klein said agreeing with Whittiker. 'We mobilized so many times recently during that Middle East bullshit that they're almost used to it. They'll think it's just another one of our never-ending drills.'

'And, to head off the papers,' Whittiker said, 'notify them. Say we're staging an unannounced alert to test the combined efficiency of our armed forces.'

'Notify the press?' asked the President in disbelief. 'Why notify those bastards of anything?'

Whittiker nodded, 'I would normally agree with you,' Mr President. But right now I feel we should be more concerned about the psychological effects this could have on our public than I am about the retaliatory aspects from the Russians.'

The President nodded approval. 'OK Vince, get Mirish in here.'

Klein nodded and picked up the phone. 'I suppose I better get back to the Capitol,' the President said as he slumped down in his worn, old leather swivel chair.

Whittiker shook his head. 'On the contrary. I think it might take the edge off the alert if you stayed here. If you went back to the Capitol, the wrong people might start getting ideas.'

The President nodded concurrence and breathed a silent sigh of relief. If there were going to be any nuclear problems, he'd sure as hell rather be here than at the White House. There was no doubt DC would be high on the list of any nuclear attack. And he sure as shit didn't want to be near any place that might be a target. He was elected to represent and govern, he thought. And that sure didn't cover dying senselessly.

Whittiker stood up and gathered his scanty reports and put them in his handsome, slim-line leather briefcase.

'One final thing, sir,' he said as the President looked up. 'I've taken the liberty of ordering the Secret Service to deliver those individuals necessary to convene an Emergency Council by this evening.'

'Here?' the President asked, wishing somehow they could keep this as far away as possible from his ranch. So it wouldn't be able to infect his private domain with the contagious problem that seemed to be multiplying by the second.

'Yes, Mr President. Inasmuch as you're staying here on a "working vacation".'

'I guess there's no alternative,' he mumbled.

'The Joint Chiefs are already airborne. Mr Ridley and his National Security Council staff, Murphy and some of his CIA brains as well as the House and Senate leaders and the three chief scientists from ARASS are right behind them.'

11

Morgan yawned and an involuntary shiver ran through his body after his short but much needed sleep on the Wardroom lounge.

Rubbing his face, he poured a steaming cup of coffee into a delicate china cup cradled in an equally delicate saucer.

He quickly set the pot down as the escaping steam from the pot spewed against his hand.

Picking up the saucer, he walked across and slumped back onto one of the overstuffed lounges.

Setting the coffee down on the table next to the lounge, he smiled at the chiming sound the cup made as it rattled against the china saucer.

'Very elegant!' he thought. Reminded him of an old English movie he'd seen on late-night TV where they'd served afternoon tea. Not like the heavy, unmelodic clunks from the crock cups in the crew's mess.

Unconsciously stirring the coffee, he looked around the lonely, deserted wardroom. Suddenly, a terrible twinge of sadness swept through his body, reminding him of the lonely trip back stateside after the bullfight on the Costa del Sol.

Still pissed off at the fat bastard for allowing the little bull to be killed, he found a bar where he hoped he could wash away some of the anger with scotch.

Inside, the air-conditioning felt refreshingly cool after the sun-filled afternoon. He was pleased at accidentally picking a place that had air-conditioning, as most European restaurants still lacked what most Americans assumed a necessity.

'Scotch and soda,' he said to the bored-looking bartender as he slid onto the cool leather stool at the end of a hand-carved wood bar.

'Si, señor. Con hielo?' asked the Spaniard, holding a handful of ice over the empty glass.

Morgan nodded, laying a large bill on the bar to show he intended to have more than one.

He was on his second drink when a reflection in the mirror in back of the bar of a shapely female passing behind of his stool caught his eye.

Turning, his face suddenly flushed like an excited teenager's.

It was the girl from the bull ring. The girl with the Givenchy scarf.

Along with dozens of other eyes, he watched as she made her way toward a table near the end of the bar.

The three men already waiting at the table stood and greeted her with warm familiarity as she returned their hellos and exchanged kisses.

The warmth from the pleasure of seeing her suddenly turned cold when Morgan saw that one of the men was the fat Spaniard who'd signaled for the bull to be killed.

He watched in disgust as the fat man placed his arm familiarly around her waist and pulled her chair closer to his.

One of the young men at the table with her was effeminate in skintight bell bottoms. His Gucci loafers looked just out of the box and his brilliantly colored silk shirt unbuttoned and tied at the navel displayed a dozen gaudy but apparently expensive chains, charms, and necklaces. He waved at a red-jacketed waiter and ordered something in Spanish that sent the waiter scurrying off toward the kitchen.

The third man at the table was a baby-faced Oriental. He had a shy, china-doll smile and was dressed very casually in his Fred Perry tee shirt, denim, and Adidas sneakers.

'Un otro, señor?' the bartender asked.

Morgan nodded. After the bartender brought his drink, Morgan's attention was drawn back to the table as bits and pieces of her melodiously seductive voice floated through the din.

Watching from behind the new ice-cold drink, Morgan could tell she had the air of wealthy but casual elegance about her. And the tailored cut of her slacks and blouse, which revealed a tanned though small bustline, seemed to confirm a young European used to the finest.

That would have ended his secret romance with her then and there had that been all there was to her. But there seemed to be a quality about her that was different from the usual spoiled rich bitches he'd run into up and down the Mediterranean. The ones who usually sneered down their expensively bobbed noses, from behind rose-tinted Dior sunglasses, with practiced looks of nonchalance.

She was darker than most Europeans. She could be a Greek, or a Turk or, God knows, even an Arab. Not that it mattered, he snickered to himself. 'This is the last time I'll ever set eyes on her anyway,' he thought with a pang of sadness.

Finishing another drink, Morgan's upper lip started to get numb from the effects of the scotch. He rubbed it several times, trying to get the blood flowing. He always thought if he could get the circulation going, it would reduce the effects of scotch.

He raised his glass and silently ordered another drink from the horse-toothed bartender.

'She come in here very much?' he asked, beginning to find it difficult to form the words.

The bartender shrugged a bored 'so-so' as he passed on his way to make another order of drinks for a waiter at the other end of the bar.

Morgan was again secretly watching from behind his frosty glass when he saw her look his way.

Before he could stop himself, Morgan raised his glass to her.

She recognized him immediately, smiled, and raised her glass in return.

As he watched her smile, he was thunderstruck.

God! Her smile was almost hypnotizing, he thought. He quickly took a sip from his drink and wiped his forehead on his wet cocktail napkin as the perspiration broke out on it in tiny beads.

Playing cool, he casually glanced back at her table and could see that although she was in the middle of a conversation, she was watching him.

He motioned for the bartender and told him to send them a round of drinks. The waiter delivered the order on his wet cork tray and Morgan could see them protesting that they hadn't ordered.

He watched, trying to act nonchalant. But when the waiter nodded in his direction, once again his face blazed bright red.

The Spaniard raised his drink in thanks as the girl whispered something in the fat man's ear.

The man roared with laughter and a moment later motioned for Morgan to join them.

The men at her table stood to shake hands as Morgan came over. And with a heavy continental accent, the fat Spaniard introduced everybody.

'Señor, may I take the pleasure of introducing Señorita Ji'lhan Adziz Riyadh,' he said, introducing her to Morgan.

In his haze, the way the Spaniard tossed out her name, it sounded to Morgan like one of those long European names that pretentiously goes on and on and on.

'What's the J. L. stand for?' he slurred through a puppy-love-filled grin.

'What?' she asked not having the slightest idea what he was talking about.

'The J. L.,' he smiled, looking around the table for help.

Everyone looked at one another, strangely puzzled.

Morgan shook his head. 'Phewww! No more for me. I could have swore your friend said your initials were J. L. something-or-other.'

She and Vasques, the Jap, and even the fag all laughed as Morgan sat in embarrassed silence.

'I'm sorry,' Ji'lhan finally said.

'They're not initials. They're part of my name. It's Arabic. It's JAY – ELL – Hahn,' she said, slowly pronouncing it phonetically.

Morgan tried to follow her. But it came out stiff and didn't sound at all like the lyrical pronounciation she or Vasques had used.

'God! This is really embarrassing.'

'Think of it as Jill. Then Hahn,' the Jap offered. 'Then just say the middle part quicker than the beginning or the end.'

He pronounced it to them a couple of times. Like a team playing charades, they drew him closer and closer until finally he was pronouncing it correctly.

'Eureka!' he proclaimed, alienating their fag friend as their game was drawing attention from the surrounding tables. 'Ji'lhan. Ji'lhan!' Morgan said proudly, ignoring the little fag's embarrassment and the Jap's reserved silence.

'You got it!' Ji'lhan and Vasques cheered.

The rest of the night was a whirlwind.

Ji'lhan was Saudi-Arabian, the youngest daughter of a Bedouin sheik, Ahmed Adziz al-Riyadh. Born in Mecca, the birthplace of Mohammed, she was the daughter of the Minister of Petroleum, the singular most powerful man in the Arab world.

The fat Spaniard was an old childhood friend of her father's and the overseer of his Spanish interests.

The Jap, Takeo Yamimura, was an old school chum of hers from the University in Paris. From a family ruled by his mother, they relied heavily on the friendship of Ji'lhan's father for economic advantages in their industrial empire throughout the far east.

Yummy, as Ji'lhan called him, had light-skinned features

which were almost European. Although 'old world' in his personal beliefs, Yummy was comfortable with any one of a half dozen languages and blended into Western society with charming ease. Though everybody believed him to be Japanese, they were only half right. A hated secret was that he actually was the illegitimate son of a Japanese geisha and a Korean religious fanatic who'd hoped to rule the world. Unfortunately, a disgruntled disciple made a martyr out of him by blowing his brains out.

Morgan learned later that the fag was an American expatriate, wasting away in Europe, the son of an American billionaire. During the rest of the evening he not only refused to acknowledge Morgan's presence at their table but would speak only in Spanish, jealously trying to exclude him from their conversation.

It was only after the man had left with friends from another table that Morgan said something to Vasques in casual, flawless Spanish.

'I've never heard an American with such a perfect accent,' Vasques complimented him.

Morgan shrugged. 'My father's name was Corona.'

'Ahh-haa! So you're really Spanish then,' Vasques said.

'No,' Morgan said. 'Mexican.'

'You don't look like a Mexican,' Ji'lhan said.

'That's because I'm a half-breed,' he smiled. 'My mother was a red-headed Irish Catholic.'

'Unusual combination,' Yummy said, briefly joining the conversation.

'It did screw me up at times,' he chuckled. 'I like scotch instead of tequila. Love chili and hate Irish stew. When I was a kid, my friends used to say that I ate so much Mexican food that I smelled like a wetback.'

'What a terrible thing to say,' Ji'lhan said sympathetically.

'Not really,' Morgan said. 'My father was one.'

There was a moment of silence.

'Well . . . whether your back is wet . . . or dry . . . it was charitable of you not to let our friend know,' said Yamimura.

Later, when they found that he was on his way further into Spain, Vasques insisted he join them, as they were driving along the route he planned to take.

'Are you sure I won't be intruding?' Morgan asked, not wanting to believe his good luck.

'Definitely!' Vasques said, smiling at Ji'lhan. 'But it's the least this fat old bastard can do.'

'She told you, huh?' asked the embarrassed Morgan.

'I'm afraid so,' Vasques nodded.

'Sorry about that.'

'Why?' Vasques asked sincerely. 'I'm sure many in the crowd felt the same as you. But the majority, well . . . they make up a forgiving animal. Especially if you offer them the right bribe.'

The thought of the bull still angered Morgan.

'You're still angry,' Vasques said, understanding.

'Man's inhumanity to just about everything . . . ' he smiled, an iciness in his voice.

'Oh dear, dear, dear!' Vasques winced.

'I realize it was just an animal,' Morgan apologized, 'but it was truly magnificent.'

'A mercenary with the heart of a poet,' Yamimura mused. 'Another odd combination.'

'Not at all odd,' Vasques said, patting Morgan on the shoulder. 'I understand exactly what my new friend here felt. I felt it every time I faced a bull, preparing to take his life,' he said, sliding Ji'lhan's chair back and shepherding them toward the door.

In the back of Vasque's Citroën, one of the last ones built, she held Morgan's hands in hers and chattered and laughed and joked to the man who was too stunned by her magical spell to do anything but listen.

Passing through the narrow streets of the little ancient town, she suddenly pointed excitedly out his window. 'Look! Look!' she whispered, pretending she didn't want anybody else but him to see what she saw.

In the dim glow from a sagging, ornamental street light, he could see a decrepit hansom cab parked in front of a cathedral with the driver slouched asleep on the box.

Morgan looked puzzled until she pointed toward the pavement under the carriage.

As they passed, Morgan caught a fleeting glimpse of two bare-assed sailors laying on top of two chunky, spread-legged whores, humping and bumping and screwing for all they were worth on top of what must have been agonizingly uncomfortable cobblestones.

'Friends of yours?' she whispered jokingly.

Passing down the black street away from the comically sad sight, Morgan grinned, 'I hope not.' He lied, having recognized the familiar hulk of Barth and the young sailor he was indoctrinating in the ways of the submariner.

'You must admire their remarkable American ingenuity,' he whispered. In the dark, she cocked her head and looked quizzically at him.

'Well . . . ' he whispered earnestly. 'Normally they'd have to pay so much for the girl and so much for the room. This way, they save enough for another girl.'

'But there's two of them,' she whispered. 'Who gets her?'

'The one with the most seniority,' he grinned.

They had almost wound their way along the dark coast to Torremolinos, when they were overtaken by a storm that ripped through the Mediterranean and engulfed them in a deluge of driving rain.

Turning off the road, they found shelter in a small hotel on a bluff overlooking a wide sandy beach.

They were warmly welcomed and quickly made comfortable in a sitting room that reminded Morgan of a country squire's library.

They sank back in the thick cushions in front of a stone fireplace as the shuffling, gray-haired concierge added logs and fanned the embers into new life.

The concierge's grandmotherly wife provided hot spicy drinks, and it wasn't long before a melancholy spell fell over their small party.

As the flickering lights from the dancing flames danced over them, they looked down onto the white sand that was bathed in floodlights hidden under the eaves of the red-tiled roof.

Mesmerized, they silently watched as wave after wave crashed onto the white sand before rushing threateningly toward the hotel that suddenly seemed perched precariously low to the sand.

Finally, Vasques and Yamimura excused themselves and shuffled off toward their warm, waiting rooms.

'You know,' said Morgan after they had gone. 'I really hated him this afternoon. I didn't even know him. But I truly hated him.'

Ji'lhan nodded and stared quietly into the flames as they danced through the crevices of the charred logs.

She reached over and took both his hands and held them close

79

to her firm breasts. 'I felt the same way. And I've known him all my life.'

Morgan didn't answer.

'It might help to know that Enrique loved Picarito, that's the bull that was killed, more than anybody,' she said, putting her arms around her knees and her feet under Morgan's leg to warm her toes.

'Unfortunately,' she continued, 'Enrique is a realist. He knew he could never breed him. He was doomed from birth by being simply . . . too small. So, by letting him die, he created two legends. One, a bull whose size and bravery will be magnified a hundred times by the time it reaches Madrid.'

'What's the second legend?' he asked.

She raised her eyebrow. 'I thought you'd never ask.'

Morgan grinned, putting his arm around her neck. 'I think I've been trapped into an old Arabian Nights story.'

'Pretty sharp for a blue-eyed wetback.'

'Okay, let's hear it,' he said, faking exasperation.

'Well. Once upon a time,' she said, taking his hand like a mother telling a bedtime story, 'Enrique was a great matador. Not like the show-off kind we have today. But truly Old World. Anyway, one day in Barcelona, one of the bulls threw him. They say twenty, maybe thirty feet straight up in the air. Before he hit the ground, the man who took care of his swords and capes – his name was Pato because he was lame and waddled like a duck – anyway, he leapt into the ring and hobbled out to try to distract the bull before it could gore Enrique. By the time Enrique regained his senses, the bull had blinded the little man. The boy today was Pato's son.'

Morgan nodded with a new respect for the man. And an understanding of why she considered him a friend.

'OK! OK!' he sighed, taking her in his arms. 'I give up.'

'Good!' she said happily, and before she could stop herself, gave him a tender, affectionate kiss.

It was a shock to them both. He reached over and gently placed the tips of his fingers on her lips. He had never felt anything so velvety soft before in his life. He kissed her very gently.

They spent the rest of the night in front of the flickering fireplace. Snuggled up in the warmth of the old sofa, they talked until dawn.

They talked about her . . . her family. The world. Hot-fudge sundaes. Politics. Arabia. Mexican food. The US Friends . . funny things that had happened to them. Their childhoods.

Hers, happy and comfortable and warm. His, as a stranger in a strange man's house.

They talked until the sky started turning a dull gray in the gloom just before dawn.

As dawn broke, the storm that had ripped through the straits died with nary a whimper and left the atmosphere still and quiet.

Their footprints along the beach were the only signs of life as they walked along arm in arm in the growing light from the newborn sun.

The sand-busting waves that had churned threateningly across the sand the night before had left the beach littered with debris.

Splintered wood, discarded bottles, crushed cans, a telephone pole, empty suntan bottles, styrofoam, a threadbare tire, and an old Frisbee lay in the sand.

It was as if the ocean had finally tired of man's litter, and vomited back on his doorstep all the things she had been unable to digest.

Down the beach, the high-rise hotels poked up toward the gray dawn like so many white tombstones.

'When I was a child, my family used to come here for holiday. It was a sleepy little village. Now it's another world,' Ji'lhan said sadly.

' 'Course there has been one rather nice improvement,' he said seriously.

She raised one of her eyebrows questioningly.

'The blondes!' Morgan smiled. 'Did you ever see any place filled with so many big-boobed blondes, and dressed in those string bikini things? I mean, mercy! This must be the world's capital.'

'Ahhh-haaa! So that's it?' she squealed as if in pain. 'You're a big boob man!' she said, pointing an accusing finger at him.

With his most innocent, little-boy look, Morgan shook his head. 'Me? Nawl!' he scoffed. 'I've never been a big boob person.'

'It's a good thing for you,' she warned, holding her tan shoulders back to be sure he saw she was definitely not one of the types.

He had been a 'boob man' once though.

In his sophomore year in college, Morgan had been asked to

crew on one of the local yachts out of Newport Beach on the annual Cinco De Mayor race to Ensenada.

Reaching Ensenada during the height of their annual Independence Day celebration, Morgan and the rest of the hundreds of crew members partied their way from one bar to another along with hundreds of other family members who had driven the 150 miles south to welcome the finishers.

Ending up at Hussong's, amid the blaring mariachis and screaming teenagers who were away from their folks and having their first drunk at the same time, he met a blonde cheerleader from a rival college.

The initial on her letterman's sweater seemed to magnify the size of her young, exceptionally voluptuous bustline.

The margueritas had numbed his brain. But, wanting desperately to get his sweaty, rope-burned palms all over her blossoming young breasts, he fed her a line of bullshit that would have made even his father proud.

It worked. Or seemed to work. Actually, she knew it was bullshit. But as she was hornier than he was she let him believe that in her eyes he seemed heroic and more worldly than his years, although later she had to teach him most of the more basic facts of life.

A month later, after seeing her almost every night, her furious father and dumpy, weeping mother paid Paul's stepfather and Aunt Claudia a visit regarding what they were going to do about her pregnancy.

'We warned her about going out with that goddamn bastard Mexican son-of-a-whore!' the man raged.

Paul's stepfather was furious. 'Like father, like son!' he cursed as he rushed Paul out of his home, past his crying Aunt Claudia and into the empty night.

Morgan's Latin blood boiled at the insults to his heritage and dead father. For a few moments he had a tremendous struggle to keep from exploding in a brutal assault on these two hypocritical son-of-a-bitching Anglos.

Finally, he stormed into the night. He didn't know what to do or where to go. But, secretly, he was delighted at the prospect of being a father. Being penniless didn't dampen his enthusiasm. He would be able to find some kind of a job without too much of a problem. And in a few weeks, he'd be able to support the cheerleader and their new baby.

It was almost two weeks before he could reach her by phone. And only then because her folks had gone to Las Vegas to help them forget the stain on their tarnished reputation and their disappointment with her.

By then Morgan had found a job and wanted her to tell him all about when the baby would be born. When could he see her? And excitedly he asked when they could be married.

'You've got to be kidding, Paul!' she giggled in disbelief. 'For God's sake, I've already had it taken care of.'

'What do you mean?' he asked, not really wanting to hear what he knew she was about to tell him.

'I had it taken care of. An abortion, dummy.'

'You killed a living child?' he heard himself whisper almost like he was detached from his body.

'Oh God! You got to be kidding,' she laughed at his juvenile, almost prehistoric beliefs.

'But it was mine too . . . wasn't it?'

'Who knows? Jesus, Paul . . . look! You were a great lay. Probably the best. But I sure don't plan to spend the rest of my life changing diapers for a little bastard and making tortillas for a guy working in a gas station.'

The anger caused a pain in the pit of his stomach. He felt as if one of the gangleaders from the barrio had run a knife through his guts.

'That was only going to be for a little while. Till I could transfer to another school and graduate,' he said.

'Oh sure!' she laughed sarcastically.

God! He just couldn't believe this beautiful girl's soul could be so dead that she'd kill her own child. He couldn't get it through his skull that she was the same person that constantly tried to engulf him with her body during her violent sexual climaxes. He couldn't believe that this was the girl who had wanted to make love everywhere. Cars. Movies. The shower in her father's bedroom. His mind felt like it was unraveling.

While she was in mid-laugh, and mid-sentence, Morgan quietly hung up. For over an hour he stood in the telephone booth watching the lights from the passing stream of traffic.

Two days later, he was sleeping on a small bunk at the Navy Recruit Depot in San Diego. With two years of college, he qualified for Officer Candidate School. Six months after boot camp he graduated at the head of his class and was on his way to Sub School in New London as an ensign.

From the time he stepped out of the phone booth to the end of his life, he never saw his grandmother, Aunt Claudia, his stepfather, the blonde cheerleader, or set foot in Newport Beach again.

'So?' Ji'lhan grinned mischievously. 'If not a "boob" man, then you must be one of those "leg" guys.'

'To be perfectly frank, I've always been . . . well . . . more interested in a woman's intellect than her physical endowments.'

Ji'lhan howled with laughter.

'I've heard of silver tongues before. But yours has to be made of gold.'

'No . . . seriously,' Morgan said, trying to defend himself.

'Come on, Paolo,' she teased.

'Well, look at it this way. Sooner or later, you're going to have to talk. And I've never known a boob . . . or a leg to talk back. 'Course, there are some who argue to the contrary.'

She shook her head as she laughed.

She was enchanted with him, and the next ten days were heaven for her and Morgan.

They swam, they laughed. They sat in the sun and rubbed suntan oil on each other. They ate *paella*. And they watched the colors of a rainbow after another thunderstorm as it laughed its way across the stormy sky. They danced. They drank the cheap musky Spanish wine. They drank two-litre beers. They held hands . . . and they made love.

When his leave was finally up, she held him tightly and cried, not wanting him to leave.

At sea once again, the place where Morgan usually felt most at home and most relaxed, he felt like he'd suffered a death in the family. And constantly fought an aching bottomless feeling that he couldn't get out of the pit of his stomach.

Three weeks later, they sailed into Piraeus, the port leading to ancient Athens. The first thing he wanted to do was find a telephone and try to reach Vasques to find out where she was.

As he searched the dock for the nearest phone, he felt his heart skip a beat. There on the end of the dock, waving her brightly colored scarf, was Ji'lhan.

For the rest of his boat's six months in the Med, at every port they sailed into, Ji'lhan would be waiting on the pier, waving one of her brightly colored scarves and happily calling out his name.

84

12

Morgan looked up as the forward torpedo room hatch, down the passageway from the wardroom, opened amid the hiss of circulating air and rhythmic whine from distant machinery.

A few moments later, Barth, his rumpled, slept-in shirt unbuttoned and hanging out, guided the Triton's captain into the wardroom.

Standing there, in a semi-drunk trance, the captain's legs shook involuntarily from the effects of the gas and from being cramped too long in one position.

With his head still shrouded in the black hood and his upper body strapped in the straitjacket, he reminded Morgan of a vibrating automaton waiting for his master's commands.

Barth loosened the straps and the captain's hands dropped heavily to his sides. Untying the drawstring, he stripped the black hood off the captain's head and quickly jerked the tape away from the scruffy growth of beard around his mouth.

The hood off, the sudden glare from the overhead lights tore through the captain's eyes. The lingering pain, which felt like someone had thrown sand in his eyes, finally passed and he could half-focus on a tan-clad figure sitting on the lounge in front of him. The captain tried to lick his dried, cracked lips with his thick, fuzzy tongue.

'Who the hell are you?' he rasped in a hoarse half whisper, still fuzzy-headed from the effects of the gas.

'Captain, I'm afraid my men have secured the capture of your boat . . . and crew.'

'What?' Clifford Seright hissed in disbelief. What did he just say? his mind screamed, while he tried to remember the Naval Intelligence indoctrination that was supposed to prepare him for situations like this. But his mind seemed bogged down in a slow-motion nightmare.

Stay calm. Damnit, stay calm until your head clears, he thought. Then find someway to signal the watch on the tender.

'Are you insane, man?' he said, trying to sound confident. 'You'll never get underway, much less to sea.'

Morgan was confused for a moment. Then he realized the captain didn't understand.

'Captain, we've been at sea for several days now,' he said, dropping the bomb.

Seright looked like someone had kneed him in the groin. 'What?' he asked weakly as the residual effects from the gas sent a chorus of bells ringing through his skull.

'Impossible!'

'Nonetheless, true,' Morgan said.

'I want to assure you that I don't want to have to slaughter your crew needlessly,' Morgan added. 'I'm an old submariner myself. And, if for no other reason, want to spare them out of sentiment. But,' he said coldly, 'don't think for a moment that that sentiment will jeopardize this mission. Are you listening?'

Seright nodded. He'd have to try to act. God knows, after eighteen years of military life, he'd been in personal danger more than once.

But he'd jeopardize the crew. Fuck the crew! he thought desperately, as he suddenly realized he was afraid to die.

No panicking, he thought to himself, crossing his arms so the man sitting across from him couldn't see his trembling. Remember! I'm an officer.

'My crew's safe, you say?' Seright croaked.

'For the time being,' Morgan nodded as he sipped from the china cup. 'But if any of them are to survive, I'm going to need your help.'

'You have to be insane if you think I'm about to help you,' Seright spat.

'It's quite simple really. When they're conscious, simply tell them that if any man moves . . . or tries to communicate with the person next to him they'll be executed.'

'That's all?' Seright asked.

Morgan nodded.

'OK,' Seright finally agreed.

'Good,' smiled Morgan as he stood and walked to the gleaming buffet. 'Now . . . how about a cup of coffee, Captain?' he asked reaching for the stainless steel pot.

'Thank you,' Seright answered. He didn't want the man to know, but the way his stomach felt, he'd just about sell his mother for a cup.

'Cream or sugar?'

'Black, please,' he answered as Morgan poured a cup of the steaming liquid.

'Of course, you'll have to kill us eventually,' Seright said matter-of-factly.

Morgan set the pot back on the electric hot plate.

'Not necessarily. To be perfectly frank, the thought of having a hundred or so corpses onboard is a problem I don't want to deal with. And I can't risk dumping you over the side. Until we're ready, no one's going to have a clue as to what's happened to your boat.'

'They'll already be searching for you. You know that, don't you?' Seright said, clumsily taking the coffee with hands still sheathed by the straitjacket.

'Not for us, Captain,' Morgan grinned confidently, 'for you. We both know how the Navy mind works. An overdue boat? The only thing they'll be looking for is debris.'

The captain slowly blew on the steaming coffee before sipping it.

'So why bother telling me all this?' he said, greedily drinking the hot, delicious coffee.

'I don't really know,' he shrugged honestly. 'I guess I'm just proud of our little accomplishment.'

'Rather dubious pride isn't it?' the captain asked.

'Barth,' Morgan said. 'See the captain to his stateroom.'

Barth looked questioningly at Morgan as the captain heaved himself to his feet.

'If it's all the same, I prefer to be with my men,' he lied, as his body subconsciously rebelled at the thought of the smelly, claustrophobic storeroom.

'That's very nice, Captain,' Morgan said at his attempt at valor. 'That's exactly what I'd want my captain to say. However, it's not out of sympathy. It's that I prefer to keep the severed head away from the serpent's body.'

Seright nodded grimly.

'Barth?' Morgan said, turning to the waiting seaman. 'Make sure the captain's snug, and I do mean snug, in his bed.'

Barth nodded his understanding and guided the captain aft toward his cabin at the end of the passageway.

13

The air around the President's ranch was heavy with the sweet smell of freshly mown hay and the sounds of feeding birds seemed to magnify the peacefulness of the countryside.

In contrast to the countryside's gentle appearance, a storm raged in a small city of double wide, air-conditioned trailers that housed conference rooms, a communications center, Marine guards, and various other Washington staffers.

Inside the largest of the conference trailers, the President sat at the head of a gleaming oak conference table, crowded with a stunned group of the country's leading advisers.

'Jesus Christ! What the hell happened to all our great, sophisticated security systems?' the President said, angrily throwing a pencil across the room. 'How the hell could someone waltz in like they owned the damned place and get away with something like this?'

'I'm afraid they took advantage of one thing,' said a grandfatherly looking man with a deep white vee-shaped hairlined mane sitting across from him.

'Which is?' demanded the President.

'Boredom. The one thing no military can defense against. Bored officers. Bored seamen who are trained for battles that never even seem likely to come. And never have during their lifetimes. Men trained for wars that are drearily informal in the first place. With enemies that are faceless. And pose no real personal threat. Sort of like the bombers in World War II, and Vietnam, who never saw the results of their missions or the faces of their enemies.'

'But surely something the size of this operation takes a lot of men. Goddammit! How the hell could they have gotten together on a Top Secret base and pulled this off without at least someone suspecting something!'

Pat Murphy, head of the CIA, a hulking former All-American tackle from Notre Dame, opened a Top Secret security file. 'Sir, only six men were used on this mission.'

'Six!' thundered the President incredulously. 'You mean six people is all it takes to steal one of those babies?'

'Well, sir . . . yes. Properly trained that is.'

'How did you come up with this magic number?'

'Well, sir,' Murphy hurriedly continued, face buried behind the folder, 'in checking the log for the Security Compound on Guam, every man . . . officers, enlisted, and civilians . . . that came in and out were accounted for. With the exception of six.'

'And they were the six . . . ' the President knew before Murphy was finished.

'Yes, sir. They were carrying I.D.s from submariners, two officers, four enlisted men, previously believed to have gone AWOL or been killed in what appeared to be muggings in San Diego, Charleston, South Carolina, and Norfolk, Virginia.'

He closed the folder and sat back heavily in the chair that strained under his weight.

'Any significance in their going as two officers and enlisted men?' asked the President.

Admiral Whittiker shook his head. 'Probably simply that once onboard, men of those ranks, spread out over a ship the size of the tender, would easily go unnoticed until they were ready to do what they planned to do.'

'Okay! Okay! Whitt . . . let's get down to the short hairs. One of the first things I want to know is do we know who the hell we are dealing with? Could it be the Soviets?'

Whittiker took off his fashionable gold-framed glasses and scratched absently at a nervous rash on his forearm. The skin felt strangely foreign. Almost as tight as the skin of a balloon that had reached its bursting point. Finally, realizing everyone was watching him, he shook his head and said, 'No. It's definitely not the Soviets. They were my first consideration. But most of their Kishkin and Krylov fleets are in transit through the Leningrad to Murmansk Canal now that the ice in the White Sea is breaking up. It would be disastrous for them to let an act of aggression like this catch these fleets landlocked in such a vulnerable canal.'

Several heads around the room nodded their agreement.

'Well, son-of-a-bitch!' thundered the President. 'Then who the hell are they?' he screamed. 'Are they sane. Or are they madmen?'

Whittiker turned back to Murphy and nodded.

Murphy opened another folder. 'They claim to be the group known as "The League of Men". That's the group that's supposedly responsible for creating an alliance between all the major terrorist organizations throughout the world.'

'Jesus H. Christ! You mean the terrorists have unionized? If so, we should have known about them then,' said the President sarcastically. 'Anything Union should be right up Klein's alley.'

Klein, sitting alone on one of the red sofas behind him, smiled uncomfortably.

'Maybe you can sell them on a pension and welfare plan,' the President chuckled.

A small, wiry general with a gray crew cut and a chest full of campaign decorations below his Marine Corps emblems stood up. 'Sir,' said General Wylie Tennyson Thatcher, III, 'have they made any demands as yet?'

The President looked at Whittiker who shook his aching head. The headaches were getting more and more agonizing, although the chief surgeon at Bethesda assured him it was nothing physiological. The never-ending pressure was just starting to take its toll, that's all. Maybe he should start thinking about retiring, the chief surgeon had suggested. Shit. After this, he doubted if there would be any alternatives. 'None. But we're sure they will, Thatch. They left a message stenciled on the case they used to sink the seaman's body with.' He tried to squeeze away some of the pain that seemed to be concentrating at the base of his skull.

'It confirmed they would contact us. It would be by mail. Directly to the White House. And that we'd know beyond a doubt the communication was authentic,' Klein added.

'Then they'll have land-based contacts,' mentioned General Thatcher, who was a third-generation Annapolis graduate and classmate of Whittiker's.

'Evidently,' said Klein. 'Unless they're planning on sending it at the end of one of the missiles,' he added with grim humor.

'Well, that's all of it, gentlemen,' Klein said, rubbing his tired eyes with both hands. 'Now what the hell are we going to do?'

One of the civilian manufacturers across from him rapped a long dead pipe into the large mirage-coloured ashtray. 'Any possible connection between them and the thefts of nuclear waste?'

Klein shrugged and turned to Allen Ridley, the grandfatherly man sitting directly across from him. 'Mr Ridley?'

Ridley, scientist and close friend of the admiral's, was also the Chief Delegate to the UN. A tall, lean bachelor in his mid-seventies, he was known as the meanest son-of-a-bitch in government. But that frugality resulted in massive donations to foundations, colleges, and charities to be used toward the goal of eliminating hunger. Thinking about the admiral's question, he finally said, 'I can't imagine anyone with twenty-four nuclear missiles being interested in nuclear waste.'

The President interrupted, drumming another pencil nervously on the table. 'Speaking about the missiles, is there any chance these people can fire the damn things?'

Klein took a sip of water from the carafe in front of his seat. 'I would think, Mr President, that it rather depends on *who* they are. But offhand, if they had the ability to make off with the submarine, then I'd bet the logistics of a launch would be one of their lesser problems.'

A murmur of agreement swept around the conference table.

'But what about the goddamn "fail-safe" system?' the President asked in frustration. 'I thought no one was supposed to be able to fire the damn things without the right codes or something like that.'

'It will be difficult,' said one of the civilian scientists, 'no doubt about that. But I have men on my staff . . . any number of bright young computer designers who could violate any "fail-safe" system as easily as hot-wiring an automobile.'

The President threw his hands up in disbelief. 'I don't understand how anything supposed to be so foolproof could be so simple to figure out.'

'Because they have one vital ingredient, sir. They have time,' a ferret-faced, pipe-smoking young scientist said. 'They can work on it at their leisure. In the normal course of a ship's operation, no one could ever have this type of access. They do.'

'How about the missiles themselves?' Klein asked. 'Don't they have a short life expectancy if they don't get serviced or something?'

The pipe-smoking scientist from ARASS, who was the prime contractor for the Poseidon, shook his head. 'I'm afraid not. The Poseidon's life cycle is virtually unlimited. The only reason we rotate them is to update the electronics. To increase their range or performance, but basically, even without regular maintenance, they'll outlive any of us.'

'Well, Jesus H. Christ! That's all I can say. Jesus H. Christ,' the President spat out disgustedly. 'A goddamn killer ship's been stolen and someone better tell me what the hell to do about it.'

Ridley, staring at the ceiling, said, 'The first problem is that we don't know what they want. They have the ability to hold the whole world hostage. I wonder if they know that. I'm sure they do, of course. But probably the most frightening aspect of all is . . . I wonder if the world's going to be able . . . or willing to pay the ransom?'

'Well, gentlemen?' the President asked, weariness and resignation in his voice.

Klein stood up and started pacing. 'I'm afraid we don't have many alternatives. One thing we have to do is alert our allies.'

'I'd like to get as much help as we can,' Whittiker added. 'Get everything that can float, fly, or wade in the water out there looking for her. We have to find her, isolate her, and destroy her by any means at our disposal.'

'I'm sure we all agree. Anyone have any questions?' the President asked, looking around at the circle of tired faces that stared blankly at him.

'Only one,' said Ridley, suddenly looking his seventy-odd years. 'If she's found and attacked,' he said, turning and directing his question to Whittiker, 'don't you think they'll fire as many of the missiles as they can?'

Whittiker looked down at the gleaming, polished conference tabletop wishing he could relieve himself from the weight of the decision he'd already made. Slowly . . . almost imperceptibly, he nodded, 'Of course they will.'

'Then I assume you've taken into consideration that if you attack and they launch those missiles, you're setting an unalterable course, the result of which will probably be casualties numbering millions of people?'

'My God . . . ' the disbelieving whisper came out before the President could stifle it.

'I don't see how we can avoid that risk, Mr Ridley,' Whittiker said, ignoring the President and pressing the point. 'From a contingency standpoint, we must assume that eventually they'll fire anyway.'

'But we don't even know what their demands will be,' Ridley said, as he weakly pounded his fist on the table.

'With the *Lewis & Clark* as the gun to our heads, don't you think they're going to be pretty severe?' asked Klein.

'I didn't assume they wouldn't be,' he said in his quiet, dignified way. 'I was merely suggesting that there was a possibility that we might be able to bargain with them.'

'Mr Ridley, God knows,' Admiral Whittiker said. 'I've tried to analyze the various alternatives. But for the life of me I can't honestly see how we can get out of this without, in the end, assuming that the world is in jeopardy of suffering great, no, staggering casualties. I feel even that may be supreme optimism.

In any event, we must go ahead. We have already accounted for seven dead, and must assume another 114 in the crew are also dead.'

'For God's sake, man,' Ridley interrupted angrily, 'a hundred or so casualties are nothing compared to what you're telling us you're willing to risk.'

'Better to risk a hundred million than mankind,' Whittiker said softly.

'Okay, Whitt. It's your ball game,' said the President finally.

'Needless to say, not a word of this can leak,' said Klein. 'Not to the press. To wives . . . or any ladies that happen to be stashed away in nice little bungalows. If I see or hear a word of this in any media intended for the public, I'll inform the President and advise that he declare Martial Law.'

'Sooner or later, preferably sooner, we're going to have to include the Russians and Chinese in this,' Ridley said, quietly resigned from his chair. 'The Allies are going to be difficult enough, and I wouldn't put too much faith in their respecting this secrecy.'

'What do you think their reaction will be?' asked the President.

'First reactions will be monumentally negative, of course. But probably fatal if missiles are launched and they haven't been informed of the situation.'

'Okay. Allen, call the Premier for me. Tell me what you want me to say. Let's get this show on the road. It seems to me that we're standing about five minutes from the edge of the biggest goddamn cliff in the world. And I sure don't want anyone pushing us the rest of the way over. At least not with me in front of the line.'

14

In the nightmarish black storeroom at the bottom of the forward torpedo room, the fourth day was agony for the Triton's crew. Arms and legs were racked with cramps. Mouths were dehydrated and lips were cracked and seeping.

The worst thing was the air. It was stifling hot and putrid. It would have been bad enough if that many men, crammed in one small compartment, had air-conditioning or even blowers circulating clean, filtered air past them. But they had neither.

For all the pain and discomfort, they were relatively quiet. But because their faces were hidden beneath heavy black hoods, it was difficult to know for sure whether they were quiet from the threat of death that had been related to them earlier by their captain or lethargic from the effects of the carbon dioxide exhaled within the confines of their individual hoods and re-inhaled with the eye-watering fumes from the urine and fecal buildup inside their once-clean dungarees.

But by now, the smell really didn't bother them. As a matter of fact, they had been exposed to it for so long, they weren't aware of it.

At the extreme forward end of the putrid, humid storeroom, Karl Beasley, the electronic technician who had been the Below-decks Watch, had to relieve himself. God knows he tried to hold it each time as long as possible. But his bladder was aching and felt like exploding and he could hold it no longer. For a few wonderful minutes the warmth from the urine felt comforting as it gushed down between his thighs, flushing out the red ugly, open sores erupting between his legs and buttocks before soaking the seat of his pants, lower back, and the legs of his dungarees.

The men on either side of him were also affected by the growing pool of acrid urine, but by now no one hardly noticed. Beasley's body basked in the momentary warmth. But all too soon it was gone, and the brief comfort was replaced by sores that burned with unanswered itching and clothes that seemed to stay damp and clamily uncomfortable.

And if that wasn't enough, almost as agonizing as anything

they were experiencing was the constant pain in their backs from lying in one position for endless black hours.

It was amazing that by now they weren't all in a state of total hysteria. Not that most weren't approaching the limits. But true to training and tradition, before they were sent to the various squadrons, the Navy knew they could endure uncommon stress as each submariner had undergone battery after battery of psychological testing that generated stress for extended periods of time.

But this was pushing it dangerously close to the brink. Each could feel even the most minute movement of the man on either side of him. Sometimes it was comforting – other times maddening. But it had one advantage. If a man started slipping into hysteria, as one of the men next to Beasley started to do, the men on either side could feel him trembling. And fearing that their captors were indeed watching and waiting to kill them, would press closer to their semihysterical mate. Until . . . hopefully he realized by the warm pressure of their bodies that they were trying to help out, and slowly the hysteria would subside.

It wouldn't be long though before it wouldn't matter. From dehydration and hunger, many – including Beasley's friend, the cook – were starting to hallucinate. You could hear him trying to force frightened animal sounds through his nose as the sticky grip of the tape kept his raw mouth bound as tightly as the straitjacket bound his body.

Several compartments aft, in the sonar shack's world of pure air, comfortable temperature, and controlled humidity, Nichols was once again training the chrome wheel back and forth on another distant bearing that signaled sonar contact. Next to him, Morgan looked up and checked his watch against the sweeping hands of the black chronometer on the bulkhead.

Sixteen-twenty hours. Still a couple of hours of daylight left, he thought. Then we can surface and start the transfer.

Nichols pushed the earphones back off his scruffy, unkempt hair until they rested in a semicircle around his neck.

In the quiet confines of the small, scientifically insulated compartment, even though partially muffled by Nichols' neck, Morgan could hear the faint *swoosh* . . . *swoosh* . . . *swoosh* . . . from his earphones as the propellers of the distant ship plowed a path through the rolling surface of the water toward their rendezvous.

Mixed in with the swooshing noises from the propellers was the *pi* . . . *ping* . . . *pi* . . . *ping* . . . *pi* . . . *ping* . . . from the distant ship's fathometer. To anyone else, it would have sounded like any other ship's fathometer, stuttering out its staccato electronic beat as its signal measured the ocean's uneven floor passing along on its unhurried journey. But the telltale sound of the *pi . . . ping* instead of the normal *ping* was the prearranged signal that was to identify this ship clearly and without a doubt to the silent Triton as it slipped effortlessly through the tropical waters 1,200 miles south of the tourist-filled beaches at Waikiki.

Morgan reached over and clicked on the intercom. 'Jonesey, three knots. Soon as we have speed, bring her up to six-five feet.'

'Six-five feet, aye,' Jones responded from the control room.

'Only the one other contact in the area?' Morgan asked.

'Affirmative,' Nichols nodded. He trained the chrome wheel locating another, more distant contact to their west. 'Only the one supertanker seventy, maybe seventy-five miles west by northwest,' he said as he shook his head to indicate that Morgan didn't need to worry about it. 'No sweat. She's definitely north of our track and hasn't varied a degree off her course. Should be clear of radar range by now. Another hour she'll even be out of sonar range,' he added reassuringly.

In the conning tower, Morgan watched as the luminous black-faced depth gauge unwound its way foot by foot toward the ocean's surface and neared periscope depth.

'Scopes are clear,' Jones yelled through the hatch that led up to the conning tower behind where he sat at the diving station.

Morgan reached into the overhead and grabbed a stubby, thick stainless lever. He pushed it and several compartments away, a hydraulic pump silently activated a cylinder which directed the hydraulic oil into the line and effortlessly and silently the periscope shot toward the surface.

Reaching its maximum height, the periscope stopped automatically with a swoosh. At the end of the smooth shaft, Morgan snapped down the round black handles used to train and focus the lens.

A remarkable instrument that hardly ever changed, Morgan thought. Out of habit, he quickly made a 360-degree sweep of their area, scanning the horizon for any possible unknown contacts or snooping aircraft.

In the old days, periscopes had just two settings, low power and high power, and were used mainly for torpedo attacks. Now, these new scopes were used mainly for navigation. Each one had a sextant built into it that was tied directly into the navigation computer. A few star sightings at twilight or sun lines at noon and within seconds, the ghostly quiet computer shot out a gleaming white card with their position accurate to within inches.

Morgan took another, slower, sweep. With the exception of the distant smoke billowing up toward the cloud-filled sky from the smoke stacks of the contact Nichols had identified, the ocean was empty.

As the periscope cleaved through the water several feet above the surface, Morgan increased the telescopic power until he could clearly see the smoke stacks and the heavy deck gear that jutted up from the ship like distant oil derricks. Increasing the power a little more, Morgan's trained eye easily saw that they were the cranes and deck gear of an aging, medium-sized cargo ship.

It was less than an hour till dark.

Astern, the cargo ship's wake formed a white crescent as it streamed in a slow, five-mile-wide circle waiting for its rendez-vous with the Triton.

Slouched in the captain's seat behind the glass wind deflectors at the far end of the flying bridge, Yummy constantly swept the horizon through a pair of powerful binoculars for a trace of the submarine.

Since the days on the Costa del Sol with Morgan and Ji'lhan, Yummy had become the absolute dictator of a business empire whose growth seemed as violent and as unstoppable as an un-checked forest fire.

The secret to Yummy's skyrocketing success in the international world of business was directly tied to his creation and patronage of the Japanese Red Army.

Bloodthirsty and seemingly devoid of all human emotions in their senseless slaughter of the innocent, the JRA had become the most feared terrorist organization in the world.

The first test of their dedication to their master's cause occurred in a holiday-crowded airport terminal in Israel – the Lod Airport massacre.

Several months later, when several lieutenants questioned Yummy's philosophical direction, they were forced to dis-embowel a family member before committing suicide in a bloody, macabre ritual on the snow-covered slopes of Mount Fujiyama.

Yummy was a megalomaniac of the most frightening kind. Recognizing no legal or moral authority higher than his own, he dreamed of the day when the rays of the Rising Sun would again shine benevolently over the Japanese empire from which he was destined to rule the world. Destined, because he was descended from the gods and was answerable only to them.

From the wheelhouse, a short, muscular Japanese captain dressed in a bright Hawaiian shirt hurried out. Bowing from the waist, he said, 'They have arrived, master.'

Yummy leaped up and rushed into the dimly lit wheelhouse. 'No mistake?' he asked. A trace of warning veiled in his voice as he spoke to the captain in the low dialect common to Japanese seamen the world over.

The captain shook his head assuring him. 'Definitely our friend,' he said with the calm assurance of an old warrior whose days at sea went back and included a warm December seventh in the Hawaiian Islands.

Yummy nodded. 'Order an electronic check of the area, surface and air. Alert the crew to stand by for the transfer,' he said to the captian as he rubbed his hands together to mask his nervous excitement.

The captain bowed and pressed a button on the bulkhead that sounded an alarm in every space onboard the ship. Turning to a junior officer, he barked out an order and the junior officer rushed aft into the compartment behind the wheelhouse which was crammed with sophisticated electronic tracking systems.

Activity burst out all over the ship as the hand-picked members of the crew rushed to their prearranged stations as efficiently as if they were members of a man-of-war clearing her decks for action.

In cabins below decks, another four men, who would be joining Morgan, gathered a few personal belongings and hurried topside to wait.

In the radar shack, the technician energized the radar's parabolic reflector in the tower high above the ship. For several minutes, he studied the sweeping beam of light that coursed around the large green radarscope.

Seeing none of the telltale blips that marked the presence of ships or planes within range, he pulled the pencil-thin microphone that dangled from his headset to his mouth and notified the bridge that the area was clear.

On the main deck, the sunset-silhouetted crew – black, faceless figures outlined by the glimmering orange light – hydraulically opened the forward cargo hatch, revealing a cavernlike space filled with heavy crates of machinery, canned foods, auto parts, televisions, and toys. Cargo that Yummy had arranged to have legitimately shipped from one company within his conglomorate to another to avoid any suspicion of the ship's zigzag route around the world.

Aft of the cargo hatch, two of the crew uncovered a shiny new diesel that would operate the huge crane with which they would take on their expected cargo. The diesel rumbled to life, spewing smoke and clattering like the engine of a huge diesel truck waiting at a truck stop for its endless journey.

On the bridge, Yummy's heart pounded with excitement as the periscope of the Triton broke the surface. Cleaving the water, it left a plume of white water spraying up behind it like the wake of a fast-moving water skier.

From the depths, a low, rumbling sound sent vibrations through the hull of the cargo ship. As he watched, Yummy could see the white water churning and boiling up around the periscope as the ballast tanks aboard the Triton were blown free of water and the massive undersea creature fought its way to the surface.

Yummy had never seen anything so beautiful. And the size of the damn thing! My God! He'd never realized how massive the Tritons really were.

He shook his head, realizing he had been suffering from a childhood condition brought on by Cary Grant submarine movies which showed them as small, fragile things, constantly in danger from deadly surface predators.

Looking down on the Triton's bridge, Yummy saw the hatch swing open and Morgan's lone khaki-clad figure emerge. Morgan raised an arm in salutation. Moments later Barth joined him and both men seemed to bask in the pure, subtropical air that they hadn't enjoyed for the best part of a week. The air inside the Triton was constantly repurified, of course, but fresh air is one thing submariners get as much of as they can any time it's available. Knowing that it might be the last for endless months to come, if not the last of all.

'Captain,' he said, without turning. Instantly the captain appeared at his side. 'Match his course and speed and bring us alongside.'

The captain bowed and returned to the bridge. With the few men Morgan had onboard the Triton, it would be the cargo ship's responsibility to do the delicate maneuvering necessary to bring both ships together.

At this slow speed and in this gentle weather, it was only minutes before the captain had his ship parallel to and yards from the Triton.

The maneuvering was a cinch for this captain and his experienced crew. They could – and had on many occasions – rendezvous at high speeds, in foul weather, and in the dead of night to pick up teams back from terrorist raids or exchange contraband, arms, and munitions for the JRA.

As the freighter moved alongside the Triton, Barth climbed down from the sail onto the main deck. One of the Japanese seamen fired a line gun toward the Triton and Barth watched the gentle arc of the small white nylon line as it fluttered down just aft of where he was standing. He grabbed the line and started hauling it in.

Attached to the line was the massive hawser which Barth slipped over one of the waiting cleats.

Quickly, the Japanese seamen threaded the heavy hawser through steel-treaded winches and ever so slowly the Triton was wound in closer and closer until finally both hulls met and were held together by the unyielding lines like two lovers locked in an embrace.

Yummy smiled down at Barth and gave him a thumbs-up sign. Arrogant bastard! Barth thought. Climbing down from the sail, Morgan went up the waiting ladder onto the ship where Yummy was waiting on the main deck.

Yummy smiled.

'Everything going OK?' Morgan smiled back.

Yummy nodded. 'There're a few things you should know about. But let's talk in my cabin. You look like you could use a drink.'

'Thought you'd never ask,' Morgan said, following Yummy up the ladder toward the bridge.

At the top of the ladder they were stopped for a minute by a creaking noise from the Triton. Looking back they could see two of the watertight hatches covering the missile tubes slowly cranking open.

Once the hatches locked open, Barth quickly punctured the filmlike diaphragm that covered the top of each tube with a razor-sharp knife. Slashing around the rubbery material, he finally flapped the eight-foot diaphragm back like the tongue of an old shoe. Once it was flipped back, a hush descended over the crew as everybody seemed hypnotized by the dull black nose of the deadly Poseidon missile, nestled comfortably within the grip of the hundreds of electronic fingers within the tube that were constantly touching it. Feeling it. Feeding it new information from the onboard computers.

100

To a man, every eye was riveted to that cold, metal symbol of brute power.

Breaking the spell, the captain clapped his hands sharply several times and brought his crew back to reality.

Barth attached the cable lowered by the crane operator to the Poseidon's stubby-looking nose.

He signaled. And ever so slowly the thick, greased cable became taut and the Poseidon started to rise slowly from its tube.

On deck, the diesel auxiliary whined its protest as it strained to haul the thirty-foot glistening giant skyward.

Finally, the missile slipped free from the gleaming steel missile tube and for a few seconds swung gently and harmlessly back and forth at the end of the cable tether like some dead man-eater at the end of a gaff.

Barth raised both arms and the crane operator hauled the Poseidon skyward until it cleared the railing of the waiting ship. Shifting gears, the operator guided the arm of the crane's orange-painted steel tower slowly over the cargo hatch, bathed from below by bright work lights.

Reviving the engine several times, the operator engaged the clutch, stood on the cable brake, and let the Poseidon slowly slide down into the waiting hold.

As it disappeared, Morgan followed Yummy into his luxurious cabin, located behind the radar shack on the bridge level.

The diesel engine from the deck crane was muffled by the heavy-paneled walls as Morgan sat forward in the comfortable modern chrome and black leather chair and flicked the ash from the expensive, aged Havana into the crystal ashtray.

Yummy returned from the heavy teak bar and handed him a generous drink in a heavy crystal-engraved tumbler. 'They found the body,' he said quietly.

Morgan's eyes narrowed in irritation.

Yummy nodded silently. 'Purely coincidental,' he shrugged. 'Some maintenance divers with a schedule known only to themselves discovered it while they were working on the tender's hull.'

Morgan sighed, 'They're sure?'

Yummy nodded his head. 'There's no mistake. They isolated the base. It's completely quarantined.'

Morgan nodded.

'That still shouldn't pose any problems for us, should it?'

'Not for the time being at least,' Morgan answered, shaking his head.

Morgan had hoped to have a few more days. But that was being greedy.

'The Air Wings, Hovercraft, and the Hunter-Killers will already be after our asses.'

Yummy nodded as he sipped a Japanese beer that, contrary to tradition, he liked over finally shaved ice. 'It's an awfully big ocean though, isn't it?' he said, raising his glass in a mock toast.

'How about our decoys?' Morgan asked.

Yummy smiled. 'We got over a ton of waste from five different sites. The papers speculated that it was the work of some "terrorist group" who were going to use it to make some kind of A-bomb with.'

'Well, they were half right.'

'We'll have it all over both oceans by the end of the week,' Yummy said, as he poured the foaming beer over another glass of ice. 'In the meantime, you will of course remain inconspicuous,' he added in a quiet authoritive manner, as a sweet though unpredictable smile crossed his face and he again raised his glass in a salute.

Morgan smiled as he studied his face for a moment. It was thinner than he remembered from the Costa del Sol. A little more drawn, if it were possible. But that could also be because of his closely cropped military-style haircut.

Morgan quickly raised his glass to return the toast and took a deep swig of the brandy so that he could look away. He hadn't been able to look at Yummy's face, or that of anyone else who had been close to Ji'lhan.

15

Morgan's last night with Ji'lhan before his boat was scheduled to leave the Med was spent very quietly at an outdoor café on the waterfront in Villefranche on the French Riviera near Nice.

Villefranche sits in a sheltered cove near the bottom of a high, rocky cliff that plunges straight down into the blue-green waters of the Mediterranean.

After dinner, Ji'lhan took a small wood case out of her handbag and sat it on the tablecloth next to Morgan's sleeve.

He looked at her as she waited like an anxious child for him to open it.

He snubbed out his cigarette and took her hands.

'I thought we promised . . . ' he said, ignoring the case.

'It's not a present. It's a secret charm. That will keep you safe from all those big-boobed blondes and bring you back to me.'

He laughed as he took her face in his hands and kissed her gently.

She took his hands and placed them over the case and waited as he picked it up and shook it gently.

'It rattles, so I guess it's not Old Spice.'

She smiled but looked puzzled.

'A cologne a lot of men have to use after their kids give it to them as a gift,' he explained.

The gleaming wood case, though small, was surprisingly heavy. He unsnapped the clasp and slowly opened the top.

Nestling snugly in the black velvet interior, a heavy gold chain that glistened like flowing lava lay entwined around a primitive medallion.

'God, Ji'lhan!' he whispered. 'It's magnificent!'

'It's Scythian,' she said proudly. 'It's the first thing my father ever really gave me. The Soviets were furious. But knowing Father, he probably looked disappointed. And they probably patted him on the back and asked his forgiveness. But I was tremendously pleased that he would risk the king's displeasure for me.'

Morgan gazed down at the heavy little treasure, hypnotized, his mind visualizing the ancient artisan who, several thousand years before, had painstakingly crafted it for his fierce nomadic masters. Masters who rewarded him by blinding him and lopping off his hands so he would never again be able to create similar beauty for a rival chieftain.

'I can't take it, Ji'lhan,' he said. 'The love that went into getting it for you . . , the sentimental value . . . '

She put her fingertips on his lips to shush him.

'Paolo,' she said through tears that welled into her eyes at the knowledge that he was leaving. 'The love that went into getting it, and my love in giving it to you, are all part of the gift.'

Morgan spotted the waiter and raised his hand to catch his eye. When he came over, Morgan quickly ordered a bottle of champagne to celebrate.

Waiting for the wine, Morgan looked up toward the dark, narrow road that snaked down the cliffs into Villefranche as an animal-like rumble beat against the rocky cliffs. The throbbing was from a powerful engine as it echoed down the cliffs and across the bay.

Reaching the base of the cliffs, the engine roared and a little gleaming car shot around the hotel at the end of the street and sped their way. The fire-engine red, phallic-looking roadster gunned over to the edge of the quay and braked to a stop next to the old heavy anchor chain that served as a guardrail.

Like a seagull's wing, the door on the driver's side swung up and a man with a graying vandyke that matched his gray business suit swung casually out. He walked briskly to the edge of the quay and stepped into a waiting sunroofed cruiser with a uniformed crew. In a spray-filled roar, they shot away toward a three-masted black yacht that glistened at anchor in the middle of the quiet bay.

As the boat roared away, the waiter poured two glasses of the sparkling, pale gold champagne.

Morgan raised his glass, 'To the Princess . . . and the Pauper.'

She raised her glass and with a mischievous grin said, 'You'd better be careful. Or I'll turn you into a frog.'

Their glasses tinkled at the touch. While in the distance, the speeding cruiser suddenly veered and roared back toward the old stone-faced quay.

Nearing the quay, it turned, throttled down, and chugged along parallel to the ancient, moss-covered stones. Suddenly the man with the vandyke broke into a wide, happy smile and waved both hands over his head.

Ji'lhan waved back like a little girl who's just seen an old playmate.

The man spoke a quiet order and the crew quickly tied the boat up.

Waiting at the table, Ji'lhan hooked her arm through Morgan's as he looked at her a little confused.

'Friend?' he asked, unconsciously intimidated by the apparent wealth of the man.

Ji'lhan looked at him and grinned. 'It's Father.'

Morgan was speechless.

'That . . . ' he choked quietly.

'You were expecting maybe a man on a camel?'

'No . . . ' Morgan shook his head. 'But I didn't think you desert people knew about boats yet.'

'Oh, that's just one of Father's "boy toys".'

'Well!' Morgan sighed. 'As long as I'm not one of your "girl toys".'

She winced, faking pain and anger. 'Of course you are, darling Paolo. But I don't usually admit it until after I've had them stuffed and mounted.'

After a joyful reunion, Ji'lhan introduced Morgan to her father. They talked excitedly and finished the bottle of champagne before he kissed her good-bye, shook Morgan's hand, and disappeared into the darkness toward the festively lit schooner.

Standing at the edge of the quay with his arm around Ji'lhan, Morgan shook his head in disbelief when he realized what the strange noise behind him had been. Walking over to the purring roadster, he reached in and turned off the ignition as everyone seemed to have completely forgotten about it.

'He likes you very much,' Ji'lhan said as they made their way toward a waiting taxi to take Morgan back to his boat. 'Even though you are an infidel.'

'But, it's your opinion I'm most interested in,' he whispered as he nuzzled her ear inhaling the beautiful aroma of the Moroccan jasmine that she always wore.

She put her arms around his waist and held onto him very tightly.

'I better take you back to the hotel,' he finally said. 'I hate good-byes at the end of piers.'

She punched him in the ribs.

'Sounds like you've done it before. I thought I was the first,' she said squeezing him even tighter. 'So, if you don't mind, I'll take you all the way to the end of your pier. Just to make sure no one else is waiting to see you off. I've heard about you sailors and your girls in every port.'

'God! I hope the crew remembered to cancel all the others for me,' he said as they squeezed into the back of a little black Peugeot taxi.

The taxi stopped at the main gate to the Navy base.

'Can a poor American sailor, and a rich Arab princess find true happiness in this cruel world?' he asked in his most solemn 'soap opera' announcer's voice.

She giggled and grabbed him.

Morgan looked at the waiting darkness beyond the brightly lit gate and hated the thought of having to leave.

'Don't look so glum,' she said softly. 'I love you.'

He kissed her gently, and said good-bye.

Through the rear window of the little taxi, he watched her disappear into the black night. An alien night that seemed like some bottomless void pulling her out of his life.

16

By the time his boat reached the States, the threat of another Middle East war blossomed.

Ji'lhan was desperate to get to Morgan in the United States.

But the war threat caught her in Mecca and travel visas for Arabs were restricted. Even though her father could have assured one, he refused, wanting to have some time to spend with her alone.

At a dinner between the two aboard his yacht at Jidda, Mecca's seaport in the Red Sea, he tried to explain the significance of her being a Saudi. And to dissuade her from the 'romantic folly' with this Westerner.

Ji'lhan respected the difficulty of this Old World predicament. Taking his hand, she tried to explain that she was more than an Arab and his daughter. She was a citizen of a modern world. A world he had given her. And after giving it to her, she wouldn't let him take it back.

He took her in his arms and held her tightly. He loved her as much as he would have a son. And as her dark, sparkling eyes looked up at him from his chest, he smiled and relented.

The following morning, from a flowery chaise in her father's walled garden courtyard, she placed an overseas call to Morgan.

Over the crackling line that she knew was probably being monitored, as all overseas calls especially during a crisis were, she told him of the dinner with her father.

Morgan was ecstatic and they talked for almost an hour, like excited teenagers planning a high-school elopement.

Morgan finally told her she was wasting her money on the expensive call and jokingly added that she should be more conservative. 'Once married, I plan on wasting a lot of it for you. And I don't think you should bother with cheap things like phone calls. Especially when there were things like Ferraris and yachts and expensive wines.'

'I'm afraid we're going to need a little of it for something else,' she shot back.

'Anything you want, kid!'

'Oh, thanks, but I'm already going to have one of those.'

'What?' he asked, not following.

'A kid.'

'A kid what?' he said after a moment of stunned silence.

'You said "anything I wanted". So I'm having one of those.'

Morgan couldn't answer. 'You're gonna . . . I mean . . . I don't . . . ' Morgan stuttered, not able to get a complete sentence out.

'Yes Paolo, I'm afraid so,' she sighed. 'And my Arab father says that if I'm not married by the time it arrives, he's sending a tribe of scimitar-bearing Bedouins to look for the father.'

'I'll be damned!' Morgan screamed, almost deafening Ji'lhan. 'You really mean it?' he asked excitedly.

'Yes. I'm sure,' she answered.

'When?' he asked, beaming.

'Six months.'

'Well! In that case, I got a little time left before I have to worry about your father's scimitar mafia.'

'You do,' she warned, 'and you'll answer to an Arab girl wielding one of her own. And I wouldn't want to think about your social life after her. As a matter of fact, I don't think eunuchs have social lives.'

'You wouldn't do that?' he gasped.

'Want to bet? I guarantee you'll be safe around any harem after I get through with you,' she warned.

They both laughed.

'Ji'lhan. God! I can't believe it.'

'It's true, my love,' she said, pausing a moment as she suddenly felt a cold loneliness without him. 'Oh, Morgan! I miss you.'

'As soon as you can, I want you to get your little butt on the first plane out of there.'

She laughed. 'By then it may not be such a little butt. My two sisters always gain at least fifty pounds when they're pregnant.'

'I'll reserve two seats for you then.'

After Morgan hung up, she dialed her father's private number to find out where he wanted to meet for lunch.

'I'm terribly sorry, mistress,' the secretary apologized profusely. 'Due to the crisis, a last minute conference in Belgium was called and your father had to fly over for the afternoon.'

Ji'lhan was disappointed.

'I humbly beg your forgiveness for not reaching you sooner,' he apologized profusely. 'But a number of calls have come in during his departure and I've been trying, without success, to reach Señor Vasques at his hotel to cancel an appointment he had with your father.'

'Vasques is here in Mecca?' Ji'lhan asked excitedly.

'Yes, Mistress,' the secretary answered.

Ji'lhan was delighted. She didn't have any close friends in Mecca, and to find out that Vasques was in for the day was a joy.

When she reached him by phone, he said, 'It's ridiculous for friends to be talking on the phone when we're so close. I insist we finish the conversation over lunch.'

'I'd love to,' she said. 'Where?'

'Where?' he replied. 'I haven't the faintest idea, my dear. The restaurants . . . like the people . . . all look the same to me. And with those terrible robes, I'm never sure if I'm talking to a man or a woman. Any country that hides a woman's legs is definitely a terrible place.'

'All right,' she laughed. 'Take a cab and meet me here. I'll see if I can't think of someplace where you can look at legs during lunch.'

'Ahhh! Female legs, my darling,' he interrupted. 'I've heard strange things about some of your Arab customs.'

'OK!' she conceded. 'Female legs.'

'Ahhh! The sight of someone to rescue me from the antichrists is indeed a joy, my love,' he laughed as he came through the ornate double doors.

'Now,' he said, hugging her in his grizzly bear embrace. 'How about a slight repast before I die of starvation? And we have a hundred . . . no, a thousand things to talk about. How are you? How's your American? How did your father take the news?' he rambled on and on, asking a new question before she had a chance to answer the last.

'You don't know how damn glad I am that you're here,' she laughed. 'And to hear someone talk more than I do is a relief. What do you want for lunch? Would you like to eat here?'

'No, no, no, my darling!' he said. 'I have no intentions of being caught in a Moslem land with a single woman in the privacy of her apartment. Besides, I want to be out in the sunshine. Where, even though they may be hidden behind sack robes, my imagination can get me into the trouble of my own choosing.'

'All right,' she said. 'I'll expose you to some marvelous local culinary mysteries. And a meal that'll fend off that desperate starvation that seems to be decimating your body.'

'Fantastic! But please, my darling, someplace where I can order something that doesn't come smelling like it's been laced with camel chips.'

'You're terrible,' Ji'lhan laughed. 'Allah will get you for talking like that,' she said.

'I didn't know what we might do, so I didn't have my taxi wait,' he said as they went out into the bright sunlight. 'Of course, I also didn't know how to ask him to wait. And I didn't want to take the chance that he might think I was trying to leave without paying . . .'

'You want to walk?' she asked.

He grimaced. 'Not one of my favorite ways to exercise,' he said, taking out a handkerchief and wiping the perspiration that was already starting to form on his forehead from the brief walk across the courtyard to the street.

'All right!' she said leading him toward a bright red Lamborghini setting in the shade of a stately tree in the middle of the circular driveway. 'We'll take one of father's.'

Stopping next to the outrageously expensive little machine, Vasques sighed.

'What's the matter?' she asked.

'I'm constantly amazed at these automobiles,' he said, wiping his forehead again. 'The last thing they consider when they design these whining little devils is comfort. Neither physically, nor financially. They make them for skinny Italian gigolos with little asses. Not masculine Spaniards. They fail to recognize that by the time the skinny-assed gigolos can afford one of these things, he's as old and as fat as this old Spaniard.'

She laughed and looked around. Her father's Rolls limousine was in the garage on a lube rack with one tire off. That left the huge American Oldsmobile station wagon used by the chauffeurs for hauling groceries and household servants back and forth to his other estates.

'OK?' Ji'lhan asked pointing at the station wagon.

'Now that's a car made for comfort,' he said, opening her door for her. 'Later in life, I can assure you, you will be pleased that you chose an American. They're the only ones who give their wives the comforts of a huge car.'

'You're insane,' she laughed.

Waddling around to the driver's side, he opened the heavy

door and slipped behind the wheel and turned the key that had been left in the ignition.

The bomb that had been attached to the ignition exploded with such force that the walls next to the courtyard were blown down.

Vasques received the brunt of the blast and he was dead before the terrible force dismembered his body and showered it toward a thousand different places.

'Sidi . . . sitti . . . sidi . . . sitti . . .' the wailing servants screamed as they dug Ji'lhan out of the smoldering rubble with their bare, bleeding hands.

In her guarded hospital room, her father's pain at what had been done to the most beloved thing in his life was worse than if he had suffered the blast himself.

The strange depressions in the white sheet that covered her were frightening testimony to the mutilation inflicted on her lithe body by the blast.

The surgeons had tried, although in vain, to suture the gaping wounds from the engine and dashboard parts that had sliced through her like shrapnel.

'Al-Riyadh?' she whispered, calling him by his Bedouin name as the pain-killing drugs made her voice almost inaudible.

'Yes, my love. I'm here.'

'You must let Paolo know. Please . . . ' she struggled to get the words out. 'Please, don't let him hear it from strangers.'

'Of course,' he promised, tears streaming down his face.

'I love him as I love you.'

'I know. Please rest now. Don't worry.'

'Thank you,' she said as, painfully, she drew her arm from beneath the sheet. Although bathed in bandages, her fingers were still beautifully delicate and still had faint traces of pale pink polish on the nails.

He took her hand and kissed her fingers.

'I'm sorry,' she whispered softly, apologizing for his pain. 'Please don't be sad.'

He squeezed her hand gently and smiled at her concern for his feelings rather than hers.

He could feel her squeeze his hand almost imperceptibly in return.

As he watched, her eyes fluttered. For a moment she seemed to be unable to focus. Finally she found his face.

'Don't be afraid,' she said softly, trying to comfort him as she died.

111

Even though the bomb hadn't been meant for her, it didn't matter. She was dead.

It was an accident. Not the bomb, but her death. Because of her father's oil policies, it had been set off to kill some of his household staff. To show how vulnerable he and his family were.

And it was successful.

At first, her father was convinced it was Western retaliation for the recent economic sanctions against them.

But his Saudian king, through his privately funded intelligence organization, found that it wasn't a Western plot. But one closer to his own household.

The information was reliable, as the informant was subjected to brutal torture learned patiently through centuries of extracting information from unwilling nomadic enemies.

His king, an old and dear childhood friend, tried to warn him. Ji'lhan's father smiled and kissed his hand.

He knew. But he was firm about handling the matter himself.

He was assassinated two weeks later together with his wife and chauffeur by a bodyguard who had been in his household since childhood. A member of an organization that, once again, refused credit.

Morgan learned of her death in a department store while shopping for a color television set for their new apartment. Watching her face on the dozens of sets on the showroom floor, Morgan felt a searing flash burn through his brain and everything went black.

It took three squad cars and two ambulance crews to get him restrained, shackled, and to the mental ward of the county hospital.

For weeks his mind raged like a wild animal whose leg had been crushed in the steel jaws of a hunter's trap every time the image of her gentle smile, lilting voice, and warm touch vibrated across his brain.

Like the trapped animal, crazed with pain, he would have gnawed off the shattered limb if he could have.

But a few friends, the bearlike Barth and the stumpy, little Jones, gathered at his hospital room and in the midst of the storm that raged within his brain, tended him and tried to soothe him until they could restore him to a semblance of sanity.

The following year, when the outrage had passed, accompanied by Barth and Jones, he tried without success to locate her unmarked, Moslem grave.

The brutal murders were never solved. And, in the end, no organization ever dared claim credit for their deaths.

But, sitting in his cheap hotel room, waiting to return to the States, a bleary-eyed Morgan read and reread an article in a national magazine.

Over and over, he reread the caption under the newsphoto by a correspondent from the midst of one of the rampaging mobs that stormed like some mindless beast through the streets of Jidda, venting hatred after the explosions.

It was only a profile, but it looked vaguely familiar.

Though dressed as an Arab, the face was strangely out of place at that time – and it was then that Morgan knew.

'Anything else?' Morgan asked as Yummy poured the last remaining drops of beer into his glass of shaved ice.

'No. Just keep yourselves well hidden.'

'Whatever you say,' Morgan answered. 'You paid for the dance, so you're calling the shots.'

Yummy nodded, pleased with Morgan's assurance. He genuinely liked Morgan. But he had a tendency to feel a little inadequate around the man. And that was something he'd rarely experienced in his lifetime.

'Once we're both clear of the area it will be an opportune time for you to dispose of the remaining members of the crew,' Yummy said. 'It shouldn't matter if their bodies are found. By then we'll both be well clear of this part of the ocean once and for all.'

Morgan nodded as he watched the ripples cast by the amber liquid in his glass. Finally, he quickly knocked back the drink and sat the glass firmly down on the bar. 'I'll take care of it,' he said as he started for the door.

Back on the bridge of the *Lewis & Clark*, Morgan and Barth watched as the cargo ship slipped toward the black horizon.

'What'd the gook have to say?' Barth asked acidly, as his dislike of the man came to the surface.

'He wants us to stay out of sight,' he said, watching the ship disappearing into the waiting darkness.

'No shit! What did he think we were going to do? Head up to Waikiki for Liberty?' Barth asked sarcastically.

Morgan shook his head in silent agreement.

'He also thinks now would be a "convenient" time for us to "dispose" of the crew. Now that we've transferred the first of the missiles.'

'Nice group of people you run with, Morgan,' Barth said in disgust.

17

Steam from the urn of new coffee hissed into the crew's mess as the Triton glided through the dark, cold depths at five hundred feet. Its aroma hung heavily in the air as Morgan joined Barth and two of his new crew members at one of the mess tables.

The shining Formica table in front of them was buried in blueprints, jigsaw-looking schematics, oversized wiring diagrams, and bulky secret Navy manuals removed, rather unprofessionally, from the captain's safe.

Watching the two smiling faces across from him, Morgan thought how far they were from what most newspapers would ultimately be picturing to the public as classic blood-crazed terrorists. They were far from the bearded, sweating, hopped up, wild-eyed anarchists of the Che Guevara or Black September mold.

On the contrary, they were clean-shaven and wore crew cuts, which was the current fashion, after the shaggy and unkempt sixties and seventies.

And why are they smiling? he thought. Maybe they're blissfully ignorant of the disaster we're heading for. Maybe they really believe they're going to be able to spend the rest of the money, or haven't yet given up that bullshit veil of immortality.

Of the four new men who comprised the balance of the crew, these were the only two that had never been aboard a submarine before.

'I hear the ocean voyage wasn't too pleasant on the way out,' Morgan said.

Herndon looked up embarrassed.

'It wasn't too bad,' said Jon Nakamoto, smiling at his partner.

'But for some strange reason every time the ship rolled, Herndon bent over a commode and yelled for someone named O'Rourke. I told him I didn't think he'd answer. But he kept yelling down at him, "O'Rourke, O'Rourke!" '

Herndon laughed at the image, but was ecstatic that they had submerged and left the rolling swells of the Pacific to those with a stronger stomach. 'God knows,' he sighed in relief, 'a couple of times I was sure I heard O'Rourke calling back to me.'

Herndon was a fat, opera-loving computer scientist. As a kid, his fat, stubby fingers had refused the conditioned reflexes demanded in piano lessons. But when exposed to the mysterious interior of a computer, they seemed lithe enough to be able to literally dance through the sensitive circuitry. Effortlessly, he could reprogram or flawlessly rebuild one of the units into a device simpler and more efficient than the manufacturing scientist had originally designed or envisioned.

His partner, Nakamoto, hadn't suffered the agony of sea-sickness. Probably because of the summers between school he'd spent on his uncle's fishing boat near Monterey. An ancient, hulking, wood-hulled seiner, it was his uncle's pride and joy. And it had helped feed the whole family, pay their rent, and put them through college after Jon's father was killed fighting with the all-Japanese 442nd in Europe while the rest of the family was split up and interned at California's Manzanar Detention Camp, and Jerome, Arkansas.

As he had always guessed would happen, one day his uncle and the boat left the old rotting pier and never came back. But it was only after his uncle had been assured that Jon was a young maths prodigy whose mind often solved lengthy formulas quicker than an operator could input them into a computer.

But for all his mental ability, he had two deep disappoint-ments in life. One was that he was Japanese. A condition brought on psychologically by the prejudice toward Japanese Americans after World War II. The second, that he was too small for football. Not only on the professional level but even as far back as his freshman year in high school. Had he been a foot and a half taller, he would have been the perfect statuesque quarterback.

But unfortunately, if he had been a foot and half taller, it would have also only increased his girlishlike lack of co-ordination. But he could dream, couldn't he?

'You got the "fail-safe" worked out yet?' Morgan asked the blond, horn-rimmed, overweight All-American who hated sports of any kind and the short, yellow Oriental un-American-looking shrimp who had both been drafted by a computer science firm to head up a very secret and highly advanced Tiger Team.

'Seems more like a mechanical than an electronic or a repro-gramming problem,' Nakamoto said, shrugging as if it was no worry.

116

Herndon nodded his unconcerned agreement.

'OK,' Morgan said. 'But I've said it a hundred times. Whatever you do, don't underestimate the Navy. They spent millions trying to anticipate something like this.'

Herndon took off his thick glasses and spun them thoughtlessly in his beefy hand. 'Oh, it's a classy system all right. I mean they have got some pretty nice security features built in. But we'll just rewire the shit out of it.'

'The rewiring's the mechanical problem I was talking about!' said Nakamoto, looking at a schematic. 'It's a three terminal system. One terminal, the master station, probably the captain's, originates from the radio shack. The other two terminals, the slaves, are in that missile control room.'

'Everyone just has to be careful not to mess with any of the wire we'll be stringing,' Herndon said. 'Outside of that, the so-called computer security is almost zero.'

'It could take, oh . . . I'd say . . . as long as . . . ' Nakamoto drew out the answer he knew Morgan was anxiously waiting to hear. Finally, he smiled. 'It could take the better part of a day at least.'

'You're sure it'll be that easy?' asked Morgan.

'If we run into a problem we'll send a masquerader through,' explained Herndon.

'A what?' asked Morgan, wondering whether or not they were trying to pull his leg the same way railroaders used to send new firemen for 'a bucket of steam'.

'A masquerader's an instruction that's sent into the system looking like the real McCoy. Or one that can come in piggyback on one that we know is authentic,' Herndon explained to Morgan.

'And if that don't work?' Morgan asked.

Herndon shrugged, 'We can always send it back to the factory. I'm sure it's guaranteed,' he said as they laughed.

'How about some kind of factory-installed booby trap device?' Morgan said, returning to a more serious mood.

Both Nakamoto and Herndon shook their heads.

'I can't find any "phantom" wiring in the schematics. Everything, all the components and systems are genuine and necessary. We'll take some meter readings though. Just to be on the safe side. But I can't imagine them taking the chance that something like that might break down and screw up a real mission,' Herndon said, shaking his head as he shuffled through blueprint after blueprint.

'Besides, did you ever hear of anything like that when you were riding these things?' asked Nakamoto.

'Never,' Morgan shook his head. 'How about target data? Can we change that?'

'No sweat,' Nakamoto said, without looking up from one of the bulky technical manuals he was leafing through. 'Although the so-called fail-safe is basically separate from the guidance EDP Bank . . . '

'Wait a minute. Hold it!' Morgan grimaced. 'Let's keep it so's the old man here knows what the hell you're talking about. OK?'

'OK. In a few simple words, for the old man, we got the "access controls" to the whole shooting match,' said Nakamoto. 'We're gonna erase the old stuff we don't want and give it what we in the biz call a contaminated program.'

Morgan nodded, pleased and looked up as Jack Marwin came through the hatch.

Marwin was a world class muscleman, an ex-guided missile technician who loved to spend his months at sea between watches working out on the ship's weight lifting equipment. Throughout the submarine service, his narcissistic vanity was legend. His dungarees were always tailored to the last thread to fit his bulging torso, his hair always sprayed to a single-haired perfection. Like Nakamoto, he also hated two things in life. Anything that got his hands dirty. And a Navy he had a grudge against.

'How's it look?' Morgan asked.

'Very, very neat and tidy. Just the way I like things,' Marwin said, standing very straight so as not to cause a wrinkle in his trousers. 'Everything's rigged. We can launch any time you give the word.'

Morgan nodded as 'Big Daddy', the last new man, came down the passageway and slinked into the compartment, dwarfed by Marwin.

Big Daddy really wasn't big in the physical sense. He got his name because he was supposed to have the biggest male organ known in Naval history. He was a snakelike toothpick of a man who usually went shirtless to show off his twenty-plus years of tattooed naval service.

One of the greatest pieces of locker art every sailor wanted taped inside his locker was a blown up snapshot of Big Daddy with a cow-breasted hooker with a bulging, rolly midsection laying at the end of a dingy double bed. The open-mouthed shock on her face was a combination of disbelief and pleasure as she lay there spread-eagled and waiting as Big Daddy's hard frog – he called it that because it could jump right out at you, was aimed down at her slit with the precision of a professional pool sharks custom cue.

Big Daddy was the oldest and saltiest man in the crew. An old-time, 'blood-and-guts' ex-submariner who remembered riding old Fleet Boats, he'd been given a dishonorable discharge after getting rip-roaring drunk at a beach party and assaulting one of the officers' wives in the back of the bus coming home. It wouldn't have been so bad but she was the wife of the base chaplain.

During his court-martial, word drifted back to his old sea buddies that she thought he had assaulted her with some kind of pornographic device.

He snickered that she must have a pussy for a husband because he'd only flashed enough of it to scare her a little.

He quickly poured a cup of coffee and dumped in several heaping tablespoons of sugar. Blowing across the hot surface, he slurped it more like a farmer than a sailor.

'You know we got cruise missiles in tubes forward?' he asked casually.

Morgan nodded and smiled. 'Didn't I promise you some nice new toys?'

'Just like Christmas!' Big Daddy smiled.

'Jesus H. Christ!' Barth muttered as Morgan walked into the control room a little later. 'Where the hell'd you find that slick-looking King Kong?'

'Marwin?' Morgan chuckled.

Barth nodded.

'He was sitting on the beach with a dishonorable.'

'Now I remember,' mused Barth. 'Wasn't he that faggot from the *Orca* they caught going down on somebody?' Barth snickered.

'No,' said Morgan. 'He wasn't the faggot. He was the "fagee". The other guy was the faggot,' Morgan grinned.

'Yeah,' Barth grinned. 'The guy said he was going through the forward torpedo room hatch and tripped. And when he landed, he accidentally fell on Marwin's hard-on.'

'That's the one!' Morgan said. 'So try to stay on your feet, OK?'

Barth grinned.

18

In the dark stateroom, Captain Seright roused slightly from a restless sleep.

Out of habit, he instinctively looked at the gauges on the bulkhead at the foot of his bunk to check the course, speed, and depth. He started to scratch his itchy crotch, but the strait-jacket dug into his shoulders, bringing him back to the reality of where he was.

He craned around and tried to see out into the passageway. But the curtain was drawn shut and all he could see through the tiny slit was a couple of feet up and down the far wall.

The boat seemed ghostly quiet and in the fog of his half-awake stupor, he stared blankly and without focus overhead until, once again, he started drifting toward the security of sleep.

Just on the upper reaches of consciousness, his mind whisked him to the six hundred acres of the Del Monte Hotel in Monterey which housed the Naval postgraduate college.

As he made his way across the campus, he passed the old tennis courts and started toward the administration office in the old Mediterranean-style building that was once the main hotel.

Passing the 'Roman plunge', he heard the sounds of the other bright young officers picked by the Navy for future command frollicking in the cool waters, enjoying a day away from the grueling curriculum of the demanding classes. The sounds from the plunge had almost faded when he heard someone whispering.

'Captain?' the voice whispered almost inaudibly.

'But I'm not a captain,' he smiled from the luxurious safety of his dream. 'At least I won't be until later . . . '

'Captain,' the voice hissed insistently.

Suddenly a hand clamped over his mouth and nose, shutting off his air. He struggled to breathe but the hand held firm.

'Captain, please don't yell,' the frightened voice pleaded.

The hand around his mouth and nose relaxed enough for him to take a breath.

In the dim glow he could make out the figure of a head peering over the edge of his bunk from someone crouched on the floor.

'Please don't yell, sir, please. OK?'

Seright nodded, the hand disappeared, and his lungs burst with relief as the air flooded in, and relieved the drowning, suffocating feeling.

He focused on a pair of frightened eyes topped by a shock of curly hair, while nervously anticipating an attack from the black phantom birds with huge eyes and powerful killing beaks that swooped down out of the black sky.

'I tried to wake you easy, sir. I shook you by the shoulder but you musta been dreaming or something and you started to yell. I had to stop you, sir. I'm really sorry,' he whispered, as Seright realized he was a young sailor suffering from the training that made it taboo to touch an officer, especially a full captain.

'Who are you?' Seright whispered, not knowing whether or not he was one of the hijackers.

'Butler, sir. Seaman Grady Butler, sir. I just came aboard in Guam the day before we were supposed to leave, sir.'

He tried to remember the unfamiliar face, but drew a blank. No doubt a new crewman that hadn't been introduced to him as yet.

'How did you get out of the storeroom?'

'They just never saw me, sir,' he whispered.

'Did anybody else get out with you?' he whispered, praying for a ray of hope that more of the normally ingenious crewmen had worked some kind of miracle.

'No, sir. They's in that storeroom up in the forward torpedo room. I was in the one under the crew's mess.'

Seright's heart sunk when he realized that the hijackers had somehow overlooked him when they took over the boat.

'How'd they miss you?' he asked.

'I don't really know for sure, sir. I was putting the ice cream we just made down in the freezer when all of a sudden my face started getting hot. The next thing I know, I woke up in the freezer almost froze. I started to skedaddle the hell out of there, but I saw a couple of guys in gas masks carrying off the cook and telling as to how if he woke up they'd have to kill him. So I just slipped back down and hid till I could figure out what was happening. At first I thought it was one of them drills or something. But then I heard them talking 'bout how they had had to kill one of the guys topside and I knew it wasn't no drill . . . '

'No. It's definitely not a drill, son,' he said, satisfied he was who he claimed to be.

'Well, I don't understand, sir. Are we at war or what?'

'In a way . . . Yes, I'm afraid we are. Now listen, son. How'd you get forward?' whispered Seright.

'Well, since they got underway, I been sorta creeping along the bilges till I could get from one place to the next without being seen. 'Course it took a while. But it was a lot easier when they surfaced. I hightailed it up here while most of them were up topside.'

Son-of-a-bitch, thought Seright. He didn't know they'd surfaced. It must have been for some kind of rendezvous. Probably for more crew, he thought, as he hadn't seen enough men, or heard enough voices to run the boat safely for long.

'Are you qualified, son?' he whispered hopefully.

'No, sir. 'Fraid not,' he smiled apologetically.

Shit, Seright thought. He tried to figure out the best way to use this green kid. 'Do you think you can reach any of the other crewmen?'

'No, sir,' Butler said, shaking his head emphatically. 'I tried a coupla days ago. I waited almost a whole day. But they got this guy with a machine gun that's guarding them. And even those guys make lots of noise and everything when they come in to make sure he hears them. 'Cuz he seems kinda crazy . . .'

The captain nodded.

'Do you want me to undo these things around your arms?' he asked, starting to undo the straitjacket tie.

Seright shook his head violently. 'No. If they find me gone, they'll know someone let me loose. And it wouldn't take them long to find us both. I'd rather have you loose and them not know about it.'

Butler nodded.

'Do you think you can get back to the missile compartment?'

'Sherwood Forest?' Butler asked, smiling that he knew some of the salty jargon.

'Yes, Sherwood Forest.'

'It might take me a while, especially since they got more guys than they did before. But I think I can.'

'Good boy. Now listen. Here's what I want you to do. And just in case you can't get back to me again . . . I want you to keep doing this, no matter what. Understand?'

Butler nodded, hoping he wouldn't disappoint him.

'I want you to make sure, no matter what, that they can't fire the missiles . . . '

'But God, sir . . . I don't know anything about . . . ' he said, but the captain interrupted.

'I know you don't. But just listen. I'm going to give you a quick lesson in sabotage.'

Butler nodded, listening intently.

'Get to the missile compartment, Sherwood Forest, and starting from the bilge level work your way up to the other levels if you can get to them without being seen – and you start turning valves.'

The young seaman nodded.

'Just start turning valves. That's all there is to it. If one is open, you close it. If one is shut, you open it. Understand? And if they catch it and change it back, after they're gone, you change it back again. The most important thing you have to do, something that might save the world, son, is to keep them from launching any of the missiles. Do you understand?'

'Yes, sir,' he whispered enthusiastically. 'Anything else?'

'Just don't get caught,' he added grimly. 'If you do, they'll kill you on the spot.'

Seright let it sink in. 'Now, get out of here before somebody comes,' he hissed.

Quickly, Butler dropped back down on hands and knees and parted the green curtains. The passageway was clear and he belly-crawled to a hatch in the deck, opened it, and disappeared into the lower depths of the boat.

Seright smiled to himself. Their first fuck-up. With any luck . . . if he happens to turn the right valves, he'll blow this baby right out of the goddamn water . . . They'd all die . . . it wouldn't be nice. But they were going to die anyway so they had nothing to lose. He didn't want to risk telling the seaman that what he was asking him to do would almost surely mean his death. Anyway, if he didn't blow up the boat, sooner or later they'd find him.

God! He was joyous at the prospects of what was going to happen. If only he could tell someone. The exec . . . the crew. The crew would cheer if they knew. They sure didn't want to die. No one did. But if they had to, which they did, and if their odds were zero, which theirs were, he knew, like all the other crews he'd commanded, they would want to make the bastards pay.

When they finally died, at the bottom of that stinking storeroom, behind those black hoods, with their mouths taped and their skivvies full of shit, he knew most of them – those that still had their minds – would know what was happening and would be cheering.

19

The President was sitting in the ranch office looking out into the star-filled night. There was a chill in the air.

In the distance, he could hear the sounds from his wife's guests enjoying one of the lavishly 'simple' buffets she was famous for. She was upset that he had declined to join them, but not as upset as she or they all were going to be in the days ahead.

As he looked into the chilly sky, it reminded him of another night, years ago, when as a teenager, his laughing-drunk father had staggered into the barn.

A towering rodeo cowboy, married to an Eastern woman, J.J. was one of the wealthiest ranchers in the West. Yet he didn't have a bull or cow to his name. The ranch's main asset was oil shale. Shale which the oil companies paid him massive amounts of cash to keep off the market.

Waiting for J.J. in the barn were dozens of ranchers from 'down the line' to make sure he paid off a recent bet.

The bet had been made at a drunken bash wherein his father promised to pay, or donate a dollar a head to their favorite charity for every live jack rabbit delivered to his barn.

Knowing the size of the local jack population, that old J.J. was a man of his word, drunk or sober, and knowing that he could afford a sizable donation to charity, within a week, every man, woman, cub, boy, and girl scout, glee club, church choir, PTA, and civic group was swarming over the hills trapping the furry varmints.

To celebrate a 'successful roundup', they got J.J. drunk and presented the seemingly chagrined rancher with truckload after truckload of crated, skittish jacks.

Standing in front of the barn, whisky bottle in one hand and stacks of dollar bills in the other, as the jacks thumped against the sides of their cages, true to his word, J.J. forked over a crisp new dollar to each one of the cheering crowd that showed up with a live jack.

The charities were overjoyed. It proved to be the best fund raiser they'd ever pulled off.

Few would have believed that after it was over, a surprisingly sober old J.J. and his young son could be found in the office at the back of the huge barn laughing so hysterically that tears were streaming down both their faces.

It seems that while old J.J. had been in Europe on one of his latest escapades away from the constant whining of his Eastern wife, he'd found out that Italians have an insatiable desire for the hunt and fruits thereof of the tasty hare.

And as J.J. and his son watched, teams of Mexican laborers were carefully loading stack after stack of the American hares into a gleaming diesel trailer rig.

'Signore,' the Italian from Milan said in his heavy northern accent once the rig was loaded. 'Fantastico! The count is complete, 35,844,' he said, taking a bank draft from his inside pocket.

J.J. punched the numbers into the ancient adding machine next to his desk. 'Comes to $179,420.'

'Well, son,' he said, returning to the office after seeing the Italian off, 'let that be a lesson to remember. Matter of fact, let it be three or four lessons. One is that that Italian fellow wants us to set up a quick freeze plant and go into the export business with him. Second is now that we kept a couple of thousand of them for breeding, we don't have to worry about "charity" no more. We paid a dollar a head for them . . . the Italian gave us five.'

'Why'd he give us so much for them?' he asked as they made their way across the dark quadrangle.

'He's gonna set them loose on his farm and charge them slickers from the cities twenty bucks apiece to hunt them. Helps them hot bloods let loose some of that macho you hear so much about.'

'So, what's the fourth lesson?'

'That's the easiest. When someone offers you a dollar for nothing, you gotta wonder why. Always look a gift horse in the mouth, son. Especially in charity and politics.'

The President remembered that more than once in his career. Especially when plotting strategy with men like Klein and understanding what big money supporters would ultimately expect.

God. How he wished he still had that proud, stubborn old son-of-a-bitch around to help. Especially now. But the dumb-ass son-of-a-bitch had died a disgustingly ridiculous death.

He'd choked to death in a classy restaurant. He'd just sat

there, without moving a muscle. Until he started turning red. Then his mother saw him and screamed.

Within minutes, he'd keeled over. People tried mouth-to-mouth resuscitation, not knowing that a half-chewed bulging piece of steak stuck halfway down his gullet prevented help.

People assumed old J.J.'d had a heart attack. The doctor who performed the autopsy would have said otherwise, but out of respect for J.J.'s pride . . . the doctor called it 'natural causes' instead of accidental. Even though 'accidental' would have brought back a whopping double indemnity from the insurance company.

'Jesus! Why couldn't he have had a little less pride,' he thought as a disheveled-looking Klein rushed into the office.

'Chapman was on the horn from Washington. He got the demands,' he said, handing the President a Top Secret folder.

Nodding apprehensively, the President quickly slid his fingers under the heavy seal. Peeling the wax from the edge of the envelope, he took it between his fingers and rolled it into a marble-sized red ball which always reminded him of playing with the cooling wax from a hot candle when he was a boy.

Taking out the report, he anxiously read the carefully worded message transmitted by the ancient Vice-President who always dutifully remained behind in Washington.

Messages from Chapman were always predictably formal and what he thought befitting the prestige of the office, since later they would undoubtedly be admitted as historical documentation from this President's tenure in office.

EO (Eyes Only) John James McGregor,
President, USA (WWH)

FROM: Chapman, Vice-President, USA, WASH., DC

Sir. Demands from *Lewis & Clark* received at White House 1530 this date by surface mail via Vancouver, BC, Canada. Verification authenticated by enclosure of Captain of *Lewis & Clark*'s standard Naval ID card. First demand directs that gold bullion equal in value to ship seized . . . approximately four billion . . . be divided in two separate but equal containers and placed at following locations.

First container . . .
Longitude 67 degrees, 25 minutes East,
Latitude 32 degrees, 45 minutes South.

Second container . . .
Longitude 178 degrees 39 minutes West,
Latitude 39 degrees 15 minutes North.

Completion of delivery no later than fourteen (14) days from
date of postmark. Lack of compliance or interference in
recovery will result in launch of missile at civilian targets.
Demand signed by Commander . . . League of Men.

20

The President laid the message on top of the red folder and picked up his phone. He dialed the number that would connect him to Admiral Whittiker's quarters, but after several rings, it was apparent he wasn't there.

Hanging up for a moment, he pushed the intercom line that connected him to the compound operator.

'Yes, Mr President,' said the crisp, militarily efficient voice.

'Locate Admiral Whittiker,' he said. 'Tell him I want to see him immediately.'

'Yes, sir, Mr President,' replied the evidently Western voice.

'Just like the cops,' Klein ventured, as the President dialed another number. 'Never around when you need them.'

The President held up his hand as Allen Ridley answered. 'Ridley, I need to see you in my office as soon as you can get here. Thank you.'

He had just hung up when the operator buzzed him on the intercom. 'Yes,' snapped the President.

'Admiral Whittiker is on his way, sir. He was here in the communication center talking to Admiral Towne in Guam.'

'Thank you,' he said, as he could already see the admiral striding briskly through the barn toward his office.

As he closed the door behind him, the President handed him the message. Whittiker read it quickly and nodded.

'I guess we can be sure it's authentic?' the President asked.

'Beyond a doubt,' the admiral nodded. 'There's only one way they could have the captain's ID card.'

'You think maybe there's any chance we can get the FBI and the Canadians to trace the letter to its source?' asked the President.

Both Klein and Whittiker shook their heads knowing it would be a waste of time.

'I don't imagine they would have put a return address on it, Vince,' the President said, shaking his head.

Ridley shuffled in, wearing an old terry-cloth robe thrown on quickly over the sleeveless tee shirt and wrinkled pants.

'Have a seat, Mr Ridley,' the President instructed, motioning the old man to the chair next to his desk.

'We've just got their demands,' the President said.

'Four billion dollars in gold, the replacement cost of the *Lewis & Clark*, delivered to two different locations, and no messing around or they set off some of the missiles,' Klein said.

Ridley nodded.

'Why two locations?' asked the President.

'Even with their warning, they know we'll have to try to destroy them,' the admiral said. 'This way they know we'll have to split our forces.'

'Better chances of recovering at least one of them,' added Klein.

'What are the locations?' Ridley asked.

The admiral looked at the message again. 'One seems to be the southern Indian Ocean. Southwest of Madagascar, I'd say. Probably between Australia and the east coast of Africa. The other looks smack in the middle of the North Pacific. Probably between Midway Island and the Aleutians.'

'As far apart as they are, it seems there's little chance they'll try to recover more than one of them,' Klein speculated, as his mind quickly calculated the distance between the two widespread locations.

Whittiker shook his head. 'I can't imagine they'd risk it.'

'Could they have already reached either one of those areas by now?' the President asked.

'Easily,' the admiral nodded. 'Although I doubt if they're anywhere near either one of them. We've concentrated a great deal of our efforts monitoring the Sea Spider. And I've added two squadrons of Hunter-Killers to the Curtain already on station. So far, nothing.'

'Then they might know about the Spider and are avoiding it,' said Klein.

'I'd say so,' nodded Whittiker. 'If not avoiding it, they've been damn lucky in missing it.'

'That might help narrow down *who* we might be looking for,' said Klein. 'I wouldn't think there would be that many men familiar with the antisubmarine defense of the United States without having access to that info from you, Admiral.'

Whittiker nodded. 'I'll have the Bureau of Personnel on it right away. Men, probably officers, recently resigned or retired, who were qualified on FBMs and who had access to Sea Spider.'

'So, they'll let us make the drop, then take their time with the recovery,' said the President, getting back to the demands.

'If they make it at all,' Ridley warned quietly.

'Why wouldn't they?' asked the President.

Ridley shrugged from the comfortable confines of the over-stuffed chair. 'I can think of a hundred reasons. If for no other they might just use this to test how far we're willing to go.'

'Speaking of going along, how are our allies and the Russians reacting?' the President asked.

The scientist sunk back into the comfortable leather. 'SEATO and NATO forces have been placed on alert under Whittiker's command. The Russians refuse to offer support,' he said from behind closed eyes. 'They won't react, or respond, unless they're attacked.'

'Bastards!' the President said. 'They're enjoying seeing us sweat.'

'Which is unfortunate as the consequences they risk are far greater than the national pride that keeps them from assisting,' Ridley added.

'Then I am to assume you gentlemen suggest we meet their demands?' asked the President.

The admiral nodded and said, 'Unless you want them to prove they can fire the missiles.'

'No . . . I don't want them to prove that. I trust your judgment that they undoubtedly can.'

'But once we pay . . . It's just the start,' said Klein.

The admiral nodded. 'That's why we've got to risk destroying them at the sites.'

'Do you really think we can?' the President asked, feeling helplessly like an outsider walking through somebody else's dream.

'I don't really know,' the admiral replied. 'The *Nimitz* is in the Med and the *Eisenhower* is in the Atlantic. I'll send them both to the Indian Ocean. The *Vinson* just left Honolulu for Japan. I'll divert her to the North Pacific, then try to slip in as many Hunter-Killers and Hover Buggies as we can. Our gamble is that we can kill her before she can retaliate.'

'And if we can't?' asked Ridley.

'We've already discussed those consequences. But we do have one definite advantage,' he said, as everyone looked up.

'If they launch a missile successfully, our missile defenses can compute the trajectory back to the original launch site. I plan to station a secondary strike force on the perimeter of each site, well within missile range. If they launch, they'll expose their position and we'll have her.'

They all nodded. 'You'll have to get the Congressional Committee rolling, Mr President,' Klein said. 'They'll have to authorize moving the gold.'

'If we're gonna end up blowing the place up, maybe we can use something else. Dummy up something to look like gold. A decoy?' said the President.

'Sure,' said Admiral Whittiker. 'But what if they're successful in picking it up and it's not the real McCoy?'

'You're right,' the President nodded.

'Besides, it's only gold,' chuckled Klein sarcastically.

21

Through the needle-thin attack periscope, Morgan could see tons of frothy spray kicking up over the bow of the huge cargo ship.

Low in the water, laden with thousands of tons, the ship plunged through the white-capped swells, sending a storm of spray into the air where the gusting winds pelted it down in a fine mist over the vast, corroding deck containers that were stacked almost as high as the flying bridge.

'Outer doors have opened,' the intercom next to the attack periscope crackled, as Nichols clicked off the mechanical procedures that were automatically occurring during the firing run.

'Angle on the bow, 30,' Morgan said quietly to Barth standing at the fire control computer, doublechecking the electronic read-out with Morgan's visual calculations.

' . . . seems like old times . . . ' Barth hummed the familiar strains of the once-popular tune.

' 'Cept this one's like a duck in a barrel,' Jones called up the hatch from his diving controls.

'No, I think it's a fish,' Morgan said, glued to the scope.

'What's a fish?' Jones asked.

'A fish in a barrel. Not a duck in a barrel.' Morgan increased the intensity of the scope and refocused on the clipper bow of the powerful ship as she bullied her way through the stormy sea.

'Well, whatever. She still won't know what the hell hit her,' Jones muttered.

'She'd better!' Morgan yelled down, his eye glued to the soft black rubber eyepiece of the periscope. 'That's why the hell we're doing it.'

'Besides, if they don't,' said Barth, raising the second scope, 'it sure as shit won't take 'em long to figure it out.'

'Jesus Kerist!' Barth whistled as he focused on the distant ship. 'That's what I call a goddamn big mawmoo!' he said, looking at one of the largest transporters ever built by man. 'A five-hundred thousand tonner,' he whispered as Morgan watched the automated giant steaming unerringly on her computer-programmed and controlled course.

'Bridge . . . Sonar,' Nichols interrupted over the intercom. 'It's her all right. COMSA readout confirms her as the *Island Queen*, a supertanker conversion. Autoguide installed a little over two years ago. Crew includes one master engineer, a master electronics mate and six seamen.'

'A crew of eight to run a whole fucking island,' Barth muttered almost inaudibly.

Since navigational electronics had become so precise, most companies had converted their fleets to the various new guidance systems, whereby the onboard crew had nothing to do with the voyage.

She was a floating robot. The engineer was onboard mainly to insure against mechanical failures and was the theoretical captain.

The master electronics mate maintained the computers and electronics. And the seamen were used mainly to operate the deck equipment to on and offload cargo, cook, and for the never-ending battle against rust.

As the floating island bulled her way through the swells, the choppy water reminded Morgan of the violent sea that rolled up the deserted beach where he and Ji'lhan spent their first night together.

For a heartbeat, he could smell the familiar aroma of her Moroccan jasmine. And his heart felt a twinge of pain that he could never seem to escape from.

'Surface!' Morgan hissed through the hatred that choked off his throat every time he thought of Ji'lhan.

At the command, Jones's hands flew across the solenoids that controlled the air valves. Instantly, air under collossal pressure roared through the air lines, forcing the water out of the flooded ballast tanks, making the Triton lighter than the seawater, and sending her shooting toward the surface.

'Seventy-five feet,' Jones called as he counted out the depth to Morgan as the Triton climbed to the surface.

'Sixty feet.'

'Forty-five feet.'

Morgan waited under the sealed hatch that led from the conning tower to the bridge. When the depth gauge indicated the conning tower was out of the water, he turned the chrome crank and opened the hatch a crack. There was a sudden blast of air as the inside atmosphere and the outside atmosphere equalized. Then he spun the crank and flung open the heavy watertight hatch.

On the wet bridge he rested his binoculars on the edge of the superstructure and trained them on the distant freighter.

For a few moments Morgan couldn't find any sign of life on the distant decks and from this angle even the bridge seemed deserted.

Suddenly he could see a young Oriental dressed in dungarees pedalling a bright yellow bicycle past the cargo containers toward the bridge. He seemed lost in thoughtless routine and was cycling along like someone on a picnic outing when he turned toward the distant open sea. He spotted the gun-metal black Triton less than a mile off their beam.

Surprised by the unexpected sight, the front wheel of the bicycle started wobbling, and the man lost control and fell in a sprawl on the wide deck.

Jumping up quickly, he limped to the ladder that led to the bridge. Scurrying up it, he flew into the wheelhouse and moments later came running back out with two men.

They watched the Triton for a few moments, talking excitedly between themselves before a fourth man joined them with a camera and together they waved in friendly salutation. It was not uncommon to see warships at sea, but a submarine was a rare treat.

As Morgan watched, the seaman with the camera clicked off shot after shot. Finally, Morgan reached over and clicked the IC button.

'Stand by,' he said calmly.

'Standing by, Skipper,' Big Daddy responded nonchalantly from the forward torpedo room.

'Fire Control locked and ready,' Nichols added from sonar.

From the bridge of the freighter, the four seagoing technicians saw the stubby-bowed Triton start a slow swing through the swells until she seemed to be heading straight toward them.

Morgan reached down and pressed the damp IC switch. 'Fire!' he said quietly.

There was a gentle shudder as the two gleaming torpedoes shot out of their steel tubes like thoroughbreds out of a starting gate.

'Torpedoes running,' Nichols' voice crackled over the intercom. In the background, while his intercom switch was depressed, Morgan could hear the sleek missiles screaming through the water like new tires whining along a hot asphalt highway.

Yummy'll really be pissed! Morgan thought, smiling to himself. He could see him raging at the old Jap captain. But he won't know why . . . There's not one clue. That'll probably put him back on his fucking pills again. With any luck he'll OD.

On the freighter, the four technicians watched the approaching submarine, speculating who she was, who she belonged to, and what she was doing.

Suddenly, about six hundred yards off their beam, two white fingers seemed to be racing toward their bulging, thin-skinned underbelly.

'Mother of God!' whispered one of the technicians as his heart seemed to explode into his throat. Without a word he raced into the wheelhouse. Frantically he knocked the automatic pilot switch to manual and spun the helm as far as she would go, praying the ship would respond before it was too late.

Two of the other technicians didn't have the faintest notion what was happening. But the fourth, an old, white-haired salt who should have retired a decade earlier, had survived this sight on two previous occasions back during World War II in the Atlantic on ships that had disappeared underneath him.

It would take at least a half mile before the sluggish freighter would respond and start its agonizingly slow turn.

He knew instinctively it was too late and rested both hands on the rail. Calmly, like a disinterested observer, he watched as the wakes from the torpedoes raced toward him.

In tandem, they disappeared almost directly under where he was standing. He felt the dull thud and was aware of the deck plates under his feet starting to bulge upward. The last thing he remembered before arching up at the spearhead of the explosion and debris was how the concussion had cleared his sinuses for the first time in years.

On the Triton the glare from the explosions was like a giant flashbulb, forcing Morgan to have to lower his binoculars until the fuzzy halo that pierced his retinas cleared.

Inside, Morgan's crew looked up as the shock waves from the explosion, magnified by the density of the water, shook the drifting Triton like an earthquake. The Triton creaked and rolled like a Greyhound Scenicruiser over rough road.

Morgan watched as the huge moving island ground to an achingly slow halt. Several secondary explosions followed, rack-ing the dying giantess with spasmodic shudders, as thousands of tons of seawater rushed into her gaping wounds.

As she started to list, the trailer-sized deck containers started spilling into the choppy sea like tiny painted toy trucks.

Through the black smoke and sooty fumes, Morgan could see the panicked survivors trying to swing out a lifeboat. Clambering in, they half lowered, half dropped it into the oil-covered sea.

'Barth,' Morgan yelled as he knelt down by the gleaming hatch.

'Speak,' Barth answered from the conning tower where he had his eye glued to the scope watching the dying ship.

'Go forward and open the forward torpedo room hatch. Give Nardulli and Marwin a hand. Get the crew topside,' he said.

Almost an hour had passed and the fires onboard the freighter were raging the full length of the ship as Morgan maneuvered the Triton close to the lifeboat.

He watched the flames as they danced macabrely across the silhouette of the huge ship that had been sent into the world in the late seventies by her Yugoslavian builders from the upper reaches of the Adriatic with a Lloyds and Norske Veritas 100-A1 rating.

They would toll the ritual Lutine Bell for her on the floor of Lloyds home office. The bell that is only rung to signify the death of another great ship.

From the bridge, Morgan could see what remained of the crew, sitting zombielike in the lifeboat staring back through soot-blackened faces at the inferno that had been their home.

The bow of the Triton looked like that of a refugee ship off Ellis Island in the early nineteen hundreds – or off Vietnam in the middle seventies – as the *Lewis & Clark*'s crew huddled together on her narrow deck.

Barth had stripped off their straitjackets while Marwin tied them into their bright orange lifejackets. Standing guard, Nardulli kept his automatic weapon trained on the limp mass of men who would have been too weak to mount any threat even if they weren't hooded.

'Do you have water and supplies?' Morgan asked the men in the lifeboat through a battery-powered megaphone.

One of the survivors nodded.

'Were you able to get off a distress signal?' Morgan asked.

The crewman nodded. He also had the film from his shattered

camera in his plastic pipe pouch safely tucked in his jockey shorts.

'Good. Then rescue should already be on its way. I'm leaving additional survivors with you. Have everyone stay close. Lash yourselves together and everything will work out.'

Morgan signaled Barth who was waiting on the bow upwind from the nauseous smell of the huddled crew. 'Okay,' he said to Nardulli and Marwin who started lowering the putridly filthy men into the water. This must be it, they thought, and the screams filled the sky like a flock of screeching seagulls attacking a school of darting anchovies.

The last man to go over the side was Captain Seright. Unhooded and untethered, he shook away Barth's hands as Barth attempted to help him. In a last attempt to save his wounded pride, he tried to climb down by himself but was too weak. Halfway down, he slipped and fell head first into the oily water.

Through the din Morgan said, 'Good luck, Captain.'

'Fuck you,' Seright yelled back in a hoarse dehydrated whisper. 'If there's a God he'll see you blown to hell before we're back on the beach,' he said, shaking his fist.

His emotions relieved, he quickly turned and started organizing his men. He started stripping away their hoods. Once their eyes adjusted to the unfamiliar brightness, like the well-trained seamen they were, they quickly turned to help others unable to help themselves.

'All ahead one-third,' Morgan said as he watched the captain locate the crew members that were in the worst shape and guide them toward the waiting lifeboat.

'Secure the forward hatch, Barth, and stand by to dive,' he said as the crew fell behind in the gentle wake of the Triton's rudder.

22

As they cleared the destruction, the memory of the lanky captain treading water against the blue waters reminded Morgan of Ji'lhan's fag friend who had been with her, Vasques, and Yummy the first night he'd met them in Gibraltar.

After her death, Morgan spent months before locating the gaudily dressed man at a sidewalk café near the Casbah in Morocco.

At first, the man was clearly on edge when he saw Morgan. He had never liked him, and was at a loss to understand what Ji'lhan saw in this common half-breed.

Later that night, however, back in his luxuriously decadent apartment, his heart pounded with lascivious excitement at the prospects of seducing the sinewy mariner who had been Ji'lhan's lover. Especially when Morgan's drunken self-pity reached the point where he seemed defenseless against a comforting, compassionate advance.

At first, the naked little man, lying on the sea-blue sheets, was excited at the prospects of what might be a sadomasochistic game. A game that many he'd seduced needed to help prove to themselves later that they were still men. And in order to maintain their heterosexual identity, they would act 'tough'. Unfortunately, this occasion was unexpectedly different.

Morgan suddenly slipped his hands through the chains around the man's neck and twisted them until they dug a white canal and he started gagging.

The man noticed too late that Morgan's drunken slur had suddenly disappeared. 'My God!' He tried to scream through the stranglehold. 'What are you doing?'

'I'll tell you what I'm doing,' Morgan said through a controlled rage. 'I'm finding out just what happened to Ji'lhan.'

'You're crazy!' the man shrieked. 'You know what happened. She was killed . . .'

'I know.' Morgan spat as he swung on top of his chest. The pressure broke most of the malleable chains, so he grabbed the man's neck with both hands. 'What I want to know,' he hissed as he put his weight against the man's throat, 'is who did it?'

The man started to wet his pants as the fear made him lose control of his bladder. 'God! How would I know? Don't you think I'd like to know, too? I loved her too you know!' he screamed, sounding genuinely convincing.

Morgan reached into his wrinkled shirt and shoved the worn magazine article into his face.

'No!' he pleaded. 'Morgan, please, it's not me.'

'Yes!' Morgan spat, bringing his knee up heavily between the bony legs. 'It is you!'

'It's not! I wasn't even near Jidda,' he said as tears flooded his eyes. He would have vomited, but Morgan's grip kept everything in his throat.

'What's that?' he asked innocently as he looked at the picture of himself that he never realized had been taken.

'It's you, my dear friend!'

In a frighteningly quiet rage, Morgan slipped off his belt and wrapped it around the man's neck. Buckling it behind one of the wood posts, he drew up the slack, pinning the man to the post so he couldn't move without strangling.

Ripping the electric wire out of a lamp on the night stand, he bound the man's soft hands so tight it felt like a tourniquet. Within moments his hands started to get numb.

'What are you doing?' he cried in terror. 'What in God's name are you going to do?'

'Every agonizing thing imaginable if you don't give me the answer . . .'

'What do you want me to say?' the man pleaded. 'Tell me, for God's sake. I don't know, but tell me what you want to hear and I'll say it,' he cried, almost convincing Morgan that he might be telling the truth.

But Morgan had to know for sure.

'I don't want you to tell me anything but the truth,' Morgan said calmly, inches from his terrified face. 'If you don't . . . ' he said, waiting to make sure the man understood, 'I'm going to cut off your balls,' he screamed as his rage grew.

The man knew without a doubt that if ever anyone was serious, this raging madman was.

'All right,' he whimpered, cringing like a trapped animal. 'All right.'

Morgan waited, staring down at him.

'It was an accident,' he said as the huge tears started flowing down his cheeks. 'It was an accident . . . I swear. He told me it was only supposed to be a warning to her father. But it went off later than it was supposed to. I don't know what happened,' he sobbed in earnest grief. 'I really don't. Either something was defective, or he lied to me,' he spat angrily at the realization of one possibility he had been avoiding. He started shivering uncontrollably as his body was suddenly cold from the heavy perspiration that was evaporating and cooling his naked skin.

'Who is "he"?' Morgan asked, a strange calm in his voice.

'Takeo,' the man said almost sadly. 'Takeo Yamimura.'

'Yummy,' Morgan said strangely quiet. Relieved at last.

The man started to nod, but the belt buckle cut into his neck causing him to gag.

'God . . . Why?' Morgan asked, tears coming to his eyes. 'She was your friend, his friend,' he said.

'Yummy needed some kind of oil guarantees from the Saudis and he heard they might not be given. And he was my friend. We were lovers. And he said he needed help. How could I say no?' he pleaded, tears streaming down his pathetic face.

'Yummy's gay, too, then?' Morgan asked.

'Yummy's anything he needs to be,' the man said sadly.

'Where is he?' Morgan asked, strangely quiet.

'I don't know,' he sobbed painfully. 'Please . . . You have to believe me. I haven't seen him since it happened. God knows I loved her so much I wanted to die when I found out she was in the car,' he babbled.

Morgan closed his eyes to try and soothe the raging anger, but he couldn't.

Several days later the little man's body was discovered. Newspapers speculated that he was evidently the victim of a brutal sexual assault by some psychopathic pervert he'd probably picked up. His friends had always known he was promiscuous and had warned him about picking up strangers.

As the *Lewis & Clark* left the burning wreck in her wake, Jones climbed up to the bridge. He and Morgan stood quietly for several minutes watching the distant black dots, the heads of the disappearing crewmen, as they bobbed up and down in the oily blue swell.

Enjoying the salty spray that kicked up from the bow and swept back over the bridge, Jones said, 'Game's going to start getting rough now.'

Morgan nodded slowly. He was suddenly too tired to answer.

141

Barth climbed up the ladder. 'Forward hatch secured. We're rigged for dive again.'

'Take her down. Let's get the hell out of here.'

'Shouldn't we tie a broom to the scope first?' Barth asked as he started down the ladder.

'Probably should use a barrel,' Jones muttered as he dropped down after him. 'Like I said earlier, that's the sign for shooting fish in a barrel.'

Morgan couldn't keep his eyes open any longer. Making his way to his bunk, he fell heavily into it and for the first time in months, dropped into a deep, refreshing sleep.

23

'Mr President.'

'It's an honor to meet you, Captain Seright,' said the President looking at the bleary-eyed and exhausted captain who had been pulled out of the oily waters barely eight hours earlier and whisked back to the States in a flurry of secrecy.

'Can we get you some breakfast – a steak, coffee?'

'Oh God, yes! . . . Thank you . . . Please, everything,' he said from a body that was so numb with fatigue he felt oblivious to everything but what his bloodshot eyes happened to be focusing on. He tried vainly to stand ridgedly at attention in the presence of his Commander-in-Chief.

'And, for God's sake, sit down,' the President said.

'Thank you, sir,' Seright said, thanking Christ he'd made the offer before he fell flat on his face.

'We'll take as little of your time as possible, Captain,' said Admiral Whittiker. 'We can appreciate your condition. But, as you know, a great many lives rest on this debriefing.'

'Admiral, I'm afraid it'll be brief from the very nature of what I will be able to tell you,' he said as his head suddenly seemed to weigh almost too much to hold up.

'Twenty-two of my men died in the water,' he went on. 'Or were dead when they went in. Until I was on the helicopter leaving the deck of the cruiser, I was never aware of how much time had passed. All I can say with certainty is that it seemed like an eternity. And always will be for some of my crew.'

'What can you tell us about the hijackers captain?' Klein asked.

'Very little, sir,' Seright answered shaking his head. 'I only saw two of them. One dressed as an officer was apparently in command. The other one was dressed in dungarees like a seaman. The officer called him Barth.'

'Any impressions or anything else about them that might help?' Whittiker asked.

'Not really,' he shrugged. 'Both were evidently technologically prepared. In control mentally and physically. I mean they weren't wild-eyed, crazy radicals or anything like that. That was the spooky part. They seemed so . . . normal. They definitely didn't seem to think or act like they were the "bad guys" in this.'

'There's not a terrorist group, or murderer, or bully who does,' said Klein.

'You never saw, or heard anything from any of the others?' the admiral finally asked, a twinge of frustration in his voice.

Seright shook his head. 'Occasionally, I heard footsteps going up and down the passageway. But I have no idea of the size of the group. Or even if this man was the leader, although he seemed to speak from a position of authority.'

There was a knock and a white jacketed steward rolled in a gleaming cart laden with white napkins, china, condiments, crystal water goblets, fruit, and a large silver coffee service. One of the cart wheels squeaked as the steward rolled it to the captain's chair, unsnapped a leaf, and folded it out into a table. From the oven underneath the leaf, he took out a hot pewter platter with a thick steak still sizzling next to a half-dozen steaming over-easy eggs and hashbrowns.

The captain looked at the bountiful feast and a sudden confused wave of sadness and joy ran through his body. Tears came to his eyes and streamed down his cheeks. 'Sorry, gentlemen,' he apologized, wiping the tears away on one of the napkins.

They nodded and waited quietly, respecting his condition.

'I guess I never really expected to see anything quite so beautiful again,' he explained, picking up the heavy silver fork and wood-handled steak knife. Even though the steak was as tender as butter, he was so weak it felt like leather.

'Neither man bragged about any of their plans? You never overheard anything?' the admiral continued.

Seright shook his head as the juices from the first bite flowed slowly down his throat like elixir. My God, he thought, as the flavor seemed to explode into his mouth.

'Do you think you could ID them from NavPer photos?' Pat Murphy, the bulky CIA chief asked. 'If we can locate any friends or relatives, that would be a big help,' he said to Whittiker.

'I think I could ID the two I saw,' he affirmed, dousing another bite in one of the golden buttery egg yolks.

Murphy nodded as the captain looked up. 'Admiral, Mr President, I'm afraid I can't really tell you shit, sorry sir, I can't tell you anything about who they are, how they came onboard, where we were, where they were going, or what their plans are.'

They looked solemnly at each other for several moments.

'However,' he added, dipping a piece of steak in another yolk. 'I can tell you we might have an ace in the hole.'

They looked anxiously at him.

'A young seaman, a member of my crew is still onboard.'

You could almost feel the crackle of optimism as the captain related the mess cook's story, his orders to him about sabotage and most importantly not to get caught, which he must have accomplished as he was not among the rescued survivors.

'Can you count on him? I mean, is he a good man, Captain?' asked the President anxiously.

'I'm afraid I can't answer that, sir,' the captain said, shaking his head. 'It was his first cruise.'

'He wasn't qualified then,' Whittiker said grimly, seeing the favorable odds starting to shrink.

Seright shook his head slowly as he wiped some of the egg from his mouth onto the soft linen napkin.

'What do you think his chances are?' Klein asked, already guessing from the admiral's expression what they would be.

'Slim at best,' the captain verified honestly. 'But to his credit, he's survived without them discovering him for as long as we were onboard.'

'And when he finds out he's been left behind?' Admiral Whittiker sighed.

The captain nodded. 'He might . . . he'll probably panic or surrender. I don't know.' He shrugged.

After Seright passed out from exhaustion and was rushed to the sick bay, the President sat quietly while Admiral Whittiker paced back and forth in deep thought.

Through the glass panel he could see Ridley hurrying across the barn toward them.

Shutting the door behind him, he shook his head and slumped down in one of the chairs. 'I just heard. I mean I just don't know what to think,' he said in bewilderment. 'It's so illogical it almost doesn't make sense.'

'I agree,' Admiral Whittiker said, 'why would they risk their mission by releasing the crew?'

'Does seem stupid,' Klein thought, staring at the faces around the office. 'But they're not stupid. Whatever the reason, this won't turn out to be as dumb as it seems.'

'Was the captain able to be debriefed?' Ridley asked.

'If you can call it that,' Murphy said.

'I suppose there's no way to keep a lid on it now,' the President asked.

Whittiker tapped the top of the desk unconsciously. 'The distress signal was picked up by too many ships,' he said, shaking his head. 'Not to mention ham operators all over the whole goddamn Pacific. Plus the Dutch and Liberian freighters that were the first ones on the scene broadcast it to half the goddamn world.'

'I guess that answers part of the question,' Klein said as the President looked at him for an explanation. 'The *why* part of why they'd risk their mission by sinking a ship and releasing the crew. Now the whole world's going to know.'

'I thought those assholes wouldn't stop at sea for anything,' the President said, ignoring the point.

'Normally they won't,' said Whittiker. 'But it seems they thought they could tow her in and claim salvage. When she broke in half and sunk, damn near dragged them both to the bottom before the two cables snapped.'

'Too bad they don't make stronger cables,' said Klein.

'At least we know where they are,' smiled the President, trying to find some solace in the situation.

'Well,' Whittiker paused. 'At least which ball park. But not which row, or which seat yet.'

'Any suggestions on how we should handle the press thing,' the President asked.

'I'm afraid for the time being I'd deny it,' Klein said. 'When the story breaks, accuse the press of scare tactics to sell newspapers and TV shows.'

'How long do you think they will buy that?' Ridley asked.

'I doubt if they'll believe it at all. But a regular bomb scare causes enough panic. Can you imagine if the whole world starts to panic at the same time. There isn't an army anywhere big enough to maintain order.'

'We've had nuclear threats from radical groups before,' said the President.

'But that's all they ever proved to be, Mr President,' said Admiral Whittiker.

'And for years, the great cities of the world have sat on their duffs and discussed and debated what to do if they were ever threatened, and we know what the results were,' Ridley said quietly.

'They're either still in Committee . . . or in the "planning stages",' Klein said disgustedly.

The communications officer from the Crypto Room knocked anxiously and Admiral Whittiker motioned him in.

'From Naval Air Pacific, sir,' he said handing the decoded message to the admiral.

'What is it, Commander?' the President asked as the admiral hurriedly read through the message.

'An American Grumman patrol bomber, and a Japanese Kawajima have confirmed two unidentified nuclear contacts.'

'Does that mean they've located them?' the President asked excitedly.

'Possibly,' Whittiker said as he studied the message. 'There could be two separate contacts, or even the same contact at two different times,' he said, handing the message to the President.

Picking up a pad, he scribbled a message and handed it to the commander who rushed out. 'I'm moving our strike force into a position to be able to intercept either contact. Hopefully one will prove to be the *Lewis & Clark*. I'll fly out myself. In the meantime, I'd like for Mr Ridley to make sure the Russians know what we've got and verify that it's not one of theirs for, unless I hear to the contrary, once on station I will attack.'

'What are their locations?' Ridley asked so that he might relay the information to the Premier.

'One is close to the area where the freighter was sunk. The other is close enough to the ransom dropsite in the Pacific to pick it up.'

'This could be the break we've been waiting for,' muttered the President.

24

Yummy's anger was uncontrollable as he glared down at the decoded message on top of his desk. He hadn't experienced anger of this severity in years and had thought he had reached a place in life where he could control it with ease.

With slow deliberation, he got up from the desk, walked to the bar, and poured a glass of beer over the ice that nestled like a snow bank in the bottom of the tear-shaped crystal tankard.

Taking out a silver case, he snapped it open. Inside were several rows of neat, brightly colored capsules to fight the staggering tiredness that followed all his psychotic outbursts.

He checked his watch. He had to be very careful with these pills. One was like riding a skyrocket. They'd relieve the agony of his rage and keep him bright-eyed and bushy-tailed for days. One too many and he'd be stoned and useless.

He popped two of the brilliantly colored tablets into his mouth and washed them down with the cold, slushy beer. A sharp pain cut his throat. He held his breath as the pain traveled slowly down his throat before disappearing into a burning sensation at the top of his chest.

He pushed a call button on the bar and his captain, who had been waiting uncomfortably outside his cabin door, hurried in.

Staring down at the message, he motioned for the captain to sit as he quickly reread the report of newspaper accounts of the recent rescue of men at sea following an explosion that involved a supertanker and a submarine.

Sitting rigidly on the edge of the seat, the captain prayed that his master would honor him by allowing him the privilege of decapitating the man who dared violate his authority. Well aware of Morgan's capabilities, Yummy thought back through their relationship to analyse what was meant by this insubordination and decide whether or not to unleash his samurai.

Even though the late morning sun was hot, the slopes were still icy as Yummy skied down the steep, twisting mountainside.

As he waited for an empty chair to round the tower to take

him back up, he heard another lone skier slide to a stop behind him.

'You ski pretty good for a gook,' Yummy heard the faintly familiar, sarcastic voice say to him.

Bristling, he looked around to see who would have the foolish arrogance to address him as a 'gook'.

'My God, Morgan!' he suddenly smiled as the skier lifted his goggles. Yummy shook his gloved hand, genuinely happy to see him.

'What are you doing in Gstaad?'

The chair lift came around and they both leaned back as it carried them toward the top of the mountain.

'Taking my hostility out on this shitty slope,' Morgan said smiling.

Yummy nodded. There was a moment of silence before he said, 'I can't tell you how sick I am about Ji'lhan,' he said. 'God! What a shock.'

Morgan nodded, silently grim.

'Have they found out anything?'

Morgan shook his head. 'I'm told they never will.'

As they came to the top without another word, Morgan roared back down toward the bottom of the slope at breakneck speed.

Spending the balance of the week together, Yummy saw the hollow-eyed Morgan was a shell of the man he'd met in Spain. Ji'lhan's death had almost destroyed him.

Over the next few nights, a drunken, melancholy Morgan hinted at a sketchy outline of his dream of revenge against the Arabs for causing her death, and the world in general for giving birth to a breed of assholes that should be slaughtered – wiped off the earth – and whose very presence was an insult to nature.

'Tell me about it,' Yummy said softly. 'Get it out. It'll help.'

Morgan smiled through his drunken stare. 'Fuck you. I'm not just talking,' he threatened.

'Talking about what?' Yummy asked.

But Morgan was adamant about not talking further. 'I can't tell you, old friend. After it's over, if anyone knew you knew, they could come after you. I won't let that happen to you.'

It took several nights for Yummy to draw out carefully his scheme to pirate a ballistic submarine. 'It's impossible,' Yummy chided, egging him on. 'Especially considering what the government spends on nuclear security.'

'They spent the bread on making sure someone can't get to

the weapons. But I'm talking about taking the whole fucking platform.'

'It sounds suicidal.'

Morgan leered at him, and said with a drunken smile, '*Au contraire*, my friend. It's so fucking simple the only thing I have to worry about is enough bread to convince men it's worth risking their lives for.'

'Enough money to get men to risk their lives. Sounds like a lot.'

'Men do it every day for almost nothing. Kids grab old ladies' purses. Guys knock over gas stations and blow out the attendant's brains for twenty or thirty dollars.'

'You should have no trouble then,' Yummy said.

The next morning, when he managed to get Morgan sober, Yummy told him he might be able to help.

Morgan smiled quietly to himself as Yummy related his relationship within the world's terrorist community.

'I might already be able to provide the manpower necessary to provide such a crew. I have access to any number of skilled seamen,' Yummy added.

Morgan shook his head. 'No. Unless they've been on an FBM, they'd be useless, unless we were taking her by assault, which we couldn't risk. If we work on this together I insist on recruiting the men that I and I alone think are qualified.'

'How many will you need?'

'Ten, including myself.'

'Ten?' Yummy shot him an incredulous look.

Morgan nodded.

'How long could you operate with just ten men?'

'Indefinitely. As a matter of fact, the stores onboard are for a crew of over a hundred. It allows them to stay at sea for ninety days with a safe margin to stay longer if they have to. We could stay at least ten times longer.'

'You're telling me you could stay gone for three years?'

Morgan shrugged. 'I hope we won't have to.'

Yummy smiled. 'All right. I'll contact some associates in Tokyo. If it's yes, then we'll move immediately.'

Leaving nothing to chance, Yummy insisted that while he was giving the project his consideration, Morgan remain his guest in Gstaad.

Morgan agreed. And for the next few months, Yummy provided him with a social life filled with endless parties, food, drink, women, and pleasure.

During one of the parties, Morgan met Jean Porret, a young Frenchman living in Switzerland. The man, who claimed to be an artist, was exceptionally bright, witty, could match Morgan drink for drink, and they soon became fast friends.

During an unseasonable snowstorm, the last of the year everyone promised, Porret stopped by Yummy's condominium and left a confidential report with him.

'Thank you, Doctor,' Yummy said, as he handed the brilliant French psychiatrist, whose hobby was art, an envelope heavy with German marks.

'A remarkable case,' said Porret, whose brilliance was matched by his greed, sitting in front of the roaring fireplace and accepting a drink from Yummy's valet.

'In what way, Doctor?' Yummy asked.

'On the surface, he's bright, witty, apparently normal. But just below this charming veneer is a man with such psycho-neurotic tendencies that he's dangerously insane.'

'Could the loss of his fiancée have caused something this drastic?'

'Possibly. But in this case, it's a composite of things dating back to childhood. He's a bastard. He lost his father. He never knew his mother. He was a half-caste. Degraded by the girl with whom he shared his first sexual contact. All these things, along with his fiancée's death, contributed to this condition.'

'He seems so normal,' Yummy shook his head slowly.

Porret nodded. 'Oh, he smiles, and jokes and cries. But actually he possesses only two emotions. Anger – and hate. Personally, if he was my patient, I'd have him committed.'

'It's hard to believe,' Yummy said, slowly shaking his head.

Porret nodded. 'He's like a . . . oh, say a nice antique lamp you bought for that special spot in your study. And when you bring it home and plug it in, it burns your house down. On the outside it was shiny and sturdy, but it had a frayed wire. There's a short circuit in his brain like that frayed wire.'

As Porret sped into the cold, icy night in his new black Porsche, Yummy was momentarily sorry that he was on his way to an encounter with a beautiful, young, large-breasted blonde with engine trouble. When he stopped to help her on the icy, twisting road, she would smile – blow his brains out before setting his car on fire and rolling it over the 1200-foot cliff.

Yummy truely liked the charming psychiatrist. But this

mission was too volatile to have a loose end in the form of this bright young man who would easily put two and two together.

It took over two years for Morgan to arrange the recruitment of the men he selected.

Once the contacts were made, over a two-week period, Yummy flew the potential crew to his estate on Tenerife, the largest of the seven Canary Islands.

Sitting around the sun-drenched patio overlooking one of the island's isolated black lava beaches, Morgan discussed, argued, debated, and diagrammed the mission to the prospective crew.

'Jeeesus Christ, Morgan!' said Barth, his legs dangling into the heated pool at the edge of the patio. 'If we don't get our fucking heads blown off, they'd blow her out of the water 'fore we cleared the breakwater.'

Morgan smiled at his old friend and shook his head. 'You were around the Navy for almost a lifetime. Were you ever stopped or questioned once you were on the tender?'

'Well, I was caught in one of those drills once where they sealed off the missile storage area. And the jarheads checked everybody's ID on the whole ship.'

Morgan nodded. 'So? Some asshole lieutenant who wants to get his drill over with as quick as possible looked at your ID card and your area tag that let you in the sub compound. Do you think he'd have known the difference if it was yours or not? Or if it was a forgery or not? Shit, no! You were a white hat. And he knew you already had to go through two gates plus the topside watch before you got onboard the tender. So the quicker he finishes his drill, the better he looks. And after the first couple of guys, he's not even looking at pictures. He's just looking to make sure they're the right color. Right?'

Barth nodded.

'How much?' asked a fatherly looking black man who after a lifetime of unsuccessful nonviolent protests had taken to burning offices filled with government workers.

'Ten per cent of the ransom. To be split equally among the crew members.'

'Jesus! You're talking millions,' said an excited Nakamoto, as his mind envisioned that with that kind of money he could own part of a pro football franchise.

'What happens if we say no?' asked the black man suspiciously.

'Nothing,' Yummy smiled. 'Absolutely nothing. You are here at Morgan's invitation because you are the best in the world in your respective fields. If you decide your interests lie elsewhere, I would only impose the condition that as this is an island with magnificent weather, wide beaches, and an unlimited supply of food, women, wine, and song that you remain as my guests until after the plan has been executed.'

Adamson asked if he and Morgan could talk later.

'I have no doubts you can pull it off,' he said in a worried voice, after the session, walking back to his bungalow. 'But if you're not going to plan on actually firing the missiles . . . I'm not sure I care to go along.'

'Look,' Morgan assured him privately. 'You know I fully intend to use the missiles. But, Christ! I can't say it to the others. Understand?'

Adamson shook his head confused.

'It's got to appear to the others, including Yummy, that it's strictly for the money,' Morgan said, telling him what he knew he wanted to hear. 'And I have to say the missiles will be a last resort. You know yourself that firing the damn things could be suicidal.'

'I understand,' Adamson smiled. 'You can count me in then,' he said, shaking Morgan's hand.

Three men, including the black man, decided that it was too dangerous and bowed out.

Several days later, seagulls flocked around the bait thrown behind one of the ancient trawlers out of Puerto De La Cruz, the resort on the opposite side of the island.

The trawler, which provided most of the fresh fish for the hotels, had great success that day. Mainly because the rare fish-attracting bait was made up from the bodies of the black leader and his two friends who had opted to take Yummy's hospitality instead of the mission.

During the next week, a sizable cash advance was transferred to each new crew's numbered account in a bank in the Bahamas.

'You have thirty days before the mission. Get your affairs in order. Spend as much of your money as you want,' Morgan said. He and Yummy decided this would give them all a 'taste' of the power and freedom that massive wealth offered.

It also gave them the assurance that the mission would be free of the normal pressures about the doubts their payoff 'might not be there'.

Some of them spent little of it . . . but the smart ones, like Jones and Barth drank as much as they could and channeled the rest off to their families, or old flames or, in Barth's case, old hookers.

Yummy shook his head.

That Morgan would dare violate his will by releasing the crew was a shock. Of course, it could be a hangover from the camaraderie that is inevitable in all military men. Regardless of whose side they're on.

Finally, he looked up at the captain.

'Confirm that everything is to proceed as scheduled.'

The captain squinted imperceptibly at the decision. But he knew better than to question his master's decision.

25

Admiral Whittiker adjusted the black pencil-thin radio mike that curved around in front of his green-shaded flight helmet. Wiping his sweaty palms on the knees of his flight suit, he sunk back in his seat aboard the anti-submarine bomber as it banked into an ever-tightening spiral through the bright, cloudless sky over the empty North Pacific.

'Admiral,' said the young pilot, a baby-faced lieutenant, as the communications officer reached over his seat and held out a decoded message from the President.

The admiral took the message and quickly scanned it.

FROM: CIC

TO: Whittiker. Chmn. Joint Chiefs Commander, Terrorist Force aboard *L. & C.*
IDd by Seright as Morgan C.E., Ex-Lt Cdr (SS).
Resigned Active Service following undiagnosed mental disorder.
Second Terrorist IDd as Barth, Richard A., Retired
Chief Quartermaster (QMC-SS).
Both missing last nine weeks.
Addition data w/b fwd on recpt.

J. J. McGregor Pres.

The second page of the message gave a brief composite of their service records, with a notation that more in-depth reports were being retrieved from inactive files and were to follow.

Morgan . . . the admiral thought. Morgan . . . hmmmm. Not an unusual name. But one with a familiar ring. Son-of-a-bitch! he suddenly remembered as the man's serious face flooded back into his memory. 'I'll be goddammed! He was that young lieutenant that tried so hard to defend one of his men. What was it for now? My God, yes! That police car thing, Whittiker thought back to the stifling little hearing room in Charleston and the sadly humorous trial that as a senior captain he had presided over, and had been instructed to bring to a speedy and un-ceremonious conclusion.

He remembered Morgan's efforts during the trial and knew that, whatever folly the man was involved in, he would be as committed to it as he was to his defendant's cause.

He wished it could be someone else. Some crazed radical. Some scatterbrained redneck. Even a group of misguided liberal scientists. Anyone but a man who was a graduate of the Navy's advanced war colleges. He'd known command and would prove to be a formidable enemy.

'Sonar . . . ' the pilot said through his helmet speaker, inter-rupting his train of thought. 'You got anything?'

'Nada . . . ' responded the sonarman nonchalantly from his cubicle in the belly of the shining jet. The admiral smiled at the familiar and relaxed jargon of a team that had trained success-fully together over a long time.

'How 'bout you Nukey-Poo?' the pilot asked to the officer responsible for all the electronics onboard equipment used in locating anything using nuclear radiating fuels.

'Oh, yes!' he confirmed. 'I see by the old geiger counter on the wall that we still got a bad guy down there.'

'What about his position?' Whittiker asked. 'Any change?'

'Position is stable. Could be a hovering nuclear submarine. On the other hand it could be a floating uranium mine,' he added, joking, not having the vaguest notion of how close he had come to the latter.

The pilot shook his head as he looked at the admiral indicating 'what can you do' with a crew who were so good they didn't bother to change their routine or show any awe when the CNO was riding with them. To them he was just another nonpaying passenger out for a joyride. The admiral smiled his understand-ing. He liked that confidence in his men and didn't want it any other way.

The pilot moved the control stick to his right and banked into a steeper turn. He pointed across the admiral out the small tinted window toward a cluster of reddish dots bobbing on the surface between them and the horizon.

'There's your loot,' he said as he turned toward the fifty bright red and white checkered sea buoys needed to keep the almost 350 tons of gold bullion ransom afloat.

The compact bomber roared toward the buoy just above the gentle swells. A mile and a half before they crossed over it, the admiral suddenly screamed in pain. 'Oh, God!' he groaned in agony as an unbelievably excruciating pain ripped through the front of his skull.

Laser flash? he thought, cursing. But before he could move a muscle to pull down the black shield used against the laser weapons, whose only purpose was to blind, the most brilliant light imaginable to man flashed through his unshaded eyes blinding him instantly.

He was wrong though. It wasn't a laser flash. The brilliant sunlike flash which passed through his and the pilot's retinas, destroying their optic nerves, was from the Poseidon ULMS-11 missile as it detonated at an altitude of 3,850 feet above the gentle blue swells of the warm Pacific.

The flash was more intense than some godlike arc-welding torch. The sun seemed dim compared to it.

The shock wave that preceded the blast was so massive that had anyone been able to take a stop action photograph of that millisecond, the ocean surface would have looked as flat and shiny as a glass tabletop. Waves, white cap swells, and wind were all stilled, flattened, and eliminated, making the mirrorlike surface as smooth and as quiet as an abandoned mill pond. Then a hole in the ocean from the ungodly force preceding the hellish maelstrom of the nuclear explosion formed and engulfed the entire area. The sea buoys, the gold, the admiral's plane, and the admiral.

From the black world of blindness, before his body ceased to exist, the last flickering thought to cross his brain was, 'It was never the gold.'

On the nuclear aircraft carrier *Vinson*, some eighteen miles from the target center, the explosion sounded like the world was splitting. The unobstructed shock wave roared across the ocean's flat surface that had no hills, or trees, or buildings to act as a buffer and hit the ship, like a stampeding herd of buffalo.

Fortunately, though unintentionally, the *Vinson* was already headed into the blast or the waves would have smashed her broadside and capsized her.

As it was, sixteen fighters and over two hundred men on the deck and walkways were blown into the ocean in a tangle of flaming jet fuel, barrels, wheel chocks, severed legs and arms, sunglasses, radar and radio antennae, as the massive island-sized ship bounced around like a pea on a china saucer.

Near the checkered sea buoys, three nuclear Hunter-Killer submarines that had spent the better part of the week creeping meter by meter, screw turn by screw turn, into the area were destroyed. Forced down to the ocean's floor by the blast like so many toy boats. Two imploded and were destroyed immediately. Which may have been a blessing for them. Inexplicably, the third survived the initial blast. Then an onboard flash fire, and the pummeling against the ocean's floor. But two flooded compartments shackled it against the bottom more effectively than had they been loaded with concrete. Although the men in the unflooded compartments survived the original disaster, all it meant was that they were to spend nightmarishly long days, dying individual agonizing deaths by suffocation, or drowning – or crazed shipmates.

26

A blissfully unsuspecting world, unaware that a danger of this magnitude even existed, sat in stunned silence.

Their condition was nothing compared to the catalepsy in the President's compound.

Finally, in a rage, President McGregor hurled a sheaf of Top Secret files across the room.

'Goddamn son-of-a-bitch!' he ranted like a spoiled child as the pages from the reports fluttered to the floor. 'I thought Whittiker promised that if they fired any of those damn things, we would follow their trajectory back to where they were fired and destroy them. Now, will someone kindly tell me just who the hell fucked up? They sure as hell fired them. So, God knows, they sure as hell must have had a trajectory,' he said as his grip on his self-control started to slip.

'Mr President,' Klein said, realizing the President hadn't understood the meaning of the decoded messages in front of him. 'Our antimissiles did follow the trajectories back. But they weren't launched from the *Lewis & Clark.*'

The civilian head of ARASS read from the message. 'They were launched from two different sites in two different oceans. One, a small archipelago in the South Atlantic. The other, a derelict ship that our missiles sunk.'

'But how is that possible? They were submarine missiles, weren't they?' he screamed angrily.

'No,' admitted the scientist. 'They're just plain missiles that happen to have the capability of being fired from a submerged platform. Actually, they can be fired from any stable site.'

'But why the hell would they bother to go to all this trouble?' the President asked, still unable to grasp the significance.

'Number one,' said Klein, 'to prove they could fire the missiles. Number two, to teach us a very expensive object lesson by showing us ransom is not going to be the ultimate purpose of this operation.'

'Also, by firing the missiles away from the sub, they've shown us that all their eggs aren't in one basket,' Thatcher, the Marine commandant, said.

'My God,' the President said. 'They could have those things hidden all over the world. Like a virtual goddamn plague.'

'It's a possibility,' Thatcher said. 'But I doubt if they'd unload them all.'

'With the success they just had, why not, for God's sake?' demanded the President.

'To offload and distribute them to twenty-four, pardon me, twenty-two separate sites requires an equal number of launch crews, and support paraphernalia. That would invite discovery. And the *Lewis & Clark*'s still the most ideal launch site. It's portable, and they maintain control.'

The President exploded in frustration. 'Well, goddammit, gentlemen,' he turned pointing an accusing finger at Thatcher and the ARASS scientist. 'Just what does Whittiker and all you tits on a boar hog Joint Staffs have to say about this now that the fat's in the fire and the shit's hitting the fan?'

'Whittiker is dead, Mr President,' Klein said softly, reminding him of something he'd been notified of at the time of the explosions. Something he'd taken tearfully hard.

The President stared at him for several seconds. 'Yes. Of course he is,' he said quietly.

'OK, so they answered the question of whether or not they can launch the damn things,' he finally said, the strain heavy in his voice. 'What about our "search-and-destroy" efforts?'

'We have the navies from seventeen countries crisscrossing the Pacific. So far, zero!' said Thatcher.

'Then maybe she's not in the Pacific any more,' speculated Klein.

'She has to be,' said the scientist, chewing on an eraser at the end of a bright yellow pencil. 'She hasn't crossed any of the Sea Spiders. So she's probably still in the mid-Pacific.'

'Any chance she got under the Pole?' asked Klein.

'No,' Thatcher shook his head emphatically. 'One of Whitt's first moves was to curtain off the entrances with a squadron of Hunter-Killers.'

'Mr Murphy?' the President said, nodding to the CIA head who was holding up a hand with a smoldering cigarette in it.

'If we can locate relatives or friends of the suspects we've identified, they might provide us with a bargaining tool.'

The President nodded. 'Good ... yes ... good. Gentlemen?' he said, looking around the table. 'We all in agreement with that?'

Mr Ridley cleared his skinny, gizzardlike throat.

'Mr Ridley?' the President asked. 'Do I recognize your throat clearing as a sign of dissent?'

'I don't disagree with Mr Murphy,' he said, 'but the men we're dealing with are butchers. The entire international community, friends and enemies alike, will condemn them.'

'So?' asked the President, wanting to bring him to the point.

'They have to expect their ultimate end to be equally as violent. So whether or not we locate their family or friends is immaterial. And heaven forbid, if we do locate them, I would suggest serious consideration as to how they are handled. If anything happened to them while in Mr Murphy's custody, the consequences could be grave.'

The President nodded, 'Good logic in that.'

'At least no one disagrees,' reflected Klein silently. Whether or not they do, none of these assholes wants to take any responsibility. He shifted uneasily in his seat. It was getting increasingly difficult to disguise his impatience with this failing group of men who were supposed to be the dynamic leaders people looked to.

'So,' the President said, 'we're back to square one. Locating and destroying the submarine.'

'That might be more difficult than we originally imagined, gentlemen,' the ARASS scientist said as everyone stared at him for interrupting. Especially when he was usually reluctant to talk unless addressed directly.

'Please elucidate,' said the President.

'Well,' he said cautiously, 'Admiral Whittiker flew to an area where a "hot contact" had been detected. A contact that was nuclear radiating, similar to a nuclear submarine.'

'So?' the general asked.

'So, we know the contact definitely wasn't one of ours. Nor a Russian. And we know it wasn't the *Lewis & Clark* because I'm sure they wouldn't do us a favor by blowing themselves up.'

'Get to the point,' suggested the President.

'The point is who, or I should say what, was the nuclear contact?'

'A decoy,' mused the general, disgusted that he hadn't been the first to recognize the possibility.

The scientist nodded as he pulled quietly on his unlit pipe.

'And it wasn't a decoy to throw us off,' Klein added thoughtfully, 'but to draw us into a baited trap.'

'Jesus . . . ' the President muttered.

'Now,' the scientist continued, 'the positive aspects of this are that it might just be the first mistake they've made.'

'How so?' asked the President.

'Someone had to bait the trap. It definitely wasn't there several days earlier.'

'His shore-based contact?' asked Klein.

'Would have to be,' said the general.

'Any way to determine who's been in that area lately?' asked the President.

'We'll backtrack through the Sea Spider's computer,' the scientist said, pleased with the acceptance of his hypothesis. 'There's no way to tell who actually dropped it. But at least we'll have a list of the vessels that are known to have passed through that area before the explosion.'

'Goddamn! That should narrow it down,' said the general with excitement in his voice at the prospects of a fox to send the hounds after.

27

Butler, the mess cook, was sweating by the time he squeezed out from behind the air and hydraulic lines which had become his main hiding place near the bottom of the bilges in the forward motor room known as MR-1. It was one of the few places he'd found where he could comfortably stretch out, with his body parallel to the pressure hull, and where his blue dungarees seemed to almost blend into the shadows.

Once out, Butler propped himself up on the metal deck plates on one elbow and listened until he was sure it was safe.

Another day at the office! he thought, as he started to crawl slowly forward toward the next compartment. There, on more than one occasion, he had crouched silently in the shadows as one of the terrorists clumped past, never suspecting he was hiding within arm's length.

For a long time now, days maybe – he didn't know because he'd lost all track of time – he'd been creeping and crawling, slithering up and down, in and out, of compartment after compartment.

He'd turned so many valves, changed so many settings on switches and gauges, he'd lost track of whether he might be turning everything back the right way again.

He'd done something in every compartment forward of the reactor compartment. There was a lot of submarine aft of the reactor, but the only way through there was through one long, dangerous passageway, dangerous in that it was a brightly lit, slick-walled tunnel, like one of the ramps in airports that lead from the waiting lounge to the airplane. Once in the tunnel, if he ran into someone coming from the other direction, there was no place to hide. So he concentrated on the forward half of the boat.

On one of his phantom sojourns, he'd picked up a pair of electric wire clippers and a couple of screwdrivers. Since then he'd become a little more efficiently devious by opening up electronic control boxes and cutting one or more of the wires before reclosing the box without leaving a trace.

Several times he came across the thick multiple-colored

strands of wires the terrorists had laid up and down the length of the boat. He'd followed them and found they ran between the computers and the missiles.

His first impulse had been to cut them on the spot. And even take out a long length like he'd seen the Indians do to the telegraph lines in an old Western movie. But luckily he'd been stopped when he'd heard footsteps coming toward him. With his heart pounding, he crammed between the air-conditioning ducts and some generator mounts. As he waited for the scruffy shoes to disappear, it gave him time to think more logically. Holding his breath so the terrorist couldn't hear him, it occurred to him that if he was going to be successful without being discovered, he'd need to be a little more calculating about what he was fucking up. And above all, to use his head.

So, after the shoes disappeared, instead of cutting and taking out a length, he carefully clipped halfway through some of the wires and laid them around a sharp corner of one of the motor mounts so it would look like some clubfooted asshole had accidentally kicked it against the sharp metal corner.

Of course if they found it, which he figured they would, the next time he'd have to change his style. That would probably be the last time he could get away with it. But shit! The boat could be gone by then. So he sure as shit wasn't going to worry about it.

As Butler slithered forward, he could hear his stomach growling.

God! I've got to get some chow this time out, he thought, his head a little fuzzy from having gone without food for God knows how long.

He knew it had been at least two days. On his way back he'd bring some extra stuff and squirrel it away. As hungry as he was, he dreaded going anywhere near the crew's mess.

Outside of the reactor, the most dangerous place was the compartment under the crew's mess where the canned goods and supplies were stored. Not so much that there weren't good places to hide. But because most of the time that's where all the terrorists gathered to play cards, bullshit, and sleep. Just like guys from any other crew in the fleet.

Another problem was, after days of bellying up and down the decks and bilges, he was a greasy mess. So he had to be careful not to leave a trail of grease or oily footprints to follow straight back to him. As new as the *Lewis & Clark* was, her bilges and below decks were like any other Navy ship.

Reaching an often-used hiding place, he stopped and waited for almost ten minutes while he watched the watertight hatch a few feet away that he had to pass through to get into the next compartment.

After waiting until he was sure no one was on the other side, he edged slowly out and crept to the hatch. Putting his hand on the spring-loaded 'dog' that unlatched it, he cautiously peered through the peephole that allowed him to see through to the other side. After making sure no one was in the next space, he unlatched the 'dog', scurried through, and dove into another hiding space. Behind him, the heavy hatch closed automatically as he listened until he could be sure no one was in the compartment or had heard him come in.

From his hiding place, he could see all the way through the compartment to the hatch at the other end. It was deserted.

Cautiously, he squeezed back out and crept toward the far hatch. He was halfway up the passageway when he saw some movement through the peephole and an instant later heard someone opening the hatch. His heart pounded as he threw himself into the waterways, banging and skinning his head against the elbows of some air lines before he could flatten himself out in the shadows.

'I'm telling you it's not the goddamn wiring!' complained a fat guy with thick glasses as he waddled through the hatch and down the passageway. Following him, Butler could see an immaculately dressed guy with the biggest muscles he'd ever seen.

'Well, it's sure not the rigging,' the muscleman said with a flat unemotional voice that reminded the mess cook of one of the many killers he'd seen on TV. 'Unless one of you's been fucking with things that don't concern you ... '

'No one's been fucking with anything of yours,' the fat man tossed over his shoulder like a vindictive child as he checked every foot of the wiring hand by hand.

'Then it's got to be your wiring,' the muscleman said with an 'I-told-you-so' attitude and overconfident smirk.

Butler exhaled a sigh of relief as they passed into the next compartment aft. He gave himself an imaginary pat on the back at his cleverness and foresight in disguising his sabotage. This was the first sign that whatever he was doing was starting to work and he was thrilled.

Flushed with his success, he forgot his hunger and thought this was something he should report to the captain.

It took him almost three hours to work his way to the hatch at the top of a ladder leading up to the passageway near the captain's cabin.

Days earlier he had disconnected the light next to the ladder so he could stand on it without feeling exposed. He was still exposed, but in the dark at least he didn't feel so outright naked.

Cautiously, he pushed against the hatch. Cracking it just a slit, he looked down both directions of the deserted, dimly lit passageway. On the bulkhead across from the hatch, he could see that the chronometer read 4.30. Butler didn't know if it was 4.30 in the morning or in the afternoon.

'God! I hope it's am,' he prayed. 'So everyone would be sacked out.'

The fates were with him. It was. After another fifteen minutes, he slowly pushed open the hatch and climbed up into the passageway. Carefully lowering the hatch, he darted up the passageway toward the green velvety curtain and slipped into the dark of the captain's cabin.

In the ghostly red glow from the lights behind the compass, depth, and speed gauges, the rumpled, soiled bunk was empty.

Staring down at the empty unmade bunk, it took a moment before he could force himself back to reality.

'Goddammit! They've moved him,' he thought, a rocklike feeling of dread hanging in his stomach. 'But where? Goddammit. Where?'

He parted the curtains with his fingertips and checked the passageway. It was empty and eerily quiet. 'They musta put him back down with the crew in tubes forward,' he thought darting back down his escape hatch.

Tubes forward wasn't hard to get to. But it was the place he dreaded most. 'Mainly,' he thought, 'because of the squirrelly little freak with the machine gun that's always there.'

It took another hour to work his way up to tubes forward. From the shadows behind a bank of computer consoles, his eyes darted back and forth, checking every shadow and glimmer, as he searched the compartment for some sign of life.

The little squirrel wasn't there. He dropped back down into the lower level and pulled himself hand over hand through the maze of high pressure lines that lead from the manifold in the control room to the trim tanks and bow buoyancy. Finally, he reached the forwardmost plates that separated the pressure hull from the cold black waters of the ocean.

Climbing up the small metal ladder between the torpedo

tubes, like a prairie dog peering up from his burrow, he looked aft.

'Jesus! Where the fuck is he?' he thought anxiously. He waited another ten minutes just to make sure he was gone and not asleep behind a torpedo or something. He'd hate to have the little son-of-a-bitch pop up and blow the back of his head away with that nasty little machine-gun while he was opening the hatch.

Son-of-a-bitch! he thought as he slowly eased himself up the final rung of the ladder. The little fox is really gone, he hummed to himself as he crawled down the middle of the compartment toward the distant hatch that led down to where the crew was being held.

Finally, laying next to it, quietly, ever so quietly, he lifted the latch and cracked the hatch.

The foul, putrid air that rose from the dark compartment below almost made him gasp. As bad as when they blow the officers' sanitary tanks, he thought, opening it halfway and peering down into the inky depths.

'Shit! It's blacker than a well digger's ass.' Slowly he reached in and felt around until he located the emergency battle lantern on the side of the ladder and snapped it on.

His mind screamed a warning the instant he snapped it on. What if the Little Squirrel's down there with them. Then I've bought it for all of us, he thought, his heart pounding.

It was difficult to say what was the bigger shock. Not seeing the frightening little killer at the bottom of the ladder waiting with a slobbery vicious smile to blow him away in a blaze of bullets. Or the shock of not seeing anything, nothing, no one in the compartment.

'They're gone!' he choked back a disbelieving scream. 'But where! They have to be here, there's no other place they could be. They couldn't have moved them. I would have known . . .'

Looking up in confusion, his eyes came to rest on a dull black submachine gun laying casually atop one of the torpedoes.

The Little Squirrel's favorite toy, he thought, and through his daze knew it was true. The man would have never left it if they weren't gone.

Between the hunger and the shock, he never remembered his return trip aft. Squeezing into the security of his cavelike sanctuary, he wrapped his arms around the deadly little weapon hoping its closeness would somehow soothe away this nightmare.

The captain was gone! And his buddies . . . his shipmates were too! But where? Either dead or over the side. Or dead and over the side. He shuddered as he thought of the old movies he'd seen where they fired dead bodies out of the torpedo tubes. He shuddered again. He was alone! Either way, whether they're alive or dead or over the side, they're gone!

His mind raced through a never-ending maze. 'What the hell am I going to do?' he cried softly as the black shadows that he had grown comfortable in suddenly seemed to be closing in, filling him with a sudden claustrophobic feeling of helplessness.

'What the hell am I supposed to do?' he cried, suddenly feeling very sorry for himself. 'No! Dammit! Stop it!' he screamed, almost to the point where he actually yelled. 'We've had it worse. Or pretty damn near,' he rationalized, 'so . . . just sit tight. Let's figure this thing out. Have a little patience.'

He did have patience. It was something he'd learned growing up in the 'Big Foot' country of northern California where his father had taken his family to get them out of the 'filth' of the big cities. Filth which to him was as much moral as it was physical.

The beautiful craggy mountains of northern California were almost like going to heaven to his father. The only thing that was a lie was the skimpy gold claims that were supposed to yield a day's pay for a hard day's work. They rarely did.

The first summer they built their cabin by hand in a beautiful meadow near the river that ran through the middle of their claim in the National Forest. They were all delighted at their accomplishment as they sat in the security of its warm interior in the cool night of the Indian summer.

But when winter came, they could get neither in or out of their claim. They were caught without newspapers or books or TV. And only occasionally had a radio, because his older sister didn't want her batteries to run down.

Alone with his younger brother and sister, they spent the long wintry days by the fire in the franklin stove while his father searched up and down the icy streams for a 'trace'.

During these lonely times, Butler had learned patience. Especially halfway through their last winter together when their father went up the river one freezing dawn . . . and never came back.

After the sixth day, they gave up looking for him. By then the snow was too high. They couldn't keep looking and they couldn't get out. So he and his brother and sister sat. And they waited through the long winter. And ate canned sardines and Spam . . . and beans . . . and oatmeal mush.

Quietly he started to sob. Goddammit!!! It wasn't fair. First Mother, then Dad, now the captain. Everybody left him. Lonely, and in some kind of trouble. His nose started running and he wiped it on one of his knees.

Dammit! Dammit! Dammit! This is the last straw! he thought fingering the submachine gun and angrily choking back a sob. I mean it, goddammit. If those bastards have run off and left me in the shithouse . . .

He buried his head in the dirty folds of his denim shirt and sobbed. Daddy . . . God . . . Daddy! Please . . . he sobbed as ever so gently the bow of the Triton slowly lifted toward the surface.

28

Dawn had just started painting a light gray stripe on the horizon when the periscope broke out of the black water. As it dipped in and out of the swells, Morgan could see the silhouette of the freighter where Yummy had collapsed after a rage when the Triton failed to keep their rendezvous the previous evening.

Less than an hour later, as the rays of sunlight bounced off the clouds and lit the surface, Morgan heard the low metallic *whooooomp*, like two huge metal drums thumping together, as the Triton was tethered once again to the side of the freighter.

When the lines were secured, the Japanese captain bowed from the bridge. 'Mr Yamimura wishes for you to join with him in his cabin,' he said, having difficulty forming the English words. Morgan nodded. From the deck he could see that several of Yummy's crew members were heavily armed. He knew it was Yummy's way of showing him he was pissed off. 'Take care of the store,' he said privately to Barth as he started up the ladder. 'If anything happens to me, take her down and get the hell out.'

'Never fear,' Barth said reassuringly.

In Yummy's cabin, the atmosphere was like ice.

'I was under the impression our rendezvous was scheduled for last night,' Yummy spoke, quietly fighting to control an outburst.

Morgan nodded. 'We ran into a small convoy of ships. My sonarman thought there might be a possibility they were military. So I took the precaution of avoiding them.'

Yummy nodded. It was a reasonable explanation. There had been ships near their location for the last two days.

Finally, he said, 'I'm terribly disappointed, Morgan.'

Morgan nodded. 'The crew,' he said quietly.

'My disenchantment at the risk you took has caused doubt in my opinions of your ability to command.'

'Sentiment,' Morgan said, staring directly into Yummy's eyes. 'Pure and simple,' he added, daring him to challenge his judgment further.

With his forefinger, Yummy picked at a hangnail on his

thumb that was sore and bleeding. 'That sentiment has me concerned. In a quandary so to speak.'

'No, you're not in a quandary. You're not concerned. What you are is pissed off,' Morgan said as his attention focused on the ivory white scalp that glimmered through Yummy's closely cropped military style haircut.

It reminded him of a night he spent with his father Remmie and some of his old golf pro buddies, relics from the 'Big War' who claimed you could crush a gook's head like an eggshell because all they ate was rice. He wondered if he could crush Yummy's.

'You have a way of cutting through bullshit and getting directly to the point, Morgan,' Yummy nodded. 'You're right, I am pissed off.'

Morgan smiled. 'Now don't you feel better getting it out in the open? Now you can tell me what it is.'

'Aside from defying my direct orders, you destroyed one of my ships.'

A grin crossed his face and he started to chuckle. 'That was one of yours?' he laughed innocently. 'I'm sorry, Yummy,' he said calling him by the name he knew he hated.

'I fail to appreciate your humor, Morgan,' he said, seething.

'So I owe you one. It's just funny, that out of an ocean full of ships, we pick one of yours to sink.'

'It has occurred to me,' said Yummy, 'to place additional personnel onboard to insure this type of violation doesn't reoccur.'

'That's your prerogative,' Morgan nodded, knowing that was the answer he wanted to hear. But what he didn't add was that he would kill the son-of-a-bitch, or bitches as the case may be, once they were underway and submerged.

Through the paneled walls they could feel the vibration from the diesel as it rumbled to life and started to offload two more Poseidons.

'Unfortunately there is much to accomplish in the next few days. The next two missiles must be transferred to the target site before we can complete our third scheduled rendezvous. Until then I shall refrain from the temptation of embarrassing you by adding to your personnel.'

Back on the bridge of the *Lewis & Clark*, Morgan watched as the second missile disappeared over the railing and down into the freighter's cargo hold. From the deck below him, Barth gave him a thumbs-up sign. 'Everything's taken care of, Skipper. We're rigged for dive,' he said.

Morgan nodded as Nichols and Big Daddy slipped the mooring lines.

'Dive the boat,' Morgan said, slipping down the hatch into the conning tower.

Barth climbed up to the bridge and rang the klaxon that signaled they were diving. From the deck, Nichols and Big Daddy clamored up to the bridge and followed Morgan down the hatch.

With the decks clear, Barth threw a salute to the freighter's captain before dropping down into the boat and securing the hatch behind him.

On the freighter, the Japanese captain could hear the submarine's hydraulics open the huge valves that sat on top of each ballast tank. Once open, tons of seawater rushed in, making the submarine suddenly heavier than the seawater and starting its controlled sinking.

As they submerged, the air hissed and gurgled out of the tank tops. It reminded him of a giant sperm whale exhaling a small storm of moisture and compressed air before diving to the ocean's bottom in search of the giant squid.

Several minutes later the dark, submerged silhouette of the *Lewis & Clark* had disappeared into the blackness.

29

'General?' Klein said into the phone. 'I think we might have something.'

'I'm on my way,' the little general said from the middle of his shave. As he hung up, he was already wiping his face clean of lather. Grabbing his jacket, he charged out of his quarters past his saluting sentries and down the sidewalk toward the distant trailers that housed the Communications Center.

Next to the Communications Center, a War Room had been set up. This was dominated by a huge electronic map of the search in the Pacific, operated by several technicians with earphones. It reminded Thatcher of a giant copy of a 'Pong' game he'd given his two daughters for Christmas years earlier. The electronic ghosts on this wall-sized mode, though, displayed the forces that were preparing for their last-ditch assault on the *Lewis & Clark*.

Klein was huddled with Captain Seright as Thatcher hurried over.

'Whatta ya got?' he demanded anxiously.

'Couple of Jap patrol bombers were flying south of Mindanao in the Philippines when they spotted a Nukey Bogie,' Seright explained. 'Couple of hours later a Russian, flying out of Anadyr in the Bering Sea spotted another hot spot about six hundred miles northeast of Japan.'

'Either of them our baby?' Thatcher asked.

'Nope,' said Seright shaking his head. 'ARASS has given us the radiation readout to look for. These are close, but no Kewpie Doll!'

'Sounds like his shore contacts have been busy,' Thatcher said, running his hand through his closely cropped hair several times. 'Either that or he's got more help than we thought.'

'Both!' said Klein with a grin. 'We been going over the readout from your Sea Spider,' he said, nodding toward the computer readout that Seright was comparing against a Maritime computer's registry that listed ships by flag, country and insuring companies.

'The bogies are near major shipping lanes,' Seright said, looking up briefly. 'Literally hundreds of ships pass through these areas every week.'

'You think you found the common denominator?' the general asked, knowing they had or they wouldn't have waved the red flag in front of his nose.

Seright smiled. Looking up through his red, bloodshot eyes, he said, 'I think so!'

'Well, dammit, Captain!' Thatcher said anxiously. 'Let's have it.'

Seright handed him a section from the computer readout. 'The only ships in common that have gone through these areas are the *Yamatori*, the *Kasagari*, the *Shitsu Maru*,' he said, pointing out the names for the general. 'And the *Island Queen*.'

Thatcher quickly studied the readout and checked it several times against the Maritime registry. Outside of having Japanese names, the ships were owned by separate companies and flew different flags.

'Other than the *Island Queen* which was sunk by the *Lewis & Clark*, I don't see the connection,' he said. He didn't like to have to figure out puzzles. He'd always hated them. Made him look stupid, he thought. He didn't even like answering the riddles his young daughters used to ask him.

'We didn't either,' said Klein as he rolled the dangling sleeve of his wrinkled shirt back up. 'Till we found that common denominator you were talking about.'

The general waited impatiently, knowing the opposite was true of Klein. The son-of-a-bitch liked puzzles, intrigue, all that shit.

Finally, Klein said, 'The ships are owned and sail for separate companies. But the individual companies are owned by Yami-mura Industries.'

'Which tells us what? The Japs gonna bomb Pearl Harbor again?'

'They might,' Klein chuckled handing him a red Top Secret folder.

There was a raft of documents in the folder. Correspondence, records, and pictures of a younger Yummy.

After reading the capsulated synopsis, the general shook his head. 'He sure as hell looks clean.'

'All we've really got to go on is rumor and speculation from CIA,' Klein nodded. 'I just finished talking to Murphy. He tells me that for years now the Japanese Red Army has had access to a stream of money that seemed to flow from the mother lode itself.'

'And you think we've found our Midas?' offered the general.

'Things seem to fit. The day prior to each postmark one of these ships was in a harbor the demands were mailed from. It's him. I can feel it in my guts,' Klein said.

'Well let's find the son-of-a-bitch then,' Thatcher said, flushed with excitement that at last he had something else to chase other than the shadowy, elusive Triton. 'Any location on him?' he asked.

'It's in the works,' Seright said. 'Murphy's taking care of it.'

Thatcher headed for the door. 'I better stand around and worry him. He'll work faster that way.'

Two hours later, Klein was buzzed at his desk in a cubicle next to the War Room which seemed to be growing with men and equipment by the minute.

'Klein, Thatch here. We think we found Midas.'

Klein took a deep breath to contain his excitement. 'Fan-fuckingtastic! Where?'

'Onboard a ship. Sort of his flag ship.'

'Where?'

'It just requested a berthing assignment in San Pedro, California.'

'Son of a bitch! That's fantastic,' Klein said, trying to contain his excitement.

'Fantastic, but not so great,' said Thatcher, his mood becoming serious.

'What's the problem?' Klein said, picking up the change instantly.

'As soon as I got his location, I authorized Murphy to get a U-4 to dog him till he got in.'

'And he made you,' Klein said, fighting to keep from erupting in anger.

'No. He's a cool bastard. He's not even using his radar. But I'm afraid he's hot.'

'Whatta ya mean, hot?'

'He's carrying some kind of nuclear radiating mass and it's not any of that "waste" shit.'

'Poseidons?' Klein whispered, his heart pounding.

'That's what it looks like.'

Klein's ears were ringing. 'Los Angeles,' he said, a nauseous feeling rushing up the back of his tongue from his stomach.

'I'm afraid so,' Thatcher said, barely above a whisper.

'Whatta ya think?' Klein asked.

'Well, if he's waiting outside the harbor we'd be foolish not to let him come on in.'

'I agree,' Klein said. 'I'll notify the President.'

'And as soon as possible. We have to move,' Thatcher said. 'Take him and the fucking ship, or blow the son-of-a-bitch out of the water.'

'Yeah. I guess you're right,' Klein paused. 'It's your ball game. Bring us the head of that gook SOB.'

'If not his head, his balls,' Thatcher said in the kind of language an ex-Marine private could understand.

'One last thing though,' Klein warned.

'Yeah?'

'Try not to blow up LA while you're at it,' Thatcher chuckled. Not at the humor. But from the real possibility of it all. He hung up and headed for the helicopter pad.

30

It was a little after 10.00 pm and a fog had fallen over the Los Angeles basin. Newcomers to the 'Southland' were confused as to whether it was fog, smog or the 'haze' the natives claimed it was.

LAX, as Los Angeles International Airport is known, would be the first to confirm its true identity by closing the airport and diverting all incoming traffic to Ontario, San Diego, Palmdale, and even San Francisco.

A few miles south of the sprawling concrete ribbons that formed the surrealistic design of the runway system, past the Palos Verdes Peninsula, lay the equally surrealistic though watery channels that formed the sprawling Los Angeles Harbor District.

Considering the massive sea traffic that travels through it and the industrial and oil complexes that border it, LA harbor is eerily quiet, in stark contrast to the hustle and bustle of New York, or the gulf ports, with their beer drinking, roster-laden stevedore crews.

From the bridge of the freighter, the Japanese captain could just barely make out his seamen through the fog as they patrolled the decks fore and aft, their automatic weapons and grenades well hidden beneath their bulky pea coats.

Across from the ship, the captain surveyed the isolated finger of land that had been built into the water to afford more ware-house space and deep-water moorings.

The captain had never been in Los Angeles harbor before. He liked it. It was clean, well laid out, and militarily efficient.

And this mooring was perfect. More than they could have hoped for. Isolated, it was evidently new, as there were lease signs on the sides of the white two-storey concrete warehouses across from him, directing potential leasors to the Port Authority in downtown San Pedro.

He walked across the bridge to the channel side. Across the deserted stretch of water, he could see the twinkling lights of San Pedro rising in the dark distance. Astern, lights from the Vincent Thomas suspension bridge formed a crescent as they twinkled in the mist between Terminal Island and San Pedro.

Slowly he paced back and forth from port to starboard, satisfied that they had safely penetrated the inner harbor.

By this time tomorrow, in twos and threes, he and half his crew would pass through the customs gate on their way to Disneyland and Knott's Berry Farm.

Once on the beach, they would melt into obscurity before heading for a regrouping rendezvous point.

His excitement was mingled with, for him, an unnatural pang of melancholy at the thought of losing his powerfully efficient little ship.

The crew didn't matter. They were faceless men who were of no consequence to his master's destiny. But his ship was a thing of beauty. A thing with a soul.

Originally he'd planned on keeping the entire crew onboard. But his master decided it would look conspicuous if no one was allowed shore leave. And as none of the crew – neither the ones going ashore nor the ones staying – were aware of the peril, the mission would remain safe.

A noise from the direction of the open sea caught his attention.

Coming up the channel, he could hear the whine of three Shark-Hooper Shadows. He watched suspiciously as the three Hovercraft effortlessly skimmed up toward them in midchannel.

Anxiously, he tapped on the bridge windshield to alert the seamen near the bow.

As the Shadows approached, they seemed to be angling toward a channel across the bay that ran obliquely toward their berthing ramps.

The first Shadow in the miniature convoy, a small 110-footer, slipped effortlessly by on the ebony surface. The second one was amidships when the captain heard a muffled popping explosion overhead and the sky seemed to light up as bright as the noonday sun.

The alarm in his head screamed and sent him springing into action as flares exploded in the sky over his ship.

Simultaneously with the flares' explosions, the gas turbines screamed to life and the Shadows darted across the black waters toward the freighter.

Throwing himself to the back bulkhead, the captain's hand pushed the alarm that roused his sleeping crew and sent them scurrying, hearts pounding, to their battle stations.

178

No sooner had he sounded the alarm when an air-jarring and vibrating sound seemed to inundate him.

It was the thundering *whooomp . . . whooomp . . . whooomp* of heavy rotor blades from three giant Sikorsky Sea Stallions as they roared in from the blackness, each loaded with a hundred battle-ready Marines.

After sounding the alarm, the captain sprinted into the Communications Center.

'Did you arm the missiles?' the captain screamed to the bewildered technician.

'Yes. At the first sound of attack,' he yelled over the *whooomp . . . whooomp . . . whooomp* of the hovering helicopters.

The captain nodded and ran back toward the bridge. Next to the radio shack he threw open a cabinet and grabbed a deadly-looking Russian Kuznetzov NK-28 and jammed a long battle clip into the breech. For a light weapon, it could almost sink a ship as each round was loaded with explosive tips.

Below the bridge, he could see one of the helicopter gunships swinging back and forth like a giant black pendulum, raking the main deck with withering cannon fire.

Two of his crewmen who had tried to return fire from their forward positions were dismembered masses. And half of one of the bodies had been blown over the side from the deadly barrage of fire from the Sikorsky's cannon.

The three Sikorskys were dipping up and down to keep from having to fire down into the heart of the freighter, when the captain opened fire.

The Sikorsky was so close to him he could see the explosive tips ripping through the thin aluminum skin. Moments later two of the external fuel tanks exploded in a brilliant orange blossom as the high-octane fuel lit the sky just above the water.

The young pilot from Chicago knew his craft was doomed. But rather than crashing onto the ship and endangering the Poseidon missiles, he tried to limp out into the channel where he hoped he could dump it safely in the water.

The captain strafed it with another burst before running out of ammo. Jamming in another clip, he watched as the Sikorsky's engine exploded and it heeled drunkenly on its side.

The big rotors smacked into the water and the ship somersaulted, tail first, into the water like a flaming Fourth of July pinwheel, consuming the young pilot, his crew, and the battle-dressed assault Marines like bacon over an open flame.

This seemed to infuriate the Shark-Hooper Shadows. With

automatic deck cannon ablaze, they zipped and skimmed back and forth over the water in a macabre ballet that looked like a Harlem Globetrotter routine.

In moments, everything above the main deck was disappearing in the tracer-laden barrage that looked like white sparks from a mad welder's torch.

The second Sikorsky swooped in over the fantail and her screaming crew swarmed out over the ship and disappeared down hatches and through passageways.

Quickly the Sikorsky lifted away and the third one settled over the freighter's cluttered fantail, spewing out the next assault company into the one-sided battle.

Little more than five minutes had passed, from the time the captain had sounded the alarm, before the Marine assault forces secured his ship.

True to their tradition, efficiently and conveniently, they left few of the enemy alive. Especially after witnessing their sister helicopter's fiery death.

Yummy's captain, true to his ancient samurai beliefs, took his deadly little weapon, put it in his mouth, and pulled the automatic trigger.

Once the firing stopped, an armored personnel carrier roared down the concrete peninsula and stopped in front of the gangway.

Thatcher squeezed out of the turret as a lanky, sandy-haired lieutenant-colonel walked up and saluted. 'Ship's secured, General. And I think we hit the jackpot you were after.'

'The missiles?' Thatcher asked unable to keep a smile from crossing his face.

The lieutenant-colonel nodded. 'Yep,' he mumbled Gary Cooperish. 'They're in airtight compartments in each side of that forward hold,' he said, pointing to where a squad of Marines was erecting battle lights and directing them down into the cargo-filled hold.

'How'd you make out, Colonel?' the general asked, suddenly serious.

The lieutenant-colonel shook his head solemnly. 'First time I ever had more killed than wounded. Seems everything or everybody was booby-trapped.'

'Prisoners?' the general asked.

The lieutenant-colonel shook his head. 'Not too many, sorry to say,' he lied.

Thatcher watched as a young lieutenant and a corporal with a radio slung over his shoulder pushed the dazed prisoners down the gangway toward them.

'My God!' the President said ecstatically over the scrambler. 'I almost wish I could have been there.'

'How about the Jap? What's his name – Yamimura?' asked Klein.

'I'm afraid we missed him,' Thatcher said from his command post in the vacant warehouse across from the freighter. 'According to one of the prisoners, he was gone long before they came into the harbor.'

'Well, son-of-a-bitch!' the President said excitedly. 'At least we got two of our missiles back.'

'I'm afraid there might be some doubt as to whether that's good news or not,' said Thatcher.

'What do you mean?' demanded the President.

'Another prisoner, one of the Jap's electronics experts, claims that if we make the mistake of moving the missiles, we risk losing Los Angeles and half of southern California.'

'So if he's telling the truth, which you're saying he is, then the missiles are armed in some way,' Klein said.

' 'Fraid so,' Thatcher answered. 'I had one of the ARASS boys give them a cursory once over.'

'And?' the President asked.

'They're connected to some sort of computer device.'

'Can we disarm it?'

'Beats the hell out of me. We have the two ARASS physicists and a couple of computer guys. Even a team from the LA bomb squad onboard.'

'For Christ's sake!' Klein said. 'If it's an arming device, why even bother fucking around. Just hook the goddamn thing up to a tug, haul her out to the middle of the Pacific, and sink the son-of-a-bitch.'

Thatcher shook his head as he stared around the dark, cavernous warehouse. 'Wish it was that easy. The computer boys say it's connected to the internal guidance system of the missiles. It's a round piece of very delicate foil with a needle in the middle of the circle. The middle of the circle's the ship's position now. If the ship's position changes . . . the needle'll move . . . the foil rips . . . and boom!'

'Son-of-a-bitch!' the President thought. 'Won't it ever end?'

'We got twenty-four hours,' Thatcher warned. 'Whatta we going to do?'

'I don't know,' shrugged Klein. 'But I'd get back here as fast as I could,' he added, looking at the suddenly lonely figure of the President.

31

DOOMSDAY ARK IN LA, the full-page headlines blazed, and within hours the suffocating panic was total.

Freeways looked like an African plains mad migration of stampeding animals running in front of a fire, as the population tried to escape. To run.

For a short time, Mexico tried to close her borders. But they were only successful for a few hours before the human wall of humanity, cars, jeeps, and RVs assaulted the border like a herd of dehydrated elephants thundering toward the smell of sweet water wafting up from some distant spring.

The quickly mobilized National Guard, Highway Patrol, and Sheriff's Department tried to make the exodus orderly. But the frenzy had the tempo of feeding sharks. And if anyone dared try to stop, or alter the flow, they knew they were risking their lives.

As one of the station wagons blazed through the heavy traffic, at breakneck speed, a young highway patrolman could restrain himself no longer.

If some idiot like this had a wreck, he'd clog the whole freeway system. And then the shit would really hit the fan.

He had to stop this asshole and make an example of him.

Yielding to the red lights and siren, the station wagon weaved its way through the clogged lanes to the shoulder.

The patrolman pulled off his sunglasses, got out, and walked toward the idling car. In the back seat, he could see two little twin girls sitting next to their older brother, trying to keep two dogs from barking. In the front seat, a frightened woman tried to soothe her diapered infant, while her husband's trembling hands fumbled with his bulky wallet, trying to get out his driver's license.

The young highway patrolman rapped on the window, and the man rolled it down and handed him the license. He looked at it a moment and was about to give him a verbal lashing, when the eleven-year-old shot him through the throat.

'Good, son,' the frightened man said.

Putting the car in gear, he roared back into the crush of traffic, leaving the dying officer laying on the shoulder, mute testimony to the lengths a normally rational man would go to save his family.

From hastily dug shelters, under the broken concrete slabs of a thousand tract homes, and from behind pitifully fragile barricades made of mattresses, books, and furniture, millions of eyes watched TV. Through zoom lenses, news crews, true to their tradition of being on the spot, kept a running account of the danger of the freighter across the quiet bay.

In front of the grainy screens, silent families clutched each other and from almost hypnotic trances, watched the scientists as they scurried around the battle-scarred deck of Yummy's ship, handing equipment up and down from the black hold that housed the waiting death.

If the screen went white, commentators reminded them, it meant their cameras and crew had vaporized and only precious seconds would remain before the shock waves, preceding the mushrooming blast, swept over them.

The already jammed highways became clogged as chain reactions to accidents mushroomed. Refusing to slow down, refusing to help each other, the system couldn't handle it, and like a clogged sewer, everything backed up. And the exodus ground to a halt.

Escape routes blocked, panicked families rushed out of their cars into strange suburbs. They broke into strange houses. Killed strange families who protested. And like much of the city they'd left behind, started burrowing into the hard, adobe clay found under most of the LA basin.

As the minutes ticked away, the hastily assembled squad of experts onboard the freighter slaved to find a solution to the fire control mechanism. But it was like a marvelous piece of modern art in that it was phenomenally complex by its pure simplicity.

The air was still heavy with the acrid smell of exploded ammunition as they tested currents, took readings, attempted to redesign circuitry to bypass the detonator, and ran all the problems via telephone hook up through the nearest computer centers.

They were scared. Terrified. They weren't heroes. And certainly, none of them wanted to die. But, hypnotically, they kept at it and wiped the thoughts of what lay at the end of the problem out of their minds.

The President was raging. His panic, though better concealed, would have easily matched any of those wild-eyed fathers on the clogged freeways leading out of Los Angeles, struggling to rescue their families from the jungle behind them.

'I don't understand who authorized any releases . . . How did this get out? I sure as hell wouldn't have allowed it . . . ' he babbled.

'It would have been impossible to suppress,' Klein said. 'There were thousands of houses on the hill across the bay. They had better seats than on the fifty-yard line at the Rose Bowl.'

'How are we for time?' asked Ridley.

'Less than twelve hours,' an exhausted General Thatcher answered.

The President felt a nervous tic on the outer edge of his eyelid. He reached up and held it. But it still kept twitching uncontrollably. 'God! If I could only do something!' he screamed at his helplessness.

'It's not your fault,' Ridley said, trying to soothe him.

'Oh yeah? Well I sure as hell don't see anyone lining up to take the responsibility,' he said, laughing. His laughter grew louder and louder until tears started streaming down his flushed face.

'God!' he thought as the emotional pressure seared agonizingly through his gut. The pain reminded him of when one of his baby teeth was loose as a child. It hurt when he wiggled it back and forth with his tongue. But at the same time, it felt good, too!

'I guarantee we wouldn't have this problem if I could get my hands on that Jap son-of-a-bitch!'

'We still have a pretty good chance of solving this,' the general tried to assure him. But it was too late.

His mind was starting to snap and he didn't know it.

His whole insides seemed to be quivering. But when he looked at his hands, they seemed calm enough.

'Jesus! What's that sound?' he thought suddenly. He looked at Ridley who didn't seem to hear the sound. He looked at Klein. He didn't seem to be aware of it either. The President put his hands to his ears as the sound got louder and louder. He started to chuckle again. As suddenly, everyone seemed to take on slow-motion qualities. Then he saw from their frightened looks that something was drastically wrong.

'What's happening? What's going on?' he gasped as everything seemed to be turning dim like a cloud passing in front of the sun.

Suddenly his body felt numb. And the pain from the tension drained away. As he looked up, he saw his father storming out of the office toward the distant barn.

Snap!

'Thank God!' he said, suddenly slapping Klein jovially on the back. 'Didn't I tell you not to worry?' he said rushing out.

Klein was momentarily stunned before quickly picking up the phone.

'Surgeon General, emergency,' he yelled angrily. 'Doctor,' he said as the President's personal physician finally answered. 'We're in danger of losing the President. We'll be in the barn. Get there as soon as you can, please,' he said, hanging up without waiting for a reply.

By the time he got to the President, he was tearing open bale after bale of hay looking for imaginary rabbits. General Thatcher grabbed the struggling, raging man who towered over him and slapped him several times across the face.

'Jesus Christ!' his heart sunk as the President grinned at him. From the glazed-eye look he knew it was too late. He was over the edge.

The Surgeon General came rushing in.

With hardly a second glance, the doctor gave him an injection. Within seconds, the President's knees grew wobbly, and the doctor led him toward his office. Kicking open the door, he led him to the leather couch and gently pushed him down onto it. By now the drug was working and the President followed instructions like an automaton.

Wiping the perspiration from the President's forehead, the doctor reached across his desk for the phone. 'Send the ambulance and inform the First Lady I need to see her immediately,' he ordered in a soft southern accent.

'Gentlemen,' Klein said to Ridley and the general. 'I think it would be better if no one knows what's happened here.'

The men both nodded their silent agreement.

'We'll just put him to bed,' Klein continued, 'and hope for the best.'

Again they nodded their consent.

'At this particular time, I don't think it's too good an idea to inform the Vice-President. Considering his age and physical condition, it would, in all likelihood, kill him. I think this situation's going to get desperate enough without having the loss of both chief executives creating another Constitutional crisis. Until this nightmare's past, as Chief Adviser, I'll assume responsibility for, say, forty-eight hours. By then, if there's no improvement in either the President, or the situation, I'll inform

Congress. We'll put the mess in their laps.'

'I'll support you on that,' Thatcher said.

Ridley hesitated. The most alien thought to his lifelong philosophy was placing total authority in the hands of one individual. The risks were infinite. But Klein had always been an honorable man and a man of action. Unpopular at times. But honorable. And they desperately needed leadership of some kind.

'Considering the options, I guess we have no alternative,' he finally said, reluctantly.

They turned as someone rushed in through the back of the barn. It was the First Lady, who was panting after having sprinted through the compound once the operator located her.

As she looked down at her husband, her eyes suddenly filled with tears. 'Oh, my God!' she whispered.

From Los Angeles, every television station had projected a time clock at a corner of their transmitted picture. In the gloom of the shelters, the round dials seemed to become grinning death heads as the sweeping second hands measured the time left for the condemned community.

As the minutes ticked into hours and the hours unwound toward infinity, the experts onboard the ship worked feverishly.

'We got to get the hell out of here now if we're going to reach any kind of safety,' one of them warned.

As scared as they were, they ignored him and kept trying to work it out.

As the second hands rounded the dial for their final sweep, families gathered together in one last tearful embrace. Hands were grasped. Wives consoled whimpering children. People made the sign of the cross and prayed to God, Allah, Buddha, or sat with vacant stares and simply waited for whichever God came. The last minutes were agonizingly long.

In the hold of the freighter, the physicists, technicians, and the support crew quietly shook hands. Sweating from their frantic effort, they sat down and waited. A few lit last cigarettes, and propped their feet up on the two stainless gleaming giants that would carry them to eternity.

The men listened as the electronics started their final cycle. They could hear the hum from the guidance systems as they rotated to get their bearings; the internal pressure systems hissed as they built up enough force for a launch; innerlocks, solenoids, and safety devices opened, closed, and clicked on or off.

They waited breathlessly, with their mouths agape. Nothing happened.

One man suffered a heart attack a few minutes later when the mechanisms clicked to life again. But after several more whirs, clicks, and the hiss of gas being cycled through tiny tubes – silence.

Nothing. Finally, as they watched, the lights on the fire control panels started twinkling out, one by one until, finally, each missile system had shut itself off.

And the numb men feverishly tried to resuscitate their stricken co-worker.

'Son-of-a-bitch!' muttered Klein under his breath as he, Murphy, the ARASS scientist, and Ridley watched the wall-sized TV monitor next to the War Room. They could see the joy as the scientists and technicians on the main deck of the freighter jumped up and down and shouted and hugged and twirled each other with delirious joy.

The Red Line phone chimed and Klein quickly picked it up. 'It's Thatcher,' he said, switching it to the conference speaker as they listened to the man talking from the warehouse across from the freighter.

'The missiles have been neutralized,' Thatcher said, tearfully, as moments before he'd thought numbly of his family outside of Arlington, convinced they would be his last thoughts before he joined Admiral Whittiker.

'That's what I call "by the skin of our teeth," ' chuckled a relieved Klein. 'Next time, if there is a next time, let's not cut it quite so close. OK?'

'Whether or not there's a next time,' muttered Thatcher, wiping his cheeks as he looked around at the Marine colonel and his troops as they filed silently out of the cavelike empty concrete warehouse, 'we had nothing to do with it. The damn things just plain didn't go off.'

Yummy stood like a statue on the metal pulpit that jutted out over the bow of the container ship in the mid-Pacific. The wind roared past him and he felt detached from both the ship and the world as, roller-coasterlike, he plunged down toward the stormy surface before swooping skyward.

The cool, misty spray that kicked past brought some relief to

188

the burning rage that ate his insides like some hungry insatiable cancer.

The missiles hadn't gone off.

The missiles that were to destroy Los Angeles as a second fiery example of the godlike power he controlled hadn't gone off.

The irreversible process of stampeding a terrified world into bestowing power to its rightful owner had been short-circuited.

'It could have been a technical flaw,' one of his young JRA lieutenants argued earlier.

'No,' he said with deadly calm. 'It was Morgan.'

'If that's true,' the lieutenant said, 'you must return to the mainland . . . '

'I agree,' said a Buddha-looking man in a black business suit. 'If he was responsible for sabotaging the detonation then he's undoubtedly jeopardized security to the point of exposing your identity.'

'No. I will remain on board. In this matter,' Yummy said, 'he must be made to suffer a most agonizing penalty.'

'But how?' asked the lieutenant. 'He has successfully eluded every naval and air unit in the Pacific. How can we hope to locate him?'

'He's created a clever game between him and I. He will play out the game by keeping our rendezvous!' Yummy said, knowing that from the beginning Morgan knew he was responsible for Ji'lhan's death and intended this macabre dance to end face to face.

'Ridiculous!' scoffed the Buddha-looking businessman who was the financial genius behind Yummy's empire.

Yummy's eyes narrowed to slits as he looked quietly at the man. 'You will never again question my judgment. My authority. Or decisions. Do you understand?'

The man bowed from the waist, realizing he was dangerously close to death.

'Yes, Mikado.'

'With the men and weapons we have onboard, there's a possibility we can disable or ram the submarine,' the lieutenant said. 'Once we accomplish that, we can take Morgan and sink it at our leisure.

'In this matter, above all, see that you do not fail.'

32

Sliding open the door to the conference room, Klein crossed quietly to the head of the table. As he moved across the room, he felt like a novice actor appearing on stage for the first time. Everyone – Ridley, General Thatcher, Murphy, Seright, and several new military and civilian scientists he didn't recognize – watched his every move as he sat down at the head of the conference table.

There were a few moments of silence before Klein, staring down at a raft of reports, finally spoke.

'The purpose of this special commission is to formulate a definitive plan between our joint forces and our allies to seek, attack and destroy the *Lewis & Clark*, the so-called League of Man, and Takeo Yamimura.'

'Thank Christ!' Thatcher thought. 'At last someone's showing some balls.'

'I'll start by saying that because of our identification of the person responsible for the hijacking, and because he's still a fugitive and the *Lewis & Clark*'s still steaming around somewhere in the middle of some goddamn ocean, we have to assume he will retaliate.

'Do we all agree,' he asked, looking around the table. 'Well, at least no one disagrees. We know we got to find the Jap and sink the submarine. So, gentlemen, how the hell do we go about it? And more importantly, what are we risking by doing it?'

'The submarine has to still be in the Pacific,' advised the ARASS scientist.

'Okay, so?' Klein pushed, trying to breath some life into the group.

'So some way isolate the Pacific. Form a cordon of warships into a noose and draw it shut. Destroy everything inside it.'

'Can it be done?' Klein asked, turning to Thatcher.

'It could be done but it would take time. Weeks, maybe even months,' Thatcher said shaking his head.

'That's a good point, General. But what the hell we got to lose but time? Besides, it may already be too late anyway, right?' Klein said as his piercing eyes flashed around the table.

The dynamics of this new personality seemed to lift everybody's spirit. And around the table minds that had been strangled the last few weeks started reviving.

'The logistics appear staggering if not impossible,' said Ridley. 'But I'm not sure I don't agree with you, Mr Klein. As well as our friend here from ARASS.'

'Besides,' injected Murphy. 'If one of the other countries in the nuclear community is attacked, there's no doubt they'll strike back. Friend or enemy alike. It's our submarine that's missing. So we have to bear the blame. They won't sustain an attack without retaliating.'

'What if they're not attacked?' asked Klein.

'How the hell would anyone know who will and who won't be attacked?' asked Murphy.

'What if we inform the various countries whether or not they're on the original strike programs of the missiles,' Klein said.

'But they've proven they can alter those targets,' said Thatcher. 'Besides, some of those targets are located in allied countries. We tell them that and the fat's in the fire for sure.'

'True, true to both your observations,' Klein said to Thatcher and Murphy. 'But if push comes to shove, we're probably on a lot of our allies' contingency targets, too. And as far as them changing the target input, does anyone here really think they'll alter all the missiles? Think about it for a minute. This sub's sitting out there somewhere waiting for orders from this Jap. Till they hear from him, chances are they won't change or alter any of the missiles. Right? If lucky, maybe we find and destroy the *Lewis & Clark* before then. Even if she does manage to fire all the missiles left, if we have our antimissiles waiting at the pass . . . to cut them off on their way to targets we know about in advance, we shouldn't risk too much.'

'There's a million ways this Jap can communicate with the submarine, though,' Murphy said. 'The *Lewis & Clark* doesn't have to be near the surface to receive transmissions. It has a floating cable-like antenna almost a mile long. When it's dragged behind them, they can pick up just about anything, anywhere in the world. From ham operators to AM radio stations.'

'Why haven't we been looking for this cable then?' asked Klein. 'Isn't that something we can look for?'

'Outside of one of our ships driving right over it, it's like looking for a needle in a haystack,' said General Thatcher.

'More like the eye of the needle in the haystack,' said Captain Seright.

'Okay, let's assume that maybe by now he's already talked to his boys sitting out there in the ocean. And they've altered or changed all the targets in all the missiles. Can we defend against both the targets we think they might hit of our allies, as well as guarantee the integrity of our own country?'

'Not without risking a lot of things like cities, dams, harbors,' said Thatcher.

'Millions could die,' Ridley said.

'True,' said Klein. 'But what happens if we tell allies and enemies alike that they're on their own. That we're looking out for number one. It could have a domino effect that could wipe the entire world.'

'What you're saying is that you're willing to risk the destruction of mankind in order to save it,' Ridley said.

Klein reached over and put his hand on the old man's shoulders. 'Allen, if you can offer me any alternative, for God's sake, do it.'

'We could give up,' he smiled.

'In a few days, maybe a few weeks, millions are probably going to be screaming from their graves, "Why the hell didn't we . . . " ' Klein said grimly.

'You're right,' Ridley conceded. 'We have to act regardless of the consequences.'

'Okay,' Klein said, rising quickly so that they would know the meeting was nearing a conclusion and to be brief. 'What're our first priorities?'

'Notification of the Soviets. The Chinese. Then the rest of the nuclear community. We'll need a profile from NATO and SEATO on every naval, sea, and air unit available through them for the cordon,' said Thatcher.

'Get on it, Thatch,' Klein said. 'In the meantime, I'd like to consult with each of you individually as soon as possible regarding the distribution of our defense missiles. Each of you be thinking about what you consider the most vital areas, industries, petroleum reserves, hydro-electric installations, science centers, etc.'

They all nodded as he rushed out.

33

An explosion reverberated through the interior of the *Lewis & Clark* like a cherry bomb through an old galvanized milk bucket.

Morgan, asleep on the Wardroom lounge, was thrown to the deck as the rumbling shock waves sent the giant ship pitching like a beach ball in the surf.

'What the fuck was that?' he screamed to no one in particular as he ran aft.

In the control room, he saw an ashen-faced Big Daddy at the diving station trying to settle the bucking ship down as smoke billowed up from below decks.

'I don't know what the hell it was, but it was aft of here,' Big Daddy yelled.

'Let's get her topside then,' he said, realizing they were both yelling even though standing next to each other. Depressing the IC button, he yelled, 'Stand by to surface! Stand by to surface!'

In the dark sonar shack, Nichols' ears were still ringing from the effects of the almost deafening noise through his earphones.

'For Christ's sake, Morgan!' he cried, clicking open his IC switch. 'We're in the middle of a goddamn shipping lane. I got contacts everywhere. One about three miles north of our track, another one about eight to ten miles astern.'

'Shit,' Morgan thought. He'd picked this heavily traveled lane so that while waiting for the next rendezvous their propeller noise would blend into the hundreds of ships passing overhead, making them almost undetectable to hovering Hunter-Killers and the Sea Spider.

'Can't help it,' he replied. 'Got no choice. Just keep tabs on them,' he clicked off as Big Daddy finally calmed the Ark back down to a gentle roll. 'Barth!' Morgan yelled. 'Barth! Where the hell are you?'

'On my way!' he heard Barth yelling back as he made his way from the crew's mess.

'Take the diving station,' Morgan ordered as Barth raced in. 'Big Daddy, stand by in tubes forward. Rig each tube for firing,' he said as he sounded the Klaxon to signal that they were surfacing.

Barth slipped down onto the seat and pulled back on the controls.

Morgan stepped to the air manifold and cycled the thundering air into the ballast tanks, blowing them empty in seconds.

As the bow buoyancy can emptied too rapidly, Barth fought to keep from taking on too steep an angle. Throughout the boat, things slid off tables, out of racks and shelves, and clattered noisily to the deck, as the Triton churned toward the distant surface.

Quickly, Morgan closed the solenoids and the raging air that whistled through the vibrating lines jarred to a stop.

'I'm gonna check aft,' Morgan said, securing the manifold.

He dropped down the ladder to the lower level and headed aft.

'Open the main induction and start the blowers,' he yelled back. 'Let's get this smoke out of the boat as soon as we can.'

Near MR-1, heavy smoke was billowing like a giant smoke ring out between the oval-shaped hatch and its watertight seal.

Jones, already wearing a breathing unit, cracked the hatch several inches, listened intently before pushing it open, and cautiously stepping through.

Through the heavy smoke, he could see hydraulic lines, air-lines, electric cables, valves – all crushed, mangled, or missing.

In the middle of the smashed debris, he could see what had been the heart of the explosion. 'Son-of-a-bitch!' he muttered under his breath as his heart sank. The two-storey-high oxygen generator was completely destroyed. He quickly made his way aft, securing valves and switches that led to the destroyed area. A hydrogen explosion, he thought as he quickly checked the pressure hull behind where the unit had stood.

Although it wasn't pierced, the hull bulged out like a balloon spot on an old rubber innertube.

He looked around and saw Morgan staring at the wreckage through the smoke, holding a handkerchief over his face so he could breathe.

'Any flooding?' Morgan yelled.

Jones shook his head.

'I'll be on the bridge. Soon as you check everything out come on up.'

Jones nodded as Morgan coughed his way out of the compartment, heading for the bridge.

In the gusty, gray world caused by the dark storm clouds, Morgan was anxiously watching two distant specks on the horizon as Jones appeared in the hatch.

Morgan set the binoculars down and leaned against the sail. 'OK. Let's have it.'

'The Oxygen Generator's gone. Scrubber's shot, too.'

'Can you jury-rig something so we can get a little something out of them?'

Jones shook his head.

'How about the pressure hull?' Morgan asked as he pulled his binoculars up to check the growing contact astern.

'Well, ain't no gaping holes,' Jones said as he unbuttoned and pulled his shirt out to cool off. 'But the way it's bellied out there's no way we're gonna get a deep dive out of her. I'll try to rig up some shoring. But even then . . . '

'Goddammit!' muttered Morgan angrily, pounding his fist down hard on the bridge cowling. 'What the hell happened?'

Jones shook his head. 'Don't know. Hydrogen built up in the lower cells. The discharge system probably clogged.'

'Maybe somebody rigged it wrong?'

'I rigged it. And I don't rig nothing wrong,' Jones warned.

'Bridge . . . Sonar . . . ' the bridge speaker crackled.

'Go ahead,' Morgan responded.

'The big guy abaft the beam just changed course.'

'Toward us?' Morgan asked.

'Affirmitive . . . 'fraid so,' said Nichols.

'Snoopy son-of-a-bitch!' said Jones, checking the after deck where the smoke was emptying out of the main induction valve. 'Maybe it's a planned course change.'

'Could be,' Morgan said as he watched the distant ship slowly change her silhouette. 'With this overcast, though, the smoke's just hanging. Probably looks worse than it is. And a minute ago we weren't on his radar. Now we are, Big Daddy,' Morgan said, pushing the IC button.

The civilian-dressed first officer and chief engineer were standing next to their captain as all three trained their binoculars on the shadowy black vessel partially hidden by the billowy smoke.

'Could be some kind of sea-going barge that broke loose during the night,' offered the Panamanian engineer as he surveyed the smoke a few miles off their starboard beam.

'Hard to tell,' the Norwegian captain nodded, 'with that smoke. Let's get a little closer.'

The three wakes from the screaming torpedoes were hidden by the choppy, white-capped waves.

The exploding cargo of liquid natural gas lifted the behemoth ship completely out of the water. Like some huge jigsaw puzzle, it broke into millions of pieces.

'Jesus Christ!' yelled Jones, ducking behind the bridge cowling as the shock wave filled with shrapnel hailed past them like a hot, metal-filled rain.

Seven miles north, the helmsman of a hundred-thousand ton container ship raced to the wing of the flying bridge to see what caused the explosion.

Astern, in the distance, he could see the dying flames as the burning debris disappeared into the gray waters, leaving a growing cloud that looked like a giant grayish brain with orange electrical charges darting across its surface seeking its dead nervous system. Running into the wheelhouse, he rang the captain's call, but the captain had heard the explosion and was already on his way from his cabin.

As the captain appeared, the seaman stammered out that the explosion came from the ship that had been dogging them since they came around the Cape a week earlier.

The captain nodded grimly. 'Come about. Radio our position to the nearest rescue forces,' he barked with the authority of years at sea. 'Have the radio operator notify our home office also. Tell them we'll probably lose six to eight hours sweeping the area for survivors.'

As they came into the bridge, the radar operator motioned for the captain. 'Sir. I have another contact.'

'Part of it still afloat?' he asked.

'I don't think so,' the Austrian technician said. 'She was here,' he said pointing to the dead ship's position seven miles astern. 'This contact's between us and the explosion. One minute, nothing, the next bloody minute, there it was.'

The captain rushed out to the tip of the flying bridge. As the wind whipped past him, he swept the gray surface with his binoculars.

There it was!

He could barely make out what appeared to be a tiny black box sticking up just out of the swells. He watched it for several moments longer. Then his heart pounded and his face flushed. He'd seen that type of black box before.

'All ahead flank!' he screamed, rushing back into the wheel-

196

house. 'Return to your original course and let's hope it's not too damn late to get the hell out of here. Move your bloody asses,' he screamed. 'That thing out there's a submarine. It's probably the one that sank that Japanese freighter last week.'

34

With the exception of Jones and Big Daddy, everyone was sitting in the crew's mess when Morgan came in. As he opened the reefer next to the coffee urn and took out a loaf of frozen bread, he felt an icy tension creeping through the compartment. Sticking the loaf in the electronic oven with a block of butter in a cup, he turned on the timer.

He took a cup and opened the spout on the coffee urn. It was the bottom of the pot and the half cup that spewed out was filled with grounds and sediment. Looking around the uncomfortably quiet compartment, Morgan leaned against the counter and blew gently across the steaming gucky liquid. Everyone's eyes avoided his.

'Well, whatta ya think old friend?' Barth finally asked.

Morgan ignored him as the timer went off. He opened the door and took out the cup of melted butter and steaming bread that smelled like it was freshly baked.

As he spooned the melted yellow liquid onto the soft hot bread he shrugged. 'I think it's gonna be thumb sucking for a while.'

Taking a bite of the bread, he threw his cup into the cold, oily dishwater in the mess cook's sink and started forward.

'So Goddammit! Let's get the hell out then,' Marwin said angrily, standing next to Herndon who had taken off his glasses to wipe the oily sweat off the top half of his thick lens.

Morgan looked down as the butter had seeped through the bread and was getting his fingers greasy. 'How?' he asked.

'Scuttle her. Get close to some place and send her down. Get the hell out,' Marwin said.

'Too late!' Morgan said, licking the butter off his thumb.

'For you, maybe.' Marwin scoffed, 'but not for the rest of us.'

'We never said we'd die for you, Morgan,' added Nakamoto.

'You never said you wouldn't either,' Morgan said quietly.

'Look! Nothing's changed,' Adamson said from the corner. 'They won't fuck with us as long as we have the missiles.'

'Bullshit!' scoffed Marwin. 'Soon as they even get a hint of our

198

position, which we just gave 'em, they'll be on us like a swarm of hornets.'

'Goddammit! We made a commitment,' said Adamson nervously. 'I say if Morgan says we have to, whatever it is, the way I see it, we do it.'

'Balls!' Marwin said angrily, pushing him against the bulkhead with a threatening finger. 'It may be a piece of shit to you, but I'm planning on keeping this body in some semblance of the condition you see it in now.'

'But we made a deal,' Adamson pleaded, putting his hand against Marwin's chest trying to push him away. His bulk made Adamson feel hemmed in and claustrophobic.

Marwin slapped it away. 'Fuck your deal, you pussy-assed officer! I didn't make no deal like that.'

Adamson couldn't take being penned against the bulkhead. Letting out a banshee wail, he tried to heave Marwin away from in front of him with both hands.

Marwin was angry. He hardly felt the skinny little giant pushing against his chest, and when he did, he saw red and started slapping him viciously across the mouth with the back of his hand.

Barth started to jump in and separate them when a sudden explosion seemed to rip through the crew's mess.

A bewildered Marwin staggered and like a rag flopped spasmatically over the terrified Adamson. Morgan lowered the small black automatic. Two decks below, the ejected cartridges bounced and clanged as they dropped through the hatch toward the bilges.

'Oh, dear God!' Herndon cried, tears welling up from behind his thick glasses. He'd never seen a dead body before, much less someone killed right in front of his eyes.

Marwin's muscular chest heaved through a gurgly spasm. He tried to lift his head to orientate himself. But he was staring up at the overhead. From his upside down position, he couldn't . . . and never would. Almost like a freeze frame in a movie, his face glazed and his eyes dilated in their last reflex action at the moment of death.

Barth finally pulled the hysterical Adamson from beneath the body. The acrid smoke from the shot drifted through the compartment, smelling like a box of sulphur-headed matches that had been accidentally lit all at once.

Morgan stared down at the light green deck plates that were turning red from the growing pool of blood. Without raising his head, he said, 'We all got into this for a lot of reasons, mostly money or revenge. Nothing's changed as far as I can see.'

For a long time no one said anything.

'You're insane, you know that?' Herndon finally said in all seriousness.

Morgan smiled, 'Hell, yes.'

He looked at Barth silently for a few moments, hoping he would understand.

'OK?' Morgan finally asked.

Barth nodded, realizing for the first time how right Herndon was.

'What about him?' Nakamoto asked. Suddenly, because of death, Marwin had become a 'him'.

'I'll take care of him,' Nardulli whispered as he stared down at the dead giant.

'I'll give you a hand,' Barth said.

'What was the ruckus?' Jones asked Morgan from the diving station.

'Little discussion about our future with Marwin.'

'Bad?' asked Jones.

Morgan nodded.

'How'd it come out?'

'Marwin didn't,' Morgan said.

The intercom crackled. 'Morgan . . . Sonar. Our friend is on his way, but I think we got big trouble.'

'Barth. Make sure all the missiles are rigged for firing,' he said over the IC as he charged off toward sonar.

'What's his range?' Morgan asked as he slithered down the ladder next to Nichols.

'Somewhere around 110 miles. But it's not just "him". It's a "they".'

'A they?'

'Yep! That's why I think we got big trouble. There's a bunch of different contacts about sixty miles beyond Yummy's ship off our starboard bow. Two possible carriers. And from the sound of it, probably the rest of the whole fucking fleet.'

Morgan stared down at the illuminated scope, listening intently at the magnified and filtered sounds of the distant contacts as they churned toward the Triton.

Morgan reached up for the IC switch. 'Jones . . .'

A moment later, Jones came on the line. 'Speak . . .'

Morgan watched Nichols' display lights blinking out the

theoretical targets from the distant noise sources. 'How deep can we get this bucket, Jonesey?'

'You got her under the surface now. Why push your luck?'

'Funny!' said Morgan.

'OK,' Jones said, trying to quickly calculate the pressure the bulging blister could withstand after shoring it up. 'I wouldn't try anything under three hundred feet,' he said.

'OK,' said Morgan as more and more lights twinkled on to the outer edges of the screen. 'Come 60 degrees to port, crank up flank speed, and make your depth five hundred feet.'

'Jesus Christ, Morgan!' he said incredulously. 'You don't think much of my opinions.'

'Sure I do, old friend. But I've seen you play cards. You always hedge your bets. Five hundred feet, Jonesey.'

'Seems like that course change sorta takes us right into the bad guys,' Nichols warned.

Morgan shook his head. 'It should take us just clear of the farthest picket ship. Once we're clear, we'll be behind them. Every minute they stay on course will take them further away from us.'

Nichols nodded. 'Then we can double back and make contact with our friend.'

'Right!' Morgan smiled, sorry that Nichols would never know the truth. 'Just make sure you and Jones hold hands for the next couple of hours. They start closing too fast, have him change course a few more degrees to port,' Morgan said as he climbed up the ladder and pushed open the hatch.

35

From Nichols' quiet black world, there was no way he could hear the hundreds of floating hydrophones that were being dropped in triangular patterns on the surface by the swarms of antisubmarine aircraft.

In an orchestrated pattern, they were eliminating mile after square mile of ocean as they chipped away the areas of empty ocean ahead of them, looking for sounds from the Triton.

Aboard an S-4B Viking, a twin to the carrier bomber Admiral Whittiker had died on, the sonar operator reached up and pushed a switch at the top of his small gray console. The switch keyed a transmitter that flashed a signal that a possible enemy contact had been established.

Admiral Towne, Commander of Pacific Forces, had just stepped out of an invigorating shower in his luxurious quarters aboard the *Vinson* and was toweling off when there was a rapid anxious knock at his door.

'Come!' he barked, not bothering to cover his paunchy, pasty white body.

The door opened and his aide, a young ruby-cheeked ensign, rushed in. 'We have a confirmed contact on the *Lewis & Clark*,' he beamed breathlessly.

'Son-of-a-bitch!' yelled the admiral in delight, dropping the wet towel on the carpeted deck. Grabbing his khaki trousers hanging behind the door, he tried to jam his still wet feet into the legs.

'Where?' he demanded almost falling comically to his knees as his legs grudgingly refused to slip past the cotton fabric.

'One hundred eight-five miles south, southwest, sir,' he said, enjoying the admiral's clumsiness. Almost falling, the admiral plopped down on to the commode so he could pull his pants the rest of the way on. Unfortunately the seat was up and he went in up to his ass.

'Anything else in the area?'

'Just one civilian container ship. About 100 miles south.'

'Where's Howard's and Sheppard's groups?' he huffed as the stubborn pants finally yielded. Standing up, he quickly brushed back his wet hair and grabbed for his epauletted shirt.

'Howard's north of Midway. About 450 miles south of our track.'

'I'll be a son-of-a-bitch!' the admiral chuckled gleefully. 'This is just too much to hope for. That puts him between us and Howard. Grab my shoes, son.'

The aide picked up the black shoes from under the king-size bunk next to the bureau and chased after him.

Charging through the carpeted passageway, the barefooted admiral smiled. 'Son-of-a-bitch!' he chuckled to himself. 'God-damn! What a way to retire, with this to my credit.'

In the dark Combat Center, behind the bridge, the admiral squinted at the plot trying to get his eyes used to the dark as the *Vinson*'s captain outlined their strike forces.

'Sheppard's about six hundred miles west. We've also got three Russian Krivak destroyer squadrons that should be within visual contact of our western pickets within three hours.'

The admiral nodded. The captain thought he was nodding acknowledgment of the facts. Actually he was nodding in dis-belief at their good fortune.

'We got him in a box,' the captain mused, looking up from the plot.

'Let's see if we can't bury him in it, Captain,' the admiral said.

'I don't see how he can possibly get out,' the captain said proudly.

'Captain, you've read their leader's profile. I won't tolerate the luxury of underestimating him.'

From the skyscraperlike bridge of the *Vinson*, Admiral Towne watched the squadron of sweptwing killers roar off in a blast of smoke and flame. As he watched, the *Vinson*'s captain came out of the Combat Center.

'The H-5s are standing by on station. They have a confirmed target,' the captain said.

Admiral Towne nodded. 'Have the President and the Joint Chiefs been notified?'

The captain nodded. 'Sir. Just a reminder. Radar still has a civilian ship in that vicinity.'

'I'm aware of that, Captain. Tell them to get on with it.'

As the helicopter gunships throbbed toward their launch zones, the crews waited nervously for authorization to attack.

Aboard the lead chopper, the weapons officer jumped visibly as the 'Attack' signal flashed on his console. He patted the squadron commander on the shoulder and held his thumbs up.

Altering his course slightly, the squadron commander reached down and pressed the firing mechanism next to his left hand and the missiles shot away from beneath the helicopter's beating rotors. As they roared off in a brilliant flash, the squadron could look down their trajectory and see them making minor adjustments as they roared off after their prey like a pack of hunting dogs after the scent.

As they neared their point of contact with the water's surface, rockets jettisoned their airframes and the torpedo sections entered the water as gracefully as a champion diver. The contact with the surface armed the explosive tips and they raced toward the depths. Homing in on the cavitation generated by the Triton's whirling propeller, they dove in a shrinking circular spiral.

In the sonar shack, Nichols' heart felt like it was exploding as he heard the banshee wail of the torpedoes coming toward them from the surface. In a panic, he reached up and pulled the battle alarm.

In the control room, Morgan realized what was happening and yelled, 'All stop!'

Jones rang it up and they breathlessly waited as, in maneuvering, Adamson fought to shut down the power.

Finally, with agonising slowness, the whirling propeller ground to a stop.

Losing contact with their noise source, the homing torpedoes switched electronically and started echoing in an attempt to keep a bearing on their target.

'Big Daddy,' Morgan shouted over the IC. 'Launch one of the March Hares, and Nichols, damnit! Turn on the Nixie,' he screamed, bringing the sonarman, immobile with fear, back to reality. Quickly, Nichols keyed the transmitting button.

In the forward torpedo room, Big Daddy ran to a small tube that angled out of the Triton. Quickly, his expert fingers flew from one valve to another as he prepared the tube for firing. When the air pressure in the tube matched the outside sea pressure, he opened the outer hatch.

As soon as the outer door light signaled open, he hit the fire button and a sleek, six-foot missile shot out of the tube.

Fifty feet from the Triton, its motor roared to life, and at a speed just faster than the homing torpedoes, it headed toward the horizon.

'Seems somebody thinks they've found our old hiding place,' said Jones. 'Come out, come out, wherever you are . . . Nichols, where's Yummy's ship?' asked Morgan, relieved.

'About 25 miles north, northwest,' he said, breathing a little easier as the decoy hissed, whirled, chugged, and clunked away from the *Lewis & Clark*, leading the missiles to a safe distance before allowing itself to be caught and destroyed.

'Bring her up to sixty-five feet and make your speed two knots,' Morgan said. 'Stand by to fire one. When the pumps have the tubes cleared, take her down to six hundred feet.'

'Five hundred was bad enough,' Jones said, to remind him of the weak spot in the pressure hull. 'Below that, we might not come back up.'

'Got no choice,' he said.

36

In the radio shack, Morgan inserted a black plastic key into the fire control panel and turned it. Next to him, Herndon and Nakamoto punched in computer orders that simultaneously violated the fail-safe system and sanctioned the new firing sequence they had devised.

Aft, in Sherwood Forest, Barth waited next to his console until the digital instructions blinked on, indicating which missile Morgan wanted fired. Lucky 7 blinked on and kept flashing until he pushed a solenoid that told Morgan he acknowledged. Quickly, Barth checked the air pressure and depth gauges. He pressed a switch that would automatically open the outer doors when the two-knot speed was reached. Reaching down to the bottom of the missile tube, he cracked open a vent. Nothing came out, which indicated the tube was dry and the missile safe. As he watched, the pressure within the tube automatically increased to match the water pressure outside. Once the outer door was opened, the thin, rubbery diaphragm would keep the water from rushing in and destroying the missile as long as the two pressures matched. He looked up at the fire control panel.

Two minutes and counting.

Jones had the boat leveled at sixty-five feet.

In maneuvering, the suddenly joyful Adamson had the speed just below two knots, so the missile wouldn't jam against the lip of the tube as it pierced the diaphragm and came shooting out of its silo into the cold waters of the Pacific.

Using an electronic computer pencil, Morgan quickly punched out an altered firing instruction card. Pulling on a pair of white linen gloves, he ejected the etched metal tab from the targeting computer and rushed aft to Sherwood Forest.

Barth's denim shirt was starting to show the effects of heavy perspiration. His eyes constantly darted up and down the clusters of gauges and dials and switches that he had only simulated firing before. But this time it was the real McCoy.

'Son-of-a-bitch! This is it,' he thought, wiping his clammy hands nervously on his pants, as Morgan came in.

Morgan quickly slipped onto the stool in front of the slave fire control station and flipped open a brass slot that always reminded Barth of one of those fancy office building letterboxes.

Slipping in the fire control disc, he pushed the sequence solenoid and the target data was electronically transferred to the missile's onboard computer controls.

As they watched, the firing sequence lights blinked from red to green as each stage automatically completed itself.

Finally, Barth looked up. 'Green Board, Skipper,' he said quietly.

Morgan nodded, heaved himself off the stool, and headed back forward to the radio shack.

As he came into the radio shack, Nakamoto and Herndon were staring at him. Both were ashen-faced and it took a moment before he realized they were staring past him, in back of where he stood.

Turning back toward the hatch, his heart skipped a beat. In stunned astonishment, he stared open-mouthed at the face of a terrified, grease-covered young sailor standing in the shadows. 'Son-of-a-bitch!' he thought as the hydrogen generator explosion suddenly made sense.

Morgan didn't move a muscle as the savage-looking barrel of the black machine gun was pointed at his chest.

'Get away from – from – from the panel,' the sailor pleaded in near hysteria. 'Please. I don't want to hurt you, but I'll kill you if I have to.'

Morgan nodded. 'Herndon, Nakamoto, step away – slowly,' he said.

As they backed off their seats, the sailor's automatic swept nervously back and forth, between them and Morgan.

'Take it easy, son,' Morgan said, trying to soothe the trembling, terrified young sailor. 'Just tell me what you want us to do.'

'You – you – you – ' he stuttered, 'aren't going to fire any of – of – of the missiles. I'm going to make sure of that,' he said quickly wiping the huge tears from his cheeks with one hand.

'OK,' Morgan said softly. 'Whatever you say.'

Herndon moaned softly in terror. He couldn't control himself. His nerves started to go, and as his knees gave out, he peed in his pants.

'Stand up! Stand him up!' the sailor screamed. 'Or I'll kill him!' he said, swinging the deadly gun down toward the moaning Herndon.

'Don't . . . please don't kill me,' Herndon blubbered as he

tried to stand back up. But the floor was wet from his urine and he couldn't rise.

Nakamoto put his arm around his partner's waist and tried to drag him to his feet. 'Don't shoot him, please don't shoot him,' Nakamoto cried, knowing the terrified, trembling sailor was almost past the stage of reason.

As he watched Nakamoto try to help the fat man up through the blur of his tears, he saw a slight movement from the tall khaki-clad man beside him.

The next split second seemed like an eternity for both Butler and Morgan.

Staring into the sad, tear-filled eyes, Morgan knew the boy wasn't a killer. The compartment seemed to vibrate as he pulled the trigger and blew away the side of his head.

Staring into each other's eyes, the boy never had time to realize he was dying.

'Dammit!' he thought, sadly feeling betrayed for still another time as he had felt an attraction to the man who vaguely reminded him of his father.

He saw the flash from the end of the man's gun, but he felt no pain. For a moment he thought he'd missed, or that it had been a warning shot.

Suddenly, he was in a lush green mountain meadow. He didn't know why, but he felt jubilant. He was positive his father was just around the next bend of the raging river that surged toward the valley below. Hurrying, he finally caught a glimpse of the familiar figure bending in the stream, panning a mother lode that would make them rich beyond their wildest dreams . . . and a family again – and he was dead.

'Green board at this panel,' Nakamoto said.

'Same here,' said the still-trembling Herndon as his eyes constantly swept over his creation of wiring that sped the firing instructions through the violated fail-safe computers.

Morgan reached for the intercom button. 'Stand by,' he said into the black enamel mouthpiece.

Throughout the boat, everybody stopped what they were doing and held their breath and waited.

In the control room, almost ghostlike, Nardulli slipped onto the bench in back of Jones where they both could watch as the automatic pilot constantly monitored the depth and course controls.

Morgan lifted the heavy, clumsy bright red guard off the firing button and rested his hand gently on top of it.

Herndon could see Morgan's jaw tighten and could almost feel the hair on the back of his neck tingling.

Quickly, Morgan pushed the heavy button.

For several seconds it stayed locked in the panel, as the electrical voltage coursed through it, igniting the various systems.

In Sherwood Forest, Barth could hear the air hissing suddenly into the chamber and the rumbling whine as the JATO bottle exploded, sending the missile shooting out of the tube. Moments later, tons of seawater rushed in the empty tube, sending the boat shooting heavily down toward the depths.

From deep in the bilges, three decks below where he stood, Barth could feel the powerful vibration as the automatic pumps roared into action to offset the onrush of water flooding the tube.

Even from a distance of almost ten miles, as Yummy watched, the missile breaking out of the waves looked like a giant fist from some legendary sea god lifting in some macabre militant salute.

The moment it cleared the swells the solid state fuel exploded, shrouding the surface in a bank of misty steam. For a split second the missile seemed to hesitate as its cumbersome body rotated in a full circle while its guidance systems reorientated themselves before streaking toward the darkening sky.

Reaching the silent, frozen edge of space, there was an explosion and the missile's main stage, now empty, jettisoned and arched gently back toward the earth's atmosphere.

Darting across the frozen polar cap, the missile headed out over the Atlantic.

By the time the antiballistic missile systems throughout the world flashed the warning that it had been launched, the Poseidon reached its final staging. With technological perfection, the missile separated from its lightweight, air frame sheathing, broke apart, and blossomed like a parasol into fourteen different missiles, and streaked toward fourteen separate targets.

Yummy had never witnessed anything so magnificently divine.

'Have the ship's engines stopped?' he asked, knowing the beauty he'd witnessed was as deadly for him and his ship as staring into the Medusa's face – and just as final.

'Six hundred feet, and we're at flank speed,' Jones said as he leveled the black Triton off. 'A rather shakey 600 feet,' he added.

In the radio shack, Morgan clicked the IC switch in acknowl-

14   209

edgment. He picked up the sound-powered phone and cranked it.

'Nichols,' he said anxiously, as the sonarman came on the line, 'what the hell's going on?'

'*Nada*, nobody's moved!' Nichols said as his visibly shaking hands twirled the wheel in a never-stopping circle across the dial. As he passed each contact, he ran their 'intensity level' through his computer to make sure their range had remained relatively the same.

'What about Yummy's ship?'

'I got no noise source. He must have come to "all-stop".'

'Time to targets?' he said hanging up and staring down at the dead seaman.

'Six minutes,' Nakamoto replied counting off the time from the digital readout over the computer console.

Morgan smiled to himself. He felt giddy. If he came to 'all-stop' it meant Yummy knew he'd been had.

Although cut off from the missiles, their computers would go through as simulated flight. Their instrumentation would correspond to the onboard flight recorders on the missiles, and when the readout counted down to zero the missiles had, theoretically, arrived at the target site.

In the Combat Center aboard the *Vinson*, Admiral Towne waited anxiously for confirmation that the Poseidon had effectively been intercepted and destroyed.

'Second stage separation confirmed by Greenland Station,' a missile technician yelled from his console as it followed the missile's trajectory.

'Blossom! I have a blossom confirmation,' a crew-cut young radarman yelled from the darkness as he peered at his green scope.

The admiral closed his eyes, suddenly nauseous. 'My God!' he thought. ABM chances for successful destruction lessened drastically after 'Blossom' time.

'Notify the President. Tell the Joint Chiefs we'll be withdrawing from the area. With what I'm going to throw in we can't risk being anywhere near it.'

His aide nodded and rushed off to the Crypto Room next to the bridge radio room.

Morgan, Nakamoto, and Herndon stared at the console as the

red digital calculator counted down the last few seconds. A few seconds later, a bright red 'Contact' light in the middle of the panel flashed.

Morgan could hear the gentle click – click – click of the solenoid as the light winked on and off like some giant's leering 'only-we-know' wink. For a few silent moments, he stared at the panel, wondering if in some way the electronics within knew that the gentle clicking of the solenoids meant that all the missiles had arrived at their targets.

Morgan thought of the targets he'd hastily transcribed onto the firing disc. Two to the Saudian oil fields, for starting the whole fucking thing to begin with. One to New Orleans for Adamson, and one to Newport Beach for his stepfather. The rest were 'passers', decoys, heading for targets that would require the ABM systems to concentrate on them because they seemed to be aimed for population centers.

37

Morgan couldn't have guessed better.

As the missiles burned back through the atmosphere, their white contrails looked like giant letter openers ripping white holes through the delicate blue sky.

When the fourteen separate warheads thundered back down from the edges of space, they were ambushed by high altitude nuclear explosions from the umbrella of defense missiles that were sent up to attack them. And after it was over, several beautiful and ancient world capitals were badly shaken. But safe.

The vast wastelands surrounding the Saudian oil fields, along with sparkling, white-washed, air-conditioned cities weren't as lucky, and after the attack, the uncontrollable oil well fires that dotted the stark landscape throughout the oil fields looked like spewing Roman candles on a hot Fourth of July night at Disneyland.

'Son-of-a-bitch!' Klein said less than a minute after the launch as he watched the feverish activity in the War Room from the President's office.

'Okay,' he said. 'So now we know they can alter the missile targets.'

'We got to figure it's open season on everything now,' General Thatcher said.

'Anyone disagree with that?' asked Klein.

Each man shook his head.

'Okay. Admiral Towne's waiting for Nuclear Strike approval. Anyone disagree with my authorizing it?'

Again everyone shook their heads.

'The *Lewis & Clark*'s got to know it's coming,' said Thatcher.

'Then why did he fire only one missile?' the ARASS scientist asked. 'Maybe it was simply a warning for us to back off. Give us time to negotiate with him.'

'Bullshit!' said Thatcher, impatiently. 'It was for us to back off, that's for sure, but it was also so he could haul ass in the confusion. We have to assume they fired to give them time to move, and to get ready to fire a "ripple".'

'Dear God!' said Ridley, quietly, almost to himself.

'So what the hell was I supposed to defend?' asked Thatcher in frustration, knowing the burden rested with him.

'It has to be the people,' said Klein.

'I agree,' said Ridley.

'What about our own defenses. Industry, our ports, dams?'

'General, if we don't offer to help the rest of the world, and if we don't at least attempt to save as much of mankind as we can, there probably won't be a world left that needs defending,' Klein said angrily.

'He's right,' said Ridley.

The general nodded. 'It's your ball game. Just tell me what you want.'

Klein nodded. 'First, authorize Towne's nuclear strike. Second, contact all allied forces, plus the Russians and Chinese. They're all on alert. I want our defense systems keyed to cities and population centers throughout the world. Especially to those areas where we doubt a defense system exists.'

Thatcher nodded.

'We could have tremendous losses from the antiballistic missiles themselves,' the ARASS scientist said. 'As a matter of fact, in some cases, may be worse than from the original Poseidons.'

'You're saying the cure is going to be worse than the disease?' asked Klein.

The scientist nodded.

'Well,' Klein said, after thinking of the alternatives for a few quiet moments, 'we have to look at it in the broadest of terms. We simply haven't got a choice. We must, at all costs, protect and direct our greatest effort to those areas of greatest populations.'

There was a moment of silence as he looked around the crowded cubicle. 'Time's awasting, gentlemen. We got too much to do to be standing around here. Let's move some ass.'

From the *Vinson*'s bridge, Admiral Towne watched as the two cruisers off his starboard beam pointed their graceful clipper bows toward the distant strike zone where, from her missile launch, the *Lewis & Clark* was last known to be.

As he watched, he could see the dots of blue-clad sailors as they scurried about topside preparing the launch.

On the cruiser's afterdeck, the missile launchers swung open to reveal the Harpoon missiles, as they automatically glided toward their launch elevation.

Glistening in the sunlight, they'd been rearmed by the weapons officers and chief missile men with nuclear depth charges instead of the ineffective acoustic torpedoes.

'What about the civilian ship?' the captain asked again.

'It's not the least bit important, Captain,' the admiral said.

Morgan leaned over Nichols' shoulder. The screen of the Target Tracking Console was empty.

'They've hauled ass. Everything's off track,' Nichols said, hoping it would mean they had backed off.

Morgan reached for the IC button. 'Jonesey. Bring her up to six-five feet.'

The earlier storm that had brought the cloudy skies had passed. Even in the bright sunlight, the Harpoon missiles looked like flashbulbs popping as they ignited and streaked toward the thin atmosphere of the heavens like a reverse shooting star.

'Six-five feet,' Jones said to Morgan as he came in from the crew's mess.

'Make you feel better?' Morgan smiled.

'Bet your ass. That bulkhead ever gives way, this water's definitely over our heads.'

'That deep, huh?' Morgan smiled.

It was a tribute to modern technology that the missiles within the massive strike didn't collide with each other as they screamed down from the atmosphere toward the target center marked by Yummy's ship like a rain of arrows from the Persians attacking the Spartans at Thermopylae.

'What an extraordinary ambush to be lured into,' Yummy thought, watching the chain reaction of nuclear explosions which was like a Titan's string of Chinese firecrackers during a New Year's celebration. Many never reached the strike zone, destroyed in the hellish inferno before having a chance to detonate.

The last conscious thought that flashed across his mind, like a neon sign as the steam from his evaporating body fluids fogged his sunglasses was, 'He always knew I'd come . . .'

The hundred-square-mile target, a thousand square miles of ocean surface, was flattened and vaporized. Yummy, his ship, porpoise, whales, sharks, coral, seaweed were all vaporized in the eyes of the maelstrom, or bubbled to the surface moments later like steamed, boiled bits of seafood in a giant cauldron of bouillabaisse.

Unfortunately, the *Lewis & Clark* wasn't there.

Between the time lost as the task forces moved away from the target area and the Triton's flank speed in the opposite direction, enough time had elapsed to take her to the edge of the strike zone.

But still, the awesome force picked up the giant submarine, just under the crest of a giant tidal swell caused by the blasts, and tossed, twisted, and racked her like a child's forgotten toy.

In MR-1, the strain was too great for the weakened bulge in the pressure hull. As it gave way, it looked like it had been ripped with a pair of pinking shears. Though the gap was only a fraction of an inch wide, the water roared in like a shower from a fireman's high-pressure hose.

Instantly, circuit breakers tripped and for a few moments, before the emergency lighting came on, or until a man here and there located an emergency lantern, the Triton was as black as a tomb.

The blast sent Morgan's head crashing against one of the rungs of the ladder in back of Jones and a searing, blinding pain sent fireworks screaming through his brain.

In the dark, Jones felt around the overhead for a battle lantern and switched it on.

'You OK?' he yelled, as he fought the controls, attempting to regain control of the submarine.

Blood was streaming down Morgan's face. His cheek was shattered as well as the bone above his right eyebrow.

'God!' he moaned as the pain seared through his battered face.

Jones gently wiped some of the blood oozing into Morgan's eye with a piece of cotton he yanked out of the first-aid kit that had fallen from the overhead.

Morgan's head started to clear. But the pain by now was becoming agonizing.

'What's our depth?' he moaned.

'Depth gauge reads ninety feet. But it's anybody's guess if it's working.'

'I'll take the helm,' Morgan moaned. 'Get back to maneuvering and find out why the hell Adamson hasn't got the breakers reset.'

'You be all right?'

Morgan nodded as he tried to focus on the gauges in the weak light of the battle lantern.

As he disappeared aft, Morgan could hear someone coming through the forward hatch. It was Big Daddy.

He came through and sagged back against the hatch. His face was white and contorted in pain and he was holding his shattered right arm.

Morgan could see by his eyes that the shock so far had cut off the pain of the compound fracture. Lucky son-of-a-bitch, Morgan thought as his head throbbed.

'That the ball game, Cap?' Big Daddy said through clenched teeth.

'Nope,' Morgan shook his head as he wiped the coagulating blood away from his swollen and blinded eye.

'Wonder if that little chaplain's wife's getting any these days,' he thought from his daze as he heaved himself painfully to his feet and stepped back through the hatch heading for the forward torpedo room.

The phone squealed and as he reached for it, he could see Barth coming in from the crew's mess.

'Morgan,' he said quietly into the mouthpiece.

'Adamson's dead,' Jones said matter-of-factly over the hissing, crackling line. 'He musta been trying to reset the breakers. And in the dark – well, he grabbed an open terminal.'

'OK, can you reset them?'

'I'd just as soon not. I'd feel a lot better if someone else did. 'S'not really my line.'

'OK. I'm on my way,' he groaned, hanging up and heaving up from the comfortable diving station cushion. 'You OK?' he asked Barth.

'Think so,' he nodded. His head was scraped and his shirt and pants badly ripped. 'Fell through a fucking hatch. Thought I'd broke my fucking back, but think it musta just been my pride.'

Morgan nodded, 'Take the helm. I gotta help Jones reset the breakers.'

As he came into the maneuvering room, a heavy, putrid stench hung in the air from the massive voltage that had seared through Adamson's body, burning it to a virtual cinder.

'Jesus!' Morgan said, almost vomiting.

Jones nodded from behind a white tee shirt he was holding over his nose to filter out the smell. He'd had the same reaction when he first came into the compartment. Only he hadn't been able to keep it down.

With a long push-broom handle, he was trying to pry Adamson's charred hand away from the shiny terminal. Finally, the tendons separated and his arm fell away from the panel, pointing rigidly up toward the overhead, like a burned wing from an overdone turkey.

Morgan's head was throbbing as he reset the electrical breakers. Instantly the lights flickered on and the air-conditioning started blowing frosty, chilled air into the by-now roasting boat.

He checked the reactor control panels. All the gauges registered in the 'Safe' to 'Marginal Safe' ranges.

The cooling water was overheated. But that was because they'd lost circulation for a while and would come down now.

In the control room, Nichols was standing behind Barth as he fought to keep the lumbering ship level.

'What brings you out of your rathole?' Jones asked.

'Got nothing left to listen to, old buddy,' he answered. 'The hydrophones are either crushed or flooded. I can't get a reading or hear a fucking thing,' he said to Morgan as he followed Jones into the dimly lit compartment.

'Doubt if we'll need them anymore,' said Morgan, his head now aching from the mere vibration of talking. The pain was unbearable. But he knew it would be relieved soon.

Admiral Towne was slouched in a cushioned seat on the bridge, drained of energy.

As he glanced around his task force, he could see that they were all still buttoned up. Not a man could be seen or would be allowed topside without protective radiation gear.

Each ship looked like a it was going through a car wash, as their fire hoses pumped seawater from the ocean back over the exteriors of the ships to flush any possible contamination off the ship and back into the sea.

'Admiral,' the *Vinson*'s captain said, coming in from the combat center. 'The helicopter squadrons have combed the area. No sonar contacts or wreckage has been detected.'

The admiral nodded. The way the bottom had been destroyed, it might be days before any of those things could be spotted. If, indeed, they ever were.

'How about the civilian ship?'

'What civilian?' the captain said, grimly, knowing the ill-fated

217

ship had been vaporized. 'Definitely in the wrong place at the wrong time.'

'Did you ever ID him?' the admiral asked.

The captain shook his head.

'Poor bastard! We'll never know now will we?'

'Second strike ready?' he asked quietly.

'Yes, sir. Standing by to launch as soon as the helicopters clear the area.'

'Captain,' the admiral said, pulling him down close so they could talk without being overheard by the crew at their nearby battle stations. 'If that son-of-a-bitch's still afloat, we can't afford to wait until they clear the area.'

The captain stared at the horizon and nodded his silent understanding.

Morgan had never known pain could be so intensely agonizing. His head seemed to be swimming as he fought to remain conscious. His remaining good eye was starting to swell shut. And everything was starting to take on a red hue as the ruptured blood vessels turned the eyeball flaming red as he swung the heavy, clumsy guard away from the firing switch.

Closing his good eye for a moment, he could feel the cool, innocent feeling switch between his fingers.

Without opening his eyes, he mustered all his remaining strength and jammed the switch down.

Leaving his fingertips resting on the switch, he felt the faint vibration as the energy pulsed through the switch on its way to the sleeping Poseidons.

'Admiral! We have a second launch!' the captain yelled from the combat center door.

'Goddamn sons-a-bitches!' Towne screamed in an unusual display of emotion. 'Assholes! Thoughtless, vicious, motherfuckers!' he raged. But subconsciously, for reasons he couldn't explain, he'd almost expected it. 'Like goddamn cannibal rats,' he thought. 'No matter how deep you drive them into their holes, they keep crawling back out.'

'Have the helicopter squadrons cleared the area?'

'No, sir,' the captain said grimly knowing he was condemning the thirty-six helicopter crews to death.

'We can't wait,' the admiral said, almost pleading for the captain's understanding.

'I know,' the captain nodded.

'Motherfucker,' Barth screamed in frightened anger as the pumps under Sherwood Forest started to clatter like a ball bearing rattling in a steel pan. The clatter grew, until he could feel the whole compartment vibrating. Finally, with their steel shafts squealing like a fear-crazed hog, they tore out the thick steel bulkhead, ripping a section out of the pressure hull as easily as if some giant had casually opened a can of sardines.

The eighth missile had just been launched as Barth sprinted forward. Diving through the hatch, he barely got it dogged behind him before the torrent of flooding waters reached the deck plates.

By the time he reached the radio shack, the boat was starting to list heavily toward the stern.

'The pumps're gone,' he yelled into the little electronics-filled space. 'Sherwood's flooding.'

Morgan pushed away from the console and stood up. Looking over at the depth gauge, he could see that they were already sinking.

The tons of flooding water had already offset their forward motion and they were sitting motionless in the water.

'I got no speed, Morgan,' Jones yelled back from the control room. ' 'Less I get some speed, I can't hold her up.'

Morgan looked around at Barth. But he already knew the answer.

As they watched, numbers thirteen, fourteen, fifteen, and sixteen finished their firing sequence. Breaking through the vellum diaphragms, they left the gaping tubes . . . with no pump to bail them out even after their outer doors automatically closed.

'All missiles away!' Nakamoto said quietly as the fire control panel lights blinked from red to green as the outer doors automatically closed after each missile had fired.

Jones appeared in the doorway of the radio shack. 'I got the trim pump trying to pump as much as I can over the side. And we ain't got no steerage either.'

'No shit!' Barth laughed shaking his head. 'Noticed that, did you?'

There was a moan from deep within the boat as the bulkhead

in MR-1 finally caved in and tons of water flooded into another dying compartment.

As the water thundered in, the added weight caused the boat to lurch toward the distant ocean floor.

Tail first, it slowly picked up speed and, like a dead whale that had wrenched free from the whaler's harpoon, pointed down toward the dark trench.

Silently, reacting from conditioned reflexes from his years aboard submarines, Jones raced forward to the air manifold and his hands flashed across the board as he depressed the switches that fed air into the ballast tanks and sent tons of water surging back out into the sea.

But the mortally wounded boat, into whose sides were gushing tons of seawater by the second, failed to respond to his feeble efforts.

She took on more and more water and a steeper and steeper angle. And a faster and faster speed. Until, finally, she headed down toward the distant trench like an express elevator shooting toward a distant black basement.

Charts, stores, clothes, Marwin's body, equipment – all crashed down onto the compartment bulkheads which, because of the growing downward angle, were becoming the deck.

The lights flickered out, and Herndon started sobbing.

A lighter flickered as Barth lit a cigarette.

In the glow from the lighter, Morgan could see that they had gone past the boat's test depth as they hurtled like a black spear down toward the yawning trench.

Barth inhaled deeply and Morgan could see the glow of the cigarette as he handed it to Jones. Jones inhaled and passed it to Morgan.

Taking two quick deep drags, the biting smoke seemed to bring some relief to his throbbing head.

'Damn, Morgan!' Barth said dejectedly through a hacking smoker's cough. 'All the years I've known you, I sorta counted on you always having an ace in the hole somewhere.'

The rapidly depleting high-pressure air was still screaming through the air lines fighting to clear the ballast tanks, but the battle was lost and they started reflooding when the seawater's pressure built up to the pressure of the air that was fighting to keep it out.

Morgan was about to answer, 'Not this time,' when the implosion occurred.

One second the compartment was dry and intact. The next split second it was gone.

The sudden compression of the atmosphere in the little space where they stood was so quick it caused a flash fire. To Morgan and his crew it was like being in a cylinder of some giant diesel engine as pressure ignited the oxygen and engulfed everything in searing flames, which lasted only a millisecond before the crushing waters snuffed the Triton and her crew like the most fragile of the hummingbird eggs.

The sound that preceded the implosion reminded Morgan of the raging surf that pounded down on the beach on the Costa del Sol and roared up toward where he and Ji'lhan stood on the beach near Marbella that first night together.

And they were gone.

Ji'lhan's smiling face and the delicate fragrance of her Moroccan jasmine cologne were the last flickering impulses that flashed across his dying brain.

In the mine-shaft blackness of the forward torpedo room, Big Daddy was vomiting at the pain from his shattered arm. Suddenly the inky blackness lit up like the noonday sun, as the oxygen ignited, mercifully ending it.

Nakamoto almost had time to smile. He'd never play for the Sea Hawks. But fuck! After this there probably wouldn't be a franchise left to play for anyway.

Herndon started to inhale, but all there was to breathe was flames. And he never exhaled again.

And Nichols, already almost deaf from the explosions, tried vainly to throw his hands up in a pathetic attempt to protect his precious ears.

Barth and Jones, old friends, looked at each other in sad amazement as flaming atmosphere engulfed them, turning their faces into grinning Halloween masks.

And Nardulli barely had time to look as the black galley range broke loose and crushed him underneath.

Like a broken match discarded in a cold cup of coffee, all life and warmth was snuffed out as the shattered Triton settled into the yawning chasm at the bottom of the black trench.

Moments later, the second strike missiles from Admiral Towne's three task forces roared down on the already dead submarine.

The whole earth shuddered on its axis as the missiles from the dead Triton rained down on the world in a cascade of fiery destruction.

Russia's thousand-foot-high Nurek Dam, where the Sere Mountains dog-leg back toward the Pamirs, disappeared. And billions of tons of water thundered into the green fertile valleys below, stripping the land of topsoil, towns, factories, and people.

One blast closed the Bosporus Straits, another destroyed the Mao-Chang Chu Science Complex in the heart of Mainland China. And the people – the people died the easiest of all.

The loss of life was staggering. But, on the whole, most of the antimissile defenses proved surprisingly effective. Almost three quarters of the 224 warheads were destroyed and knocked to the ground like fiery dead pheonixes.

After the massive tremors and shock waves disappeared, parts of the world were left looking like desert wastelands as the mushrooming clouds rose majestically toward the cold, hurricane force winds of the clear upper atmosphere. The clouds reached the upper layers of the clear air and it was several days before they started dispersing, leaving the sky filled with what looked like a giant, mad skywriter's artwork on a windy afternoon.

38

Klein leaned back in the President's old leather swivel chair in office.

Rubbing his eyes with both hands, he looked at the cluttered desk in front of him, piled high with briefs and secret communications on the global damage from the Poseidons.

He knew, when the world recovered from the shock, they would be blamed. After all, it had been the United States' missiles and they had been fired from a United States submarine – regardless of who had been at the controls. They would have to set up a massive aid and relief program to reconstruct the damage, rebuild the cities and countries.

It was only fair. Particularly since the Russians, Chinese and Europeans had sustained staggering military and economical losses.

The United States was top dog again. Only this time Klein intended for them to stay at the top of the heap.

He looked over at Ridley who had been poring over one report after another.

One of the red phones on his desk chimed and he reached over and picked it up.

'Klein,' he barked.

Putting his hand over the mouthpiece, he looked over at Ridley.

'It's Admiral Towne,' he said.

'Yes, Admiral,' he said, returning to the phone. 'I see,' he nodded. 'There's absolutely no doubt?' he said as the admiral confirmed they had located the wreckage of the *Lewis & Clark*. 'Good. Very good. Keep me informed,' he said hanging up.

'They found the *Lewis & Clark*. Or what's left of it,' he smiled. 'The Navy's already got some ships on location. By this time tomorrow they'll have made sure nothing's left that can do anybody any harm.'

Ridley slowly leaned forward. Very deliberately and methodically he laid the reports he'd been studying into a series of neat piles.

'It's remarkable,' the old man said. 'As a matter of fact, it's positively uncanny.'

Klein looked up but didn't speak.

'The world has just survived a holocaust that threatened every living thing on the face of the earth, and we've come out virtually unscathed,' he said, looking at Klein.

Klein nodded silently. Once he discovered through Thatcher that they could knock down some of the Poseidons and let others appear to penetrate the defenses he couldn't justify not allowing it to happen. He wondered if Ridley would guess.

Klein rubbed his tired eyes. Probably sooner than anybody else, he thought, giving the old man the credit he deserved.

'The explosion in the Bosporus cut off Russia's access to the oceans. Their missile complexes . . .'

Klein waited patiently without replying.

'China lost their leaders . . .'

'Do you realize there's not a person, or a country, no one, ally or enemy alike, that won't have to come to you?' Ridley said, shaking his head. 'Do you realize they . . . ' He stopped as Klein's distant stare turned toward him.

Ridley felt his heart suddenly pounding.

'Of course . . . ' he said, realizing how easily he and the other advisers had supported Klein's missile deployments. His logic had seemed so innocent.

Chill bumps ran down between the old man's shoulder blades.

'I don't suppose you'll be informing Congress . . . '

'What Congress?' Klein asked without bothering to look up as he penned a note to one of the reports.

'Hail, Caesar,' Ridley said softly.

Klein quietly looked at him for a moment with a slight smile before turning back to the desk full of reports.